Mike Smith

THE
HUNDRED
DECKER
ROCKET

MACMILLAN
CHILDREN'S
BOOKS

Ivy had just finished making a telescope.
She was trying it out for the first time when
Mum shouted from downstairs.

"Have you tidied your bedroom yet?"

Through the telescope, Ivy saw something
strange and beautiful, glistening very far away.

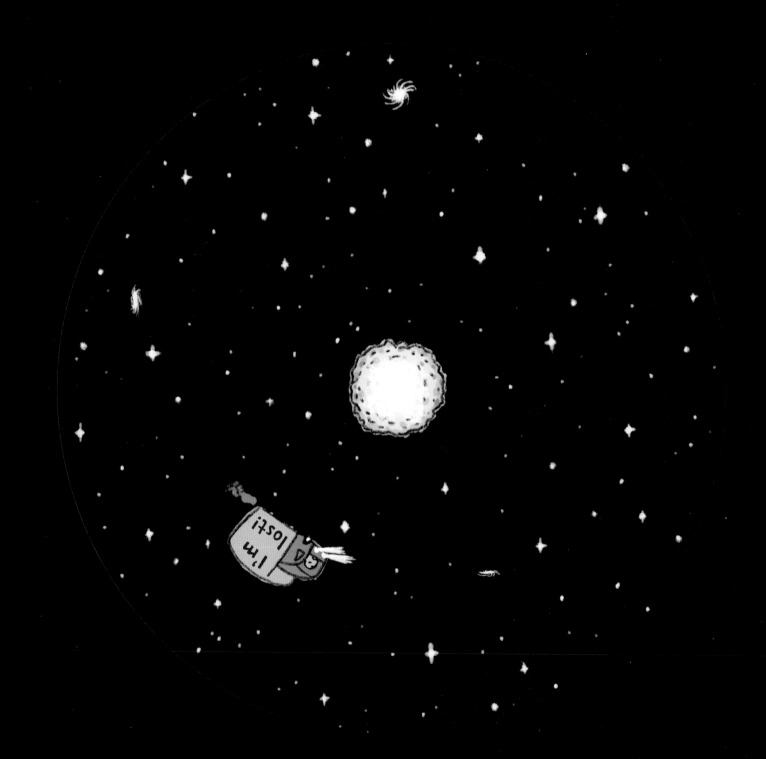

"Let's go there!" said Ivy.
"What do you think, Eddie?"

"I'm up for it," said Eddie.

It took a few days to find the bits they
needed to build a rocket.

But before long, they were ready.

They gobbled breakfast,
made a packed lunch and . . .

As they shot through the clouds,
Earth got smaller and smaller.

They drifted in space for what
seemed like forever.

After half an hour, they decided
to eat their sandwiches.

Eddie was just finishing
the crumbs when . . .

DONK!

they landed on a strange planet.

Eddie found some aliens to chat to.

"What off Earth are they saying?" asked Ivy.

Eddie explained that they had made a mess of their
planet and wanted to leave.

"They saw our spaceship and would
like our help to build one."

"I'm up for it,"
said Ivy.

So they all set to work.

The more they worked, the
bigger the spacecraft grew.

The bigger the spacecraft grew,
the more aliens appeared.

The more aliens that appeared,
the more rubbish was collected.

And the more rubbish that was collected,
the cleaner the planet became.

But everyone was too busy to notice.

Finally, with 100 decks, there would
be enough room for everybody.

They all climbed aboard
the rocket and strapped
themselves in.

BOING!

As they travelled in space, the aliens looked out for a new planet.

They landed gently on
the soft orange grass.

While they were admiring their new home,
Ivy discovered that it wasn't new after all.

It was the same planet – just cleaner!

The aliens thanked Ivy and Eddie and promised
to look after their planet this time.

Ivy and Eddie were very excited to be on their way back home.

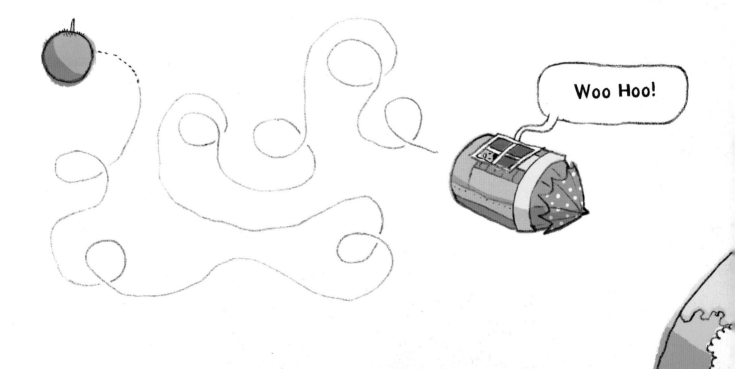

As soon as they landed, Ivy rushed
straight to the telescope.

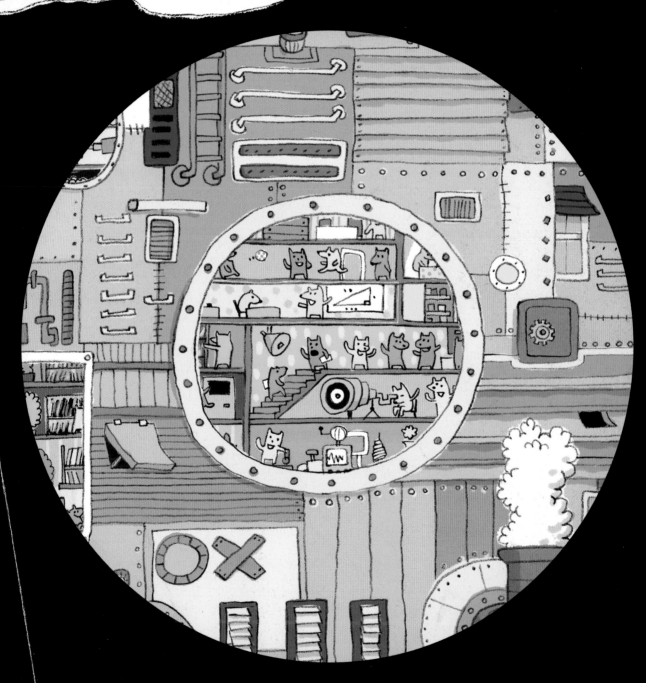

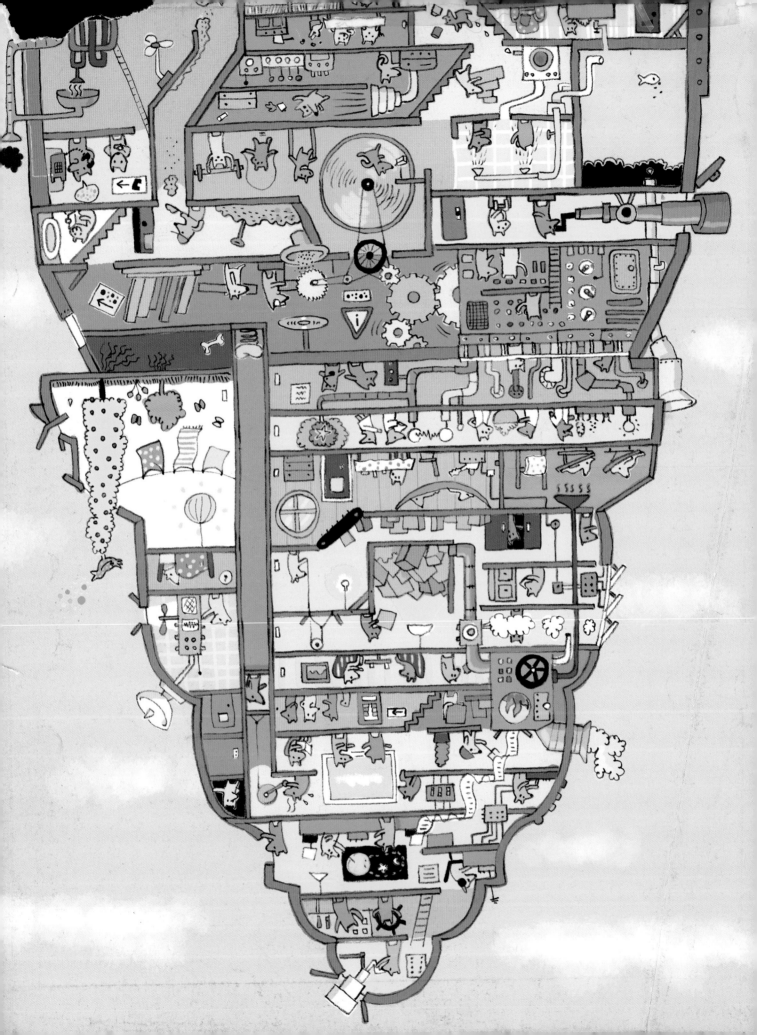

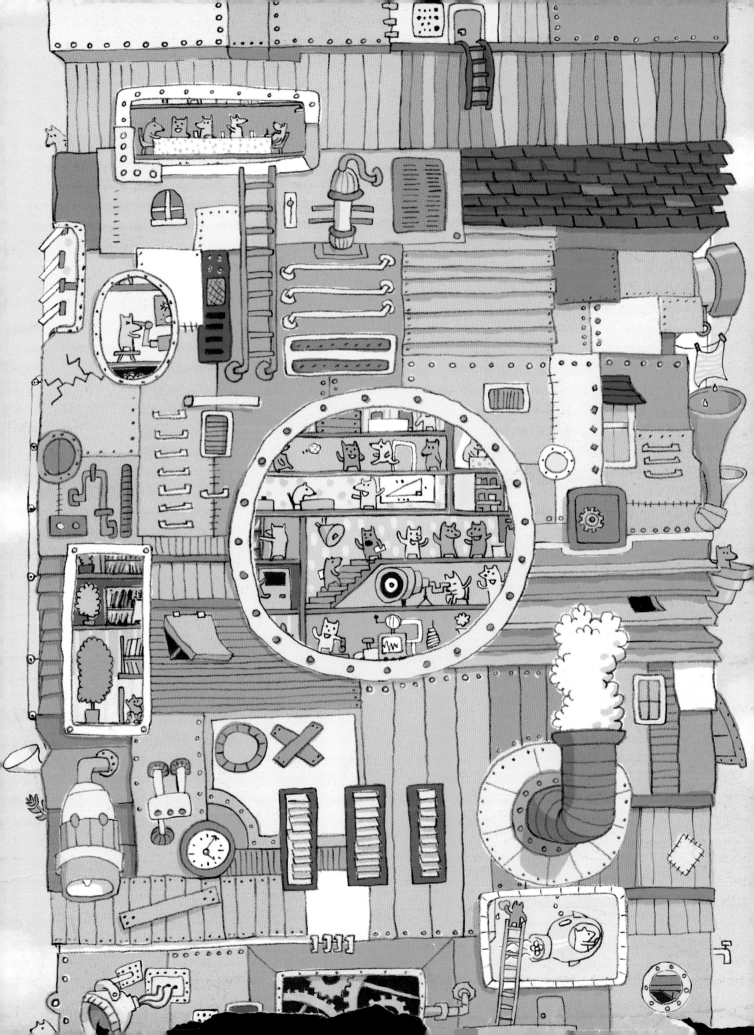

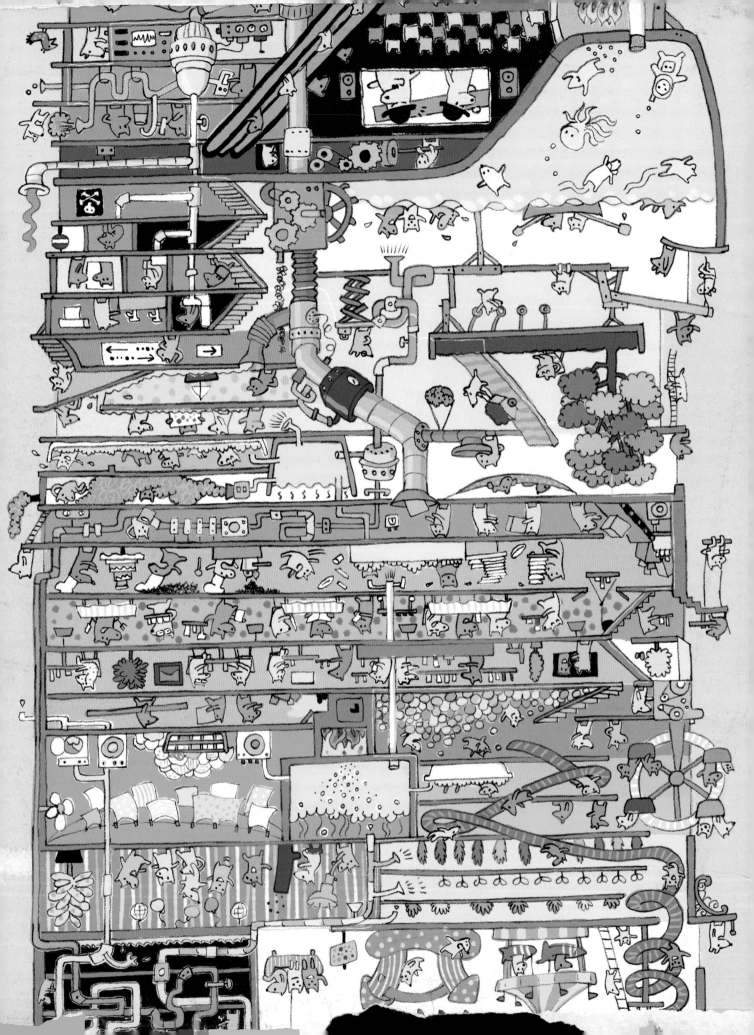

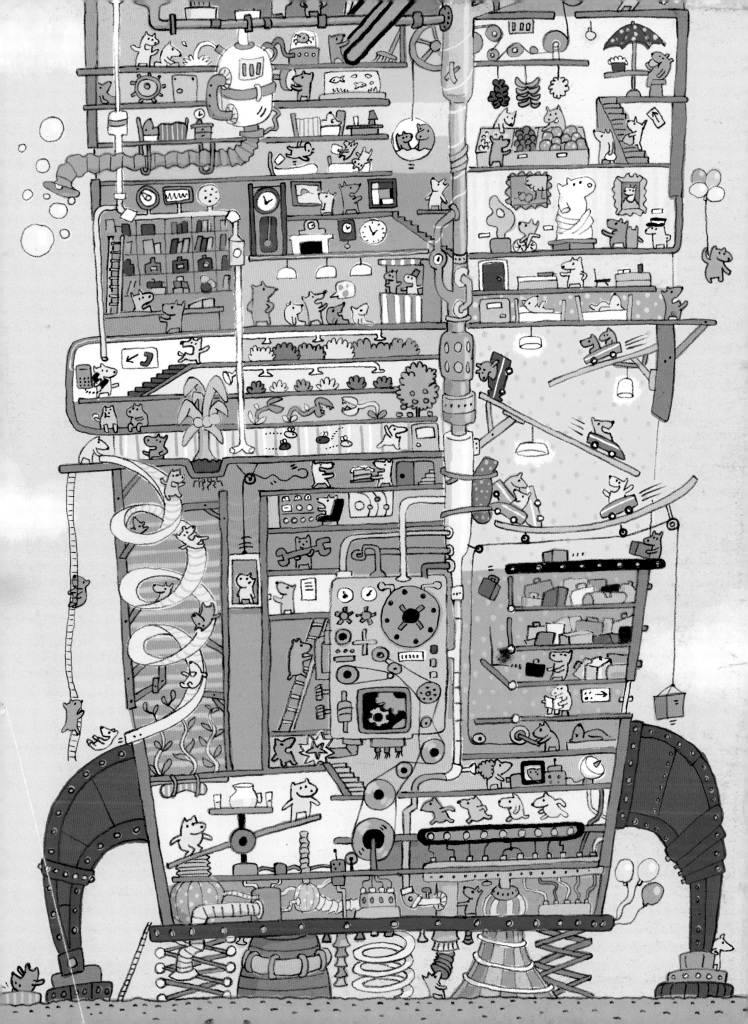

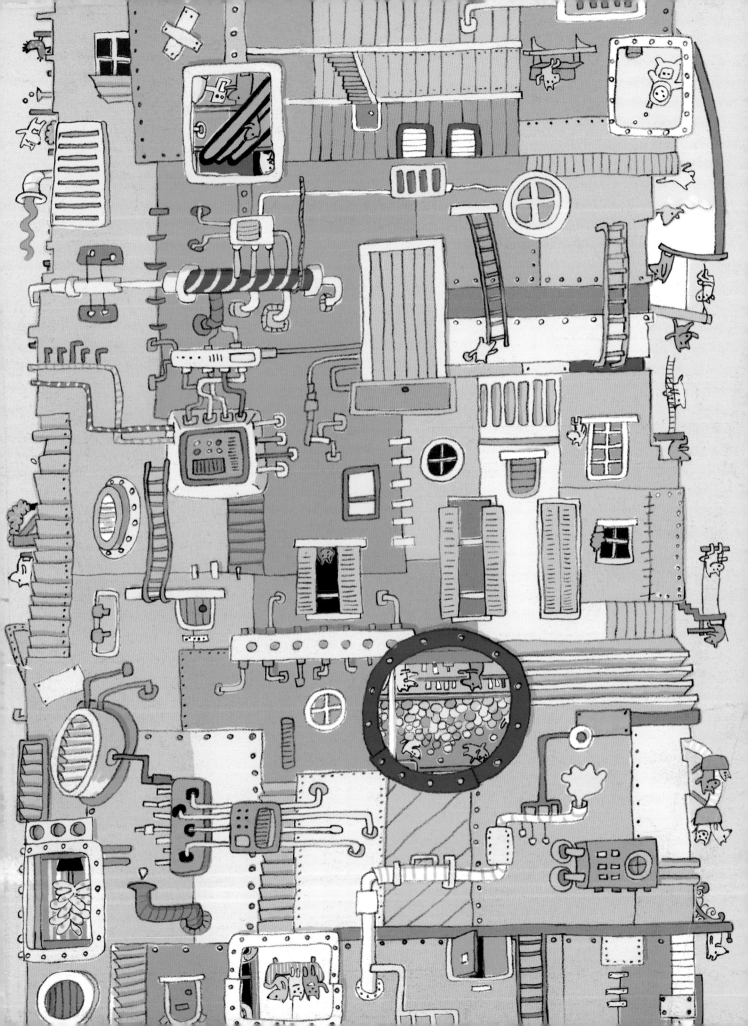

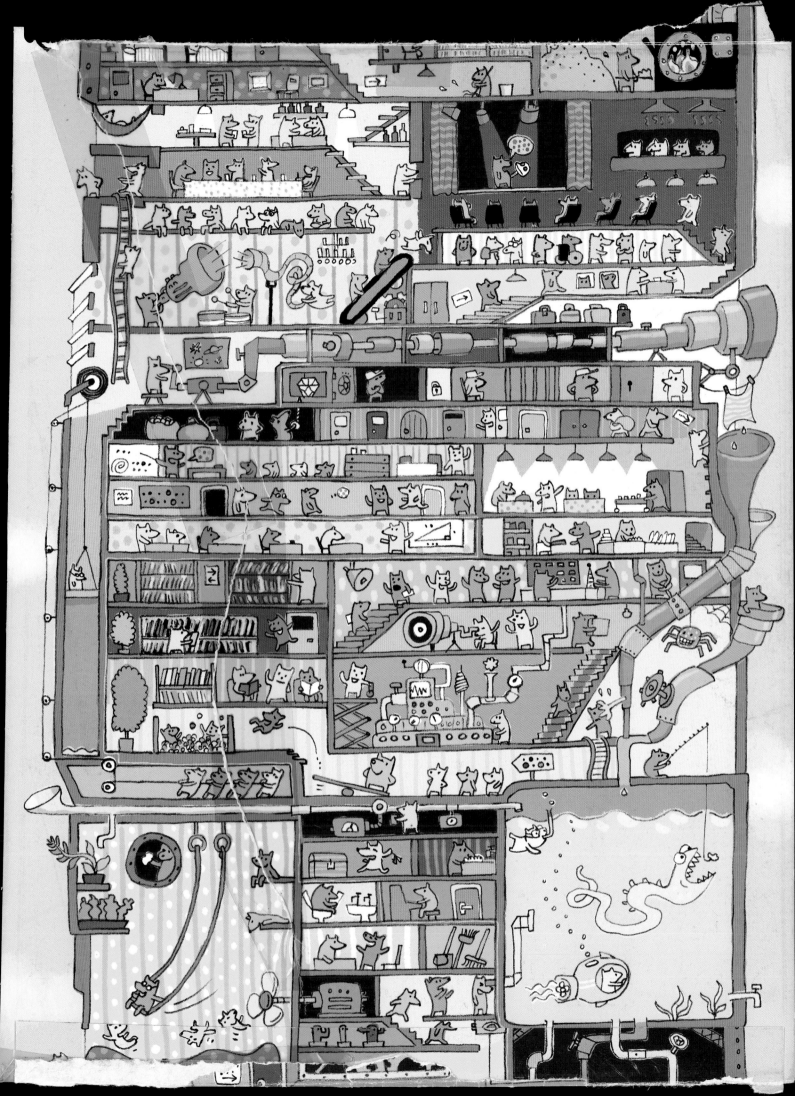

MICROWAVE

M·E·N·U·S

MICROWAVE
M·E·N·U·S

CECILIA NORMAN

First published in 1985 by
Octopus Books Limited
59 Grosvenor Street
London W1

© 1985 Hennerwood Publications Limited
ISBN 0 86273 204 2
Printed in England by
Severn Valley Press Limited

CONTENTS

Notes

1. All spoon measurements are level.
2. All eggs are size 2 or 3 unless otherwise stated.
3. All sugar is granulated unless otherwise stated.
4. Preparation times given are an average calculated during recipe testing.
5. Metric and imperial measurements have been calculated separately. Use one set of measurements only as they are not exact equivalents.
6. Cooking times may vary slightly depending on the output of the microwave cooker, the type and shape of the container used and the temperature of the food, therefore always observe your manufacturer's instructions.
7. The recipes in this book were tested in a cooker with an output of 700 watts. Food will need to be cooked for a few minutes longer in a cooker with a lower output.

INTRODUCTION

MEAL AND MENU PLANNING

Cooking ahead is so much more satisfying when you know the food can be reheated without deterioration. Here the microwave oven comes into its own. At once life becomes easier as the cooking workload can be spread and the final touches, such as combining meat and sauces or reheating, do not necessarily have to be done by the cook but can be completed by the helpers. And once the meal is over any food remaining need not be thrown out, as it can be reheated in the microwave with excellent results.

Meal planning requires a certain amount of care in deciding what goes with what, which dishes can be served cold and which must be hot. You should have a variety of texture and colour and cost must be considered according to the importance of the occasion. It is virtually impossible to plan dishes for a menu without first considering what the microwave oven can cope with as it may not be able to undertake all the cooking required for the whole menu. So to get the most out of the microwave and produce appetizing food, you should use it for all those things that it is best at and combine those processes with conventional cooking where that would be advantageous.

This book of menus will give you a good idea of what the microwave will cook and reheat. Many of the dishes have been prepared ahead of time so that they can be either served cold or reheated and brief instructions on setting about the preparation and serving are given at the start of each menu.

STORAGE

The keeping qualities of various foods both cooked and uncooked are obviously a vital factor in planning specific menus. The microwave oven in conjunction with the freezer considerably widens the range of foods instantly available.

The advance preparation notes with each menu give details of which dishes can be frozen, how long for and how to reheat them.

A refrigerator is an equally important companion to the microwave oven. It is used for short-term storage and storage of items which cannot be frozen but which would deteriorate at room temperature.

Reheating, except for soups, is best done in a microwave oven and although it is preferable to serve immediately after reheating, this is not always possible. In this case it may be more practicable to transfer the reheated food to a conventional oven to maintain the temperature.

HOW THE MICROWAVES WORK

So how does a microwave oven work? Leaving aside the technical details, what you really need to know is how the microwaves affect and cook the food.

It is really very simple. The microwaves, which are invisible, are produced when the electricity supply is connected and the oven is switched on. The microwaves activate the food or liquid particles, so that they move rapidly one against another, causing friction, which in turn causes heating. The longer the microwave oven is switched on, the hotter the particles become, so that eventually cooking takes place. Some kinds of food cook more quickly than others, which is equally true with conventional cooking, for example fish is quick, whereas swede is slow and anything that has to take in water to swell, such as rice, is slow, whereas pasta is quick.

When the microwaves enter the food they have to divide themselves up through the total quantity or weight. Thus if the amount in the microwave oven is small, cooking will be quick but if there is a great volume of food being cooked at one time, this will be relatively slower. Also certain foods attract microwaves more readily than others, for instance microwaves are particularly drawn towards water, fat and sugar.

Cooking times are frequently much faster than conventional cooking times but not in every case. For example one jacket potato may take 4 minutes in the microwave oven, two 7 minutes and six 17 minutes but if you wanted to cook, say, 30 potatoes for a party it would be quicker to cook them all at once in the conventional oven for one hour, as to do them in the microwave oven, six at a time, would take 85 minutes.

All microwave ovens have certain hot and cold areas and this pattern will remain constant in that particular appliance (it is only a matter of the microwaves congregating in clusters in particular spots). Before buying it is not possible to determine exactly where these hot spots will be: they are different in every oven and is not a question of model or type. It is as well to find out where your hot and cold spots are in the oven, so that you can take advantage of them. To do this you need nine ramekins or small dishes of exactly the same size, shape and material. Fill them with exactly the same amount of water at the same starting temperature. Place the dishes evenly spaced on the oven floor or turntable and switch on. In ovens without a turntable, you will be able to see that dishes in the hottest spots will come to the boil first. In those with a turntable you will observe that as the dishes pass through the hot spots bubbles will appear, which subside as the dishes move into a cooler region.

VARIABLE CONTROL

Most microwave ovens have a Defrost setting in addition to Maximum or Full power. Many others are equipped with a selection of power settings enabling a stronger or weaker microwave requirement to be used and allowing greater flexibility in cooking certain foods.

The power levels on microwave ovens are marked in many different ways according to the manufacturer's style. They may be numbered 1 to 10, or have descriptive controls such as Roast, Simmer, Keep Warm and, yet again, on others percentages are used – these you may or may not have to programme yourself. Microwave ovens vary not only in their declared output, i.e. 500 watts, 600 watts, 650 watts or 700 watts, but each model has its own personality and the power level on any setting may vary by 10% above or below, all of which will affect the cooking time.

As a guide to the description of the settings used in this book, Maximum (Full) means 100% on an oven rated 650 to 700 watts; Medium High, 70%; Medium, 50%; Medium Low 35% and Low, 10%. It is important, however, to compare the manufacturer's recommendations for power levels with those given here and adapt according to the terms or numbering given in your own guide book.

The settings of a microwave oven can be compared with a gas or electric oven, where the heat is made more or less intense. In the majority of microwaves, the reduction in energy is achieved by the automatic turning off of the microwaves for a few seconds. The switching on and off has many advantages, for example, when cooking poultry the resting period gives the flesh a chance to relax and when cooking delicate items such as eggs, milk or cheese, the risk of high temperature curdling is reduced.

There is no appreciable difference in the result when using numbers 9 and 10, but some foods do cook more successfully on Medium (50%) whilst others are better on Defrost (35%). Warm (10%) is useful for very delicate defrosting, proving yeast mixtures and keeping food warm. Milk which boils over easily can be controlled by reducing the setting when the milk is seen to rise.

In this book the recipes were tested on our two faster 700 watts ovens, but due to the imponderables mentioned above, the timings will not be totally accurate for every appliance. We used one microwave oven with a turntable and one without and we turned the dishes where even cooking was important. It is worth turning dishes even if they are on a turntable. If the dish is too large to turn, just pushing it slightly to one side, forwards or backwards will all aid the evenness of the cooking. Whenever dishes are covered, this is also noted in the recipe method and the power levels are listed at the beginning of each recipe. Do not change the power during the cooking of each recipe unless instructed to do so in the method.

As I have used my fastest ovens the timings may be shorter than you find necessary, but it is far better to be cautious in the cooking times. You can always put a dish back in the microwave to cook a little longer but overcooking cannot be remedied.

COOKING TECHNIQUES

Though I am totally devoted to microwave cooking, I am realistic enough to take a balanced view of its capabilities. It will not entirely eliminate the use of conventional methods and a conventional cooker in many instances, but a better understanding of the ways in which the microwave works will prove to you just how invaluable it can be.

Microwave cooking is different from conventional cookery in that although you do not have to stand over it, you do have to stand by. Stirring is as important for microwave cookery as it is for conventional and just as food can spoil through lack of care with saucepans burning on the bottom, so can microwaves spoil food in a different way. To avoid this, in addition to stirring, it is necessary to be careful with turning, covering and the greatest mistake is overcooking.

Stirrable dishes, such as soups, stews and vegetables, should be frequently stirred, as microwaves otherwise tend to cook more around the outsides of the dish than in the centre. This is because the outside gets extra power as the microwaves enter from the top and the sides, while the middle receives the microwaves mainly from the top.

Non-stirrable foods should be turned two or three times during cooking, to even out the effect of the hotter and colder areas in the cavity.

Food that cannot be stirred or repositioned should not be cooked in a rectangular dish, as the portions in the corner will overcook, due to the fact that the microwaves enter from both angles as well as from the top. Choose containers which readily hold the food but are not bigger than necessary. Shallow foods must sometimes be arranged in a single layer and fillets of fish or chicken breasts for example will cook quickly because they are so thin, but they must be repositioned during cooking or you will find that the outsides cook while the middle remains raw. Overlapping is only desirable if the food is manageable enough to be repositioned – gammon steaks respond well to this.

Covering foods helps to hasten cooking by trapping the heat and moisture – but because of the rather violent nature of microwave cooking, it is inadvisable to cover too tightly. Starchy liquid from potatoes, high-water content fruits, such as plums or rhubarb, will boil up and over, pushing their way between the lid and the dish. It is a good idea in some instances to place the lid slightly on one side. Cling film will balloon up. It rarely bursts but when cooking is completed, lids will be difficult to lift off and cling film gets sucked down on to the food in the dish. Although cling film does not need to be pierced it should be vented by pulling back one corner before cooking commences.

Sometimes the method for a recipe, such as the Steak and Kidney Pudding on page 71 states that a dish should be covered loosely in cling film. To do this, fix the cling film on one side of the dish, then lift it high above the dish, drawing off twice as much as you would normally use. Fix the other end of the cling film on the opposite side of the dish and allow the cling film to drop into natural folds. If during cooking you find that the folds are sticking together, thus preventing the food from rising, clip them in one or two places with scissors or make a slit in them with a sharp knife.

If the wing tips, legs and thinner parts of poultry, such as the breast become dark in colour or appear to be drying up, they should be covered with small pieces of aluminium foil (provided the manufacturer of your microwave recommends its use), then overwrapped with cling film to shield the foil. Make all the usual tests for cooking but do this in several places instead of the usual one. Thick items should be turned over halfway through cooking. This applies both to joints of meat and also to jacket potatoes and large baked apples.

Foods that you wish to keep as crisp as possible should be covered only by greaseproof paper or paper towels. Paper towels can also be used underneath rolls, bread or pastry, when they are being defrosted or warmed, to absorb the excess moisture.

To keep food hot while standing outside the microwave, it is sometimes covered with foil. To do this make a tent out of the foil but put a small slit in the top to allow steam to escape, otherwise the condensation will drop back and soften the food. Jacket potatoes, however, are best wrapped in a clean ovenglove or teatowel when standing, to keep their skins crisp.

One difference between cooking on the hob and cooking in a microwave is that in the first the container heats up to such an extent that it is sufficient to continue cooking food after the gas or electricity has been turned off. Containers in a microwave should only become hot if they are in prolonged contact with hot food (see page 10). To allow for this, undercook rather than overcook food, so that after a short standing time, the food can be tested and if necessary further cooking undertaken.

Because the microwave oven is slow to heat water-based liquids (apart from milk), soups should be cooked in concentrated form and extra liquid added afterwards or use *hot* stock or water to start with.

Vegetables normally requiring water in cooking need only half a cup of water in the microwave oven. Salt the water but do not sprinkle salt directly on the vegetables.

When pieces are cut up uniformly or sliced thinly they will cook more quickly whether by conventional or microwave means, thus a food processor can be a particularly useful adjunct.

If your microwave oven is fitted with a turntable you will find spills are contained by the raised edge but some ovens have a fitted shelf which is level. In this case any spills must be wiped up immediately. The reason for this is that although spillage is a nuisance in any case, the microwaves cannot tell the difference between the food and the wasted liquid and will continue to cook the residue, baking it on to the shelf.

LIMITATIONS
The microwave will carry out most cooking processes that are otherwise done conventionally. It will take the place of the hob for boiling, steaming and poaching and for cooking most foods in liquid in a saucepan. It will not, however, deep fry, because the temperature of the fat cannot be adequately controlled and the risk of fire will be dangerously high. Shallow frying is also not possible because the microwaves will cook the fat and the food simultaneously – in conventional cookery the fat seals the food first and cooking is completed by conduction.

Microwave frying is a special kind of cooking requiring the use of a treated dish, which is specially designed to become very hot and transmit this heat to the underside of the food. Microwave frying, being unique, keeps fat absorption to the minimum.

Grilling must be carried out conventionally, but the baking, braising and casseroling of most foods is both fast and successful in the microwave oven.

On the whole, the microwave oven should be used for cooking moderate quantities – that is to say up to four to six portions at a time. This will involve a saving in fuel particularly when heating liquids – you have to cover the element of most kettles with water so that you probably are heating more than you need. It is not more economical to heat large quantities of a large weight of high density vegetables in the microwave. It would be just as quick or quicker to do this in a saucepan – but the colour, of course, will not be as bright and there will be a greater loss of vitamins due to the higher proportion of water used. However, do not put very small quantities into the microwave, for example, don't try to blanch one onion. The microwave power would be too strong for this and may cause sparks.

The microwave oven cannot cook foods that have to be crisp outside and soft inside. If you are reheating crisp foods, such as chips, make sure that they are covered with a paper towel and not cling film, which would cause softening.

USING THE RECIPES
In common with other forms of cookery, the progress of the cooking is determined by the look and sometimes the feel of the food: you cannot rely solely on the timings given in any book. When making sauces look for a thickening band of sauce around the edge of the bowl and each time this appears open the door and stir the sauce briskly. Fish will change colour and if it appears white outside, yet glassy in the centre, turn the pieces over, cover and rest the fish before continuing cooking. There is hardly ever any harm done to the food if you open the door, look, make any adjustments necessary, close the door, then continue with the cooking.

The chapters within this book are designed to serve a specific number of people but the recipes may be adapted within certain limitations using the following guidelines.

When reducing or increasing quantities of food, cooking times cannot be exactly halved or doubled. There is little difference in the time taken to melt, say, one or two ounces of butter or a small or large lump of chocolate, but a double quantity of vegetables will need nearer twice as long. As a general rule when doubling a recipe, increase the cooking time by 75% and when quadrupling, increase by 225%. For example if one quantity takes one minute, then double will take $1\frac{3}{4}$ minutes and fourfold will take $3\frac{1}{4}$ minutes. When reducing allow half the time plus a little e.g. if one quantity takes 4 minutes, half the quantity will take approximately $2\frac{1}{2}$ minutes and a quarter the quantity will take $1\frac{1}{2}$ minutes.

Where possible use smaller or larger dishes when reducing or increasing the quantity and small dishes should be turned during cooking even when the oven is fitted with a turntable.

If you have prepared part of the menu in advance, the microwave oven, set on Low (10%) will keep food hot for one hour or if fitted with the probe, will automatically keep food at a given temperature for about the same length of time.

Microwaves cook shallow items more quickly, so that gravy around the food will dry up and congeal while larger items in the middle may remain quite cool. Therefore when reheating dishes which consist of solids and liquids always use a container which just fits, for otherwise the gravy will separate and run away from the food to the side of the plate. This is equally important when using the microwave for defrosting.

Another technique when reheating is to put the thicker density items towards the outside of the dish or plate and remember that items that take longer to cook will also take longer to reheat.

CONTAINERS
Containers have a great influence on the evenness of cooking and on the cooking times. They must be made of a material suitable for the microwaves to pass through and not include those that will react to microwaves.

Glazed pottery and china are excellent choices for use in the microwave provided that they do not have any metal decoration or printing above or underneath. However, some pottery has impurities in its manufacture and even a small fleck of metal may cause problems. To test for this put the empty dish in the microwave together with a glass half-filled with water. Switch on for about 30 seconds. If after this the water is hotter than the dish, then the dish is safe to use. If the dish is hotter it is not safe. If they are the same temperature, then the dish is not suitable for prolonged heating, but may be used for short periods of, say, 2 minutes.

Plastic dishes and containers now being sold specifically for microwave use have various advantages but have disadvantages too. The main advantage is that foods can cook more quickly as there is no obstruction to prevent the microwaves readily reaching them. The disadvantage is that the containers can become soft and distort from the effects of hot liquids following prolonged cooking. Most plastics will develop holes and sear if very hot fats or sugar syrups are cooked in them. Also, some plastic containers discolour if coloured substances, such as tomato sauces, are prepared in them.

Plastics are only suitable for microwaving when they can stand up to average cooking temperatures. Generally speaking you can use them for warming food.

Foam dishes should not be used because there is a

possibility that they will melt. Foam also acts as an insulator, slowing down thawing if you attempt to defrost on dishes of this material.

Boilable plastics often sold in the form of pudding basins are excellent for all cooking, except when sugar or fat are in the ingredients.

There are ranges of thermo-plastics that can be used in the conventional oven, the microwave or the freezer and are indestructible unless dropped on a hard floor. Paper containers are also available, specially treated, so that they too can be used both in the microwave and a cool-to-medium conventional oven. Check the manufacturer's instructions before using.

Heat-resistant clear glass basins and mixing bowls are ideal for microwaving. A 2.8 litre (5 pint) bowl can be used to make about 2 kg (5 lb) jam or enough soup to serve twelve. Like any other product they will break if misused, for example placed on an ice-cold surface when just having been used for making caramel. Most ovenglass and ceramics are not suitable for use under the conventional grill and plastic and paper must *never* be used for this type of browning.

Specially designed glass ceramic ware is now available which is suitable for the microwave, the freezer, the refrigerator and on the hob as well as at a suitable distance under the grill. But remember that you should not put a small dish on the hob because the heat on either side would make it impossible to lift.

All forms of metal are excluded because items which have a metal trim will damage the magnetron (the microwave source) and possibly the oven lining. This is immediately detectable because sparks occur audibly and visibly. Secondly, dense metal, such as stainless steel, cast iron and enamelled dishes, do not allow microwaves to pass through them, so that food contained inside will not heat. Beware of casseroles that appear to be ceramic, when in fact they are enamelled cast iron. These should not be used.

Never use any container having metal in it and this includes lead crystal, gilt-edged glass and staples (sometimes used to secure straw baskets). Never use metal tags from polythene bags. The only time that aluminium foil can be used is to shield parts of the food, that would otherwise overcook and this can only be done provided your manufacturer's instruction book confirms its use. The aluminium foil is of a higher density metal than the fine particles of metal decorating plates or twist-ties and therefore can be used. The pieces of aluminium foil must not touch the sides of the oven. If in doubt, you can overwrap with cling film or greaseproof paper. When aluminium foil is used to shield the top of food, it is unlikely that it will reach anywhere near the top oven lining, but it must not stick up in a twisted point as this turns it into a sort of lightning conductor which will cause sparking. Aluminium foil dishes, provided they are shallow (less than 2 cm (1 inch) deep), are completely filled with food and fit in with all the other requirements of using metal in the microwave, are safe, but any foil lid must first be removed. Sometimes ready-prepared dishes are sold in a foil dish inside a cardboard carton. To use these, take out the foil dish and remove the lid, then replace the foil dish in the carton but leave one end open. The cardboard will help to hold in the heat, making reheating faster but will also protect the foil. As described above for small foil pieces used to shield food, the foil carton must not touch the sides of the oven.

See-through roasting bags both hold in the heat and enhance browning, particularly if they are domed, so that the bag is not in direct contact with the food. Use them for poultry, when you will find it convenient to split the bag open to make a kind of tent, or use it for vegetables, sealing the top loosely with an elastic band. You must leave a sizeable gap at the neck of the bag for steam to escape.

Whenever you cook in a roasting bag make sure that it is resting on a lipped shelf or removable plate, because the bag becomes very hot and limp due to the heat from the contents and spillage can occur as you take it from the microwave.

Paper is useful as a covering, e.g. greaseproof, non-stick silicone and paper towels which will also absorb excess fat and moisture. Cling film is now regularly used for microwave cookery and also for freezer wrapping. When using it for cooking it should be vented to prevent ballooning, see page 8. Cling film wraps snugly around all but plastic dishes. If you wish to use it in conjunction with these, you will have to wrap it so that the cling film overlaps and sticks to itself. Buy a large or catering pack if you are going to do a lot of microwaving. The weight of the pack ensures that it will remain steady when you tear off the cling film and this makes it much easier to use.

The shapes and sizes of dishes also have a marked effect on both the evenness and the speed of the cooking. Deep-sided dishes slow down the cooking times because the microwaves get weaker as they go through the food. They also allow room for boiling liquids and their rounded sides make it easy to stir and mix the ingredients thoroughly.

Shallow dishes are useful when little liquid is involved and also when drier results are needed, but moist items can be cooked in shallow dishes provided they are suitably covered. Casseroles also have their uses and a large chicken roasting dish with shallow lid is essential.

Always use deep dishes when making crumbles, for dishes with toppings which cover the food, such as Shepherd's Pie, and particularly when the base food is watery. Use jugs and bowls that are large enough to contain the food even after they have boiled up. Cake dishes should only be two-thirds filled.

When making cakes, quiches or custards choose ring moulds, round dishes no more than 23 cm (9 inches) in diameter or rectangles that are about twice as long as they are wide. Cakes and tarts cannot easily be unmoulded when freshly cooked but after freezing they turn out without any trouble.

It is inadvisable to leave utensils, such as wooden spoons, in the bowl while cooking in the microwave oven. Painted wood handles will crack and the handles of ordinary wooden spoons can become very hot due to residual moisture or grease that has become ingrained. Plastic spoons may melt but there is a special range of utensils specifically designed for microwave use.

MENUS
FOR
ONE

The recipes in this chapter are all designed for one serving but they can all be increased to serve more if you wish, see page 9
As described, you must allow more time and possibly use larger containers when increasing the recipes. When individual items are being cooked at the same time they must be turned during cooking.
If you have freezer space many of the recipes in the other chapters can be served as meals for one – just cook as directed and freeze in small portions. Food for one need no longer be boring and tedious to prepare. With a little forethought you can have a different menu every night and have the bonus of enjoying even faster reheating.

BABY'S MENUS

LUNCH

FILLET OF PLAICE WITH TOMATO

GROUND RICE PUDDING

DINNER

CHICKEN AND VEGETABLE DINNER

MASHED BANANA

These menus are designed for a baby aged about 6 months.
The fish dish can be prepared up to the end of step 2 three hours
before cooking and chilled.
Ground Rice Pudding can be made in advance. Add a few tablespoons
of homogenized milk, then reheat to boiling point and allow to cool
before serving.
The Chicken and Vegetable Dinner can be prepared in advance in a
larger quantity if preferred and frozen in suitable portions. Store for up
to 1 month. Reheat on Maximum (Full), stirring every 15 seconds to
make sure the hot and cold parts of the dinner are equally mixed. Test
the temperature before offering to the baby.
The banana is quick to prepare and must be mashed at the time of
serving as it discolours on standing.
Although you can freeze food in sterilized glass baby food jars, only
three-quarters fill the jars to allow for expansion. Do not put lidded jars
in the microwave oven. Baby foods for freezing can also be sealed in
special bags using a bag sealer. Slit the pouch before heating and turn
the food into a small bowl as soon as it is manageable.

FILLET OF PLAICE WITH TOMATO

PREPARATION TIME: *5 minutes*
COOKING TIME: *1 minute*
MICROWAVE SETTING: *Maximum (Full)*

1 × 50g (2oz) piece of
fresh plaice fillet, skinned
1 tomato, skinned

Make absolutely sure there are no bones in the fish fillet.

1. Put the plaice fillet on a saucer.
2. Seed and chop the tomato and spread over the fillet.
3. Cover with cling film, pulling back one corner to vent and cook for 45 seconds. Leave to stand for 1 minute, then carefully remove the cling film and test to see if the fish is completely cooked in the centre. Give an additional 20 seconds' cooking time if required.
4. Mash, chop finely or press through a sieve according to the baby's age.

GROUND RICE PUDDING

PREPARATION TIME: *5 minutes*
COOKING TIME: *4 minutes, plus standing*
MICROWAVE SETTING: *Maximum (Full); then Medium Low (35%)*
MAKES 5 TABLESPOONS

6 tablespoons homogenized milk	*$\frac{1}{2}$ teaspoon caster sugar*
	pinch of nutmeg
2 teaspoons ground rice	*$\frac{1}{8}$ teaspoon butter*

1. Mix the ingredients thoroughly together in a 1.2 litre (2 pint) basin and cook on Maximum (Full) for 1 minute or until boiling.
2. Stir, then reduce the setting to Medium Low (35%) and cook for 3 minutes.
3. Stir, then cover and leave to stand for 5 minutes. Stir again before serving.

CHICKEN AND VEGETABLE DINNER

PREPARATION TIME: *10 minutes*
COOKING TIME: *5 minutes*
MICROWAVE SETTING: *Maximum (Full)*
MAKES 100g (4oz) OR 4 TABLESPOONS

75g (3oz) raw chicken breast, skinned and diced	*1 small carrot, peeled and finely chopped*
100g (4oz) potato, peeled and diced into 5mm ($\frac{1}{4}$ inch) cubes	*3 tablespoons water*

1. Combine the ingredients in a 1.2 litre (2 pint) bowl. Cover with cling film and cook for 5 minutes, stirring once during cooking.
2. Purée or chop finely and sieve. (F)

MASHED BANANA

PREPARATION TIME: *5 minutes*
NO COOKING REQUIRED

1 ripe banana
$\frac{1}{2}$ teaspoon orange juice

1. Peel the banana and mash with the orange juice.

Top: Fillet of plaice with tomato; Ground rice pudding; bottom: Mashed banana; Chicken and vegetable dinner

TODDLER'S TREAT

FISH FINGERS, BAKED BEANS AND MASHED POTATO

BLACKCURRANT AND APPLE DUNK DESSERT

The potato may be prepared ahead of time and kept chilled but the fish fingers must be cooked directly from frozen.
Do not leave any remaining baked beans in the can but store in a covered bowl in the refrigerator.
The blackcurrant dessert may be prepared several hours in advance but if it is going to stand for any length of time, add extra milk when cooking. The apple can be put in at the last minute.

FISH FINGERS, BAKED BEANS AND MASHED POTATO

PREPARATION TIME: *5 minutes*
COOKING TIME: *about 6 minutes*
MICROWAVE SETTING: *Maximum (Full)*

1 × 100g (4 oz) potato
2 fish fingers
2 tablespoons baked beans in tomato sauce
2 teaspoons milk

1. Scrub and dry the potato and prick thoroughly. Put on a paper towel and cook for 2 minutes. Turn the potato over and cook for a further 1½ minutes or until soft.
2. Put the fish fingers and baked beans on a plate and cover the baked beans with cling film. Cook for 1 minute. Leave to stand while finishing the potato.
3. Peel the potato and mash with the milk. Place on the fish finger plate.
4. Without removing the cling film from the baked beans, replace the plate in the microwave and heat for 30 seconds. Test to make sure that the fish fingers are cooked and the potato and beans are at a suitable temperature before serving.

Fish fingers, baked beans and mashed potato; Blackcurrant and apple dunk dessert

BLACKCURRANT AND APPLE DUNK DESSERT

PREPARATION TIME: *5 minutes*
COOKING TIME: *about 3 minutes, plus cooling*
MICROWAVE SETTING: *Maximum (Full)*
MAKES 6 TABLESPOONS

7 tablespoons cold milk
2 teaspoons custard powder

4 teaspoons concentrated blackcurrant drink
1 sweet dessert apple

1. Put 6 tablespoons of the milk in a 1.2 litre (2 pint) basin and cook for 1 minute or until steaming.
2. Blend the custard powder with the remaining milk and 2 teaspoons of the blackcurrant drink. Pour into the hot milk and cook for 2 minutes, stirring twice during cooking. (It is important to cook for the full length of time to eliminate any powdery taste.)
3. Beat in the remaining 2 teaspoons of blackcurrant drink and leave to cool, stirring once or twice during cooling to prevent a skin forming.
4. Quarter and core the apple, peel if preferred and cut into bite-size pieces. Stir into the custard. To eat, scoop out the piece of apple with a spoon. This dessert is also pleasant cold. To prevent a skin forming cover tightly with cling film, pressing it against the surface of the custard.

SOUP PLUS

VERMICELLI SOUP

WELSH RAREBIT WITH BACON

MINTED GREEN PEAS

The Vermicelli Soup can be prepared ahead of time. Reheat for 3 minutes in a partly covered bowl and stir thoroughly before serving. It may be necessary to add a little extra stock to thin the soup.
Cook the bacon rashers, then set the peas to cook.
Meanwhile toast the bread and prepare the cheese topping.
Complete the cheese topping after the peas are removed from the microwave oven, then pile on to the toast and slip the bacon on top. Drain the peas and serve.

VERMICELLI SOUP

PREPARATION TIME: *5 minutes*
COOKING TIME: *7 minutes, plus standing*
MICROWAVE SETTING: *Maximum (Full)*

300ml (½ pint) well-flavoured chicken stock	*salt*
50g (2oz) vermicelli	*freshly ground black pepper*
½ teaspoon soy sauce	*chopped parsley, to garnish*

1. Pour the stock into a medium bowl, partly cover with cling film and cook until boiling, about 3 minutes.
2. Stir in the vermicelli, three-quarters cover and cook for 4 minutes without stirring.
3. Carefully uncover, stir in the soy sauce and add salt and pepper. Leave to stand for 3–4 minutes before serving, garnished with chopped parsley.

WELSH RAREBIT WITH BACON

PREPARATION TIME: *about 5 minutes*
COOKING TIME: *about 5 minutes, plus browning*
MICROWAVE SETTING: *Maximum (Full); then Medium Low (35%)*

2 bacon rashers	*pinch of mustard powder*
1 thick slice bread, freshly toasted	*few drops Worcestershire sauce*
1 tablespoon milk	*75g (3oz) grated stale cheese*
½ egg yolk or 1 yolk (size 5)	

1. Snip the rind off the bacon to prevent it from curling during cooking and place on a plate or piece of greaseproof paper, cover with a paper towel and cook for about 30 seconds per rasher. Remove from the paper immediately to prevent sticking and set aside.
2. To prepare the cheese topping, combine the milk, egg yolk, mustard powder and Worcestershire sauce and stir until thoroughly blended. Mix in the cheese, reduce the setting to Medium Low (35%) and cook for 1 minute, then stir. The cheese should not be completely melted.
3. Pile the cheese on the toast, then snip the bacon into small pieces and sprinkle on top. Brown under a preheated conventional grill and serve at once.

MINTED GREEN PEAS

PREPARATION TIME: *1 minute*
COOKING TIME: *4 minutes*
MICROWAVE SETTING: *Maximum (Full)*

7 tablespoons water	*75g (3oz) frozen petit pois*
¼ teaspoon salt	*1 sprig fresh or frozen mint*

1. Put the water into a small dish and stir in the salt.
2. Add the peas and the mint sprig, cover with cling film, pulling back one corner to vent and cook for 4 minutes. The peas will keep hot for a few minutes provided the cling film is not removed. When ready to serve, pull back the cling film and drain or remove with a slotted spoon.

Vermicelli soup; Welsh rarebit with bacon; Minted green peas

PACKED LUNCH

GOLDEN CHICKEN DRUMSTICKS

MIXED SALAD†

PINWHEEL COOKIES

HOT DRINKING CHOCOLATE

Cook the Pinwheel Cookies up to a week ahead of time and store in an airtight container. Wrap tightly in foil an hour or two ahead of time. Cook the drumsticks up to 12 hours in advance, cover and chill.
†Serving suggestion
Prepare the mixed salad including lettuce, cucumber, cress, tomatoes and quartered hard-boiled egg a few hours ahead of time or overnight and store covered in the bottom of the refrigerator. For extra speed the drumsticks and salad can be put into a picnic box ready for serving. Prepare the Hot Drinking Chocolate at the last minute.

GOLDEN CHICKEN DRUMSTICKS

PREPARATION TIME: *about 4 minutes*
COOKING TIME: *about 3 minutes*
MICROWAVE SETTING: *Maximum (Full)*

2 × 90g (3½oz) drumsticks, rinsed and dried	*¼ teaspoon mustard powder*
10g (¼oz) butter, softened	*¼ teaspoon salt*
1 teaspoon paprika	

1. Rub the drumsticks with butter and sprinkle on all sides with a mixture of paprika, mustard and salt.
2. Arrange in a small dish, making sure that a thin end is next to a thick end. Cook, uncovered, for 3 minutes.
3. Cool rapidly, then place in the picnic box with a mixed salad (see preparation notes).

PINWHEEL COOKIES

PREPARATION TIME: *about 10 minutes*
COOKING TIME: *about 4 minutes, plus cooling*
MICROWAVE SETTING: *Maximum (Full)*

100g (4oz) soft margarine	*1 teaspoon coffee essence*
50g (2oz) caster sugar	*1 tablespoon cocoa powder, sifted*
150g (5oz) plain flour	

1. Beat the margarine and sugar together in a mixing bowl with a wooden spoon, then gradually sift in the flour and mix to a fairly firm dough.
2. Roll out half the dough between sheets of greaseproof paper to a 15 × 15 cm (6 × 6 inch) square.
3. Knead the coffee essence and cocoa powder into the remaining dough. Roll out in a similar way.
4. Place the unflavoured square on top of the chocolate section and roll up Swiss roll fashion. Cut into 18 slices.
5. Cut a large circle of greaseproof or non-stick silicone paper to fit a turntable or into the microwave oven. Place on the oven shelf and arrange 9 of the pinwheels around the outside edge. Cook for 3 minutes, then test with a cocktail stick which should come out clean. Cook the remaining biscuits in the same way. Cook for a further 30 seconds if necessary. During cooking the pinwheels puff up and spread.
6. Leave until cool, then separate the biscuits and, if preferred, sandwich with jam, melted chocolate or cream. The pinwheels are delicious as they are and can be kept in a sealed container for a few weeks. Should they have softened, they can be crisped in the microwave oven, allowing about 20 seconds for 6 biscuits.

HOT DRINKING CHOCOLATE

PREPARATION TIME: *1 minute*
COOKING TIME: *about 2½ minutes*
MICROWAVE SETTING: *Maximum (Full)*

300ml (½ pint) milk
2–3 tablespoons powdered drinking chocolate

1. Put the milk in a large jug or lipped bowl and heat for 1½ minutes.
2. Whisk in the powdered chocolate. Cook for a further 30–60 seconds or until the milk is boiling. (It is important to use a large jug or bowl because milk rises considerably when boiling.)
3. Whisk the drink once more, then pour into a heated vacuum flask.

Hot drinking chocolate; Pinwheel cookies; Golden chicken drumsticks and mixed salad

FAST FARE

CHILLI CON CARNE

POTATO IN ITS JACKET

CHINESE LEAF SALAD AND FRENCH DRESSING

CHOCOLATE BLANCMANGE

Prepare the blancmange ahead of time. Cover to prevent a skin forming and chill in the dessert dish.
Prepare the French dressing in an individual salad bowl in advance. Add the shredded leaves and toss just before serving.
Cook the potato in its jacket just before the meal. Then wrap in a clean cloth to keep it hot while the Chilli con Carne is cooking. The Chilli con Carne can also be cooked ahead of time and refrigerated. Reheat on Maximum (Full) in a small cereal bowl, covered and vented, for about 3–4 minutes if starting from cold.
Precook the potato in its jacket and keep chilled. Reheat for 3 minutes. A whole potato can be left uncovered but if the potato has been halved and ready mashed, cover the top with cling film.

CHILLI CON CARNE

PREPARATION TIME: *5 minutes*
COOKING TIME: *about 8 minutes*
MICROWAVE SETTING: *Maximum (Full)*

½ onion, finely chopped	1 tablespoon tomato purée
¼ green pepper, cored, seeded and diced	pinch of dried basil
	1–2 pinches chilli powder
75 g (3 oz) minced raw beef	salt
	freshly ground black pepper
3 tablespoons fully cooked canned red kidney beans	cucumber twist, to garnish
2 tablespoons liquid from the can	

1. Put the onion and green pepper into a 1.2 litre (2 pint) pudding basin and cook for 2 minutes to soften.
2. Add the minced beef, kidney beans, bean liquid, tomato purée, basil and chilli powder to taste. Stir thoroughly, then three-quarters cover with cling film and cook for 5–6 minutes or until the beef is cooked and the mixture is still moist.
3. Remove the cling film, add salt and pepper to taste and serve hot, garnished with the cucumber.

POTATO IN ITS JACKET

PREPARATION TIME: *5 minutes*
COOKING TIME: *about 4 minutes*
MICROWAVE SETTING: *Maximum (Full)*

1 even-shaped 175 g (6 oz) potato, scrubbed and dried	salt
	freshly ground black pepper
butter or margarine	watercress sprigs, to garnish

Jacket potatoes will keep hot for at least 30 minutes provided they are wrapped. During this standing time they will soften further. If standing for more than 5 minutes, reduce the cooking time by about 1 minute.

1. Prick the potato thoroughly and deeply. Put on a paper towel and cook for 4 minutes, then squeeze gently on top and bottom. If parts of the potato are still hard, turn it over and cook for a further minute.
2. Halve the potato, mash with butter or margarine and sprinkle with salt and pepper. Garnish with watercress.

Left to right: Chilli con carne; Chocolate blancmange; Potato in its jacket; Chinese leaf salad and French dressing

CHINESE LEAF SALAD AND FRENCH DRESSING

PREPARATION TIME: *5 minutes*
NO COOKING REQUIRED

1 tablespoon salad oil	$\frac{1}{4}$ teaspoon freshly ground
1 teaspoon wine vinegar	black pepper
$\frac{1}{4}$ teaspoon salt	2–3 Chinese leaves

Chinese leaves are an ideal salad ingredient as they will keep in the bottom of the refrigerator for about a week. They provide a good texture contrast to the chilli and jacket potato. Substitute cos lettuce leaves if a Chinese cabbage is unavailable.

1. Combine the oil, vinegar, salt and pepper in an individual salad bowl. Cover and set aside until required.
2. Shred the Chinese leaves just before serving. Beat the salad dressing in the bowl with a fork, add the leaves, toss to coat evenly and serve at once.

CHOCOLATE BLANCMANGE

PREPARATION TIME: *5 minutes*
COOKING TIME: *1$\frac{1}{2}$ minutes*
MICROWAVE SETTING: *Maximum (Full)*

3 teaspoons cornflour	$\frac{1}{4}$ teaspoon vanilla essence
1 teaspoon cocoa powder	$\frac{1}{2}$ teaspoon butter
2 teaspoons caster sugar	strips of orange, to
150ml ($\frac{1}{4}$ pint) milk	decorate

This can be served hot but will be more custard-like.

1. Blend the cornflour, cocoa and sugar together in a large jug or 900ml (1$\frac{1}{2}$ pint) pudding basin. Gradually stir in the milk, adding the vanilla essence. Cook, uncovered, for 1 minute. Stir and cook for a further 30 seconds or until the mixture thickens. Stir briskly, then mix in the butter.
2. Pour the blancmange into an individual dish, cover with cling film to prevent a skin forming and put in a cool place to set. Decorate with orange strips before serving.

TV DINNER

SCRAMBLED EGG WITH CHEESE AND HAM

MIXED DICED VEGETABLES

APPLE CHARLOTTE

Prepare the Apple Charlotte in advance but do not cook. Cover the ramekin tightly with foil to prevent the apple from blackening. Cook to the end of step 3 while eating the main course, then brown under the grill just before serving. Alternatively, cook completely and brown just before the meal, then reheat, uncovered, for 30 seconds before serving.

Prepare the ingredients for the scrambled egg and combine the eggs, milk, salt, pepper and butter just before the meal.

Cook the vegetables first, then complete the scrambled egg dish while the vegetables are standing and before they are drained.

SCRAMBLED EGG WITH CHEESE AND HAM

PREPARATION TIME: *about 5 minutes*
COOKING TIME: *about 2 minutes*
MICROWAVE SETTING: *Maximum (Full)*

2 eggs	1 teaspoon butter
2 tablespoons milk	25 g (1 oz) slice lean
salt	cooked ham, diced
freshly ground black	25 g (1 oz) grated one-day
pepper	old cheese

1. Break the eggs into a 600 ml (1 pint) jug or bowl. Beat in the milk, then add salt and pepper to taste and the butter.
2. Cook for 1 minute, then stir vigorously, breaking up the bracelet of egg that forms around the sides of the mixture.
3. Stir in the ham. Cook for 1 minute, stir in the cheese and cook for a further 15 seconds, or until the egg is cooked to the desired consistency. Do not overcook as the egg will continue to coagulate over the next 30–60 seconds. Serve on a warmed plate with Mixed Diced Vegetables.

MIXED DICED VEGETABLES

PREPARATION TIME: *30 seconds (frozen mixed vegetables); about 5 minutes (fresh mixed vegetables)*
COOKING TIME: *4 minutes, plus standing (fresh or frozen)*
MICROWAVE SETTING: *Maximum (Full)*

100 g (4 oz) mixed diced	salt
vegetables, fresh or frozen	freshly ground black
(see below)	pepper
sprig fresh mint or thyme	1 teaspoon butter
6 tablespoons water	(optional)

Use a combination of any of the following vegetables cut into small equal-sized portions, so that they will cook evenly; carrots, peas, runner beans, potatoes, sweetcorn, red and green pepper.

1. Put the vegetables, sprig of herbs and water in a 600 ml (1 pint) jug or basin, cover with cling film, pulling back one corner to vent and cook for about 4 minutes. Leave to stand for 2 minutes, then drain carefully.
2. Remove the cling film, discard the sprig of herbs, add salt and pepper to taste and stir in the butter if liked.

If using vegetables in a sealed microwave-proof bag, put the bag on a paper towel in the microwave oven and slit the top with a sharp knife or scissors. Cook without adding water for about 3 minutes, carefully lift the paper towel and bag from the microwave oven. Open the bag carefully and turn the vegetables on to the serving plate. Add salt and pepper and stir in the butter if wished.

APPLE CHARLOTTE

PREPARATION TIME: *10 minutes*
COOKING TIME: *about 1½ minutes, plus browning*
MICROWAVE SETTING: *Maximum (Full)*

15 g (½ oz) shredded suet	½ small cooking apple,
25 g (1 oz) fresh white	about 50 g (2 oz)
breadcrumbs	2 tablespoons blackberry
pinch of ground nutmeg	jam

1. Mix the suet, breadcrumbs and nutmeg together.
2. Peel, core and slice the apple finely.
3. Put a layer of crumb mixture in the base of a ramekin dish, cover with a layer of apple followed by a layer of jam. Repeat the layers, finishing with crumbs. Pat the crumbs down firmly, then cook for 1½ minutes until the apple is soft.
4. Brown under a preheated conventional grill.

Scrambled egg with cheese and ham; Mixed diced vegetables; Apple charlotte

ELEGANTLY ALONE

POUSSIN WITH STILTON

BUTTERED TAGLIATELLE

FRUIT BRÛLÉE

Prepare the base for the Fruit Brûlée 24 hours in advance and chill in the freezer. Transfer to the refrigerator 2 hours in advance. Put the sugar on top of the Fruit Brûlée and caramelize while the poussin is cooking, then return to the refrigerator until ready to serve.
Prepare but do not cook the poussin until just before the meal.
Cook the tagliatelle while the poussin is at step 5. Alternatively, the tagliatelle may be cooked in advance. To reheat, run the pasta under cold water in a colander, add the butter, put on to a serving dish and cover with cling film. Cook for 1 minute on Maximum (Full).

POUSSIN WITH STILTON

PREPARATION TIME: *about 5 minutes*
COOKING TIME: *about 14 minutes*
MICROWAVE SETTING: *Medium Low (35%); then Maximum (Full)*

15 g (½ oz) butter	½ teaspoon cornflour
pinch of cayenne	1 tablespoon white wine
pinch of salt	1 tablespoon water
25 g (1 oz) Stilton cheese	parsley sprigs, to garnish
1 × 400 g (14 oz) oven-ready poussin, fully thawed	

1. Put the butter, cayenne and salt into a small bowl and cook on Medium Low (35%) for 1 minute or until melted.
2. Put the piece of Stilton cheese into the cavity of the poussin, then put the poussin into a small shallow dish.
3. Pour the melted butter evenly over the poussin, then cover with greaseproof paper and cook on Medium Low (35%) for 6 minutes.
4. Turn the poussin over, replace the cover and cook for a further 6 minutes or until cooked.

5. Transfer the poussin to a serving plate and keep warm.
6. Transfer the cooking juices to a bowl. Blend in the cornflour. Add the wine and water and stir well to mix.
7. Put the bowl in the microwave oven and raise the setting to Maximum (Full). Cook for 30 seconds, stir, then cook for a further 30 seconds or until thickened. Pour over the poussin and serve at once, garnished with parsley, or reheat the sauce just before serving.

BUTTERED TAGLIATELLE

PREPARATION TIME: *5 minutes*
COOKING TIME: *about 4 minutes, plus standing*
MICROWAVE SETTING: *Maximum (Full)*

about 300 ml ($\frac{1}{2}$ pint) water	*2 teaspoons butter or margarine*
$\frac{1}{4}$ teaspoon salt	
$\frac{1}{2}$ teaspoon salad oil	*chopped parsley, to garnish*
50–75 g (2–3 oz) or 2 to 3 nests tagliatelle	

Some varieties of pasta take longer to cook, so if the tagliatelle is undercooked, allow a further minute's standing time.

1. Put the water, salt and oil in a 900 ml (1$\frac{1}{2}$ pint) basin, put in the tagliatelle and turn the nests over so that the top is just moist. Cover with a lid or completely with cling film piercing a small hole in the centre, and cook for 4 minutes.
2. Leave to stand for 1 minute, then carefully remove the covering. Drain if necessary and mix in the butter or margarine, then garnish with the parsley.

FRUIT BRÛLÉE

PREPARATION TIME: *about 10 minutes, plus chilling overnight*
COOKING TIME: *about 2$\frac{1}{2}$ minutes, plus browning*
MICROWAVE SETTING: *Medium Low (35%)*

5 tablespoons double cream	*2 teaspoons caster sugar*
	$\frac{1}{2}$ dessert pear
1 egg yolk	*1 tablespoon caster sugar, to decorate*
$\frac{1}{4}$ teaspoon cornflour	

The quantities in this recipe may be increased but allow extra time at each cooking stage.

1. Put the cream in a 600 ml (1 pint) jug and cook for 1$\frac{1}{2}$ minutes, until the cream bubbles and boils at the edges.
2. Using an electric beater, whip the egg yolk, cornflour and sugar together until pale and thick.
3. Pour the egg mixture into the hot cream, beating thoroughly. Cook for 1 minute, beating every 15 seconds until the mixture is mousse-like and thick enough to form a channel when a spoon handle is drawn through the centre.
4. Peel and core the pear, cut up coarsely and put into the base of a flameproof ramekin dish. Pour the cream mixture over the fruit, then cool and chill overnight. (F)
5. Sprinkle the top of the dessert with a generous layer of caster sugar, pressing it well down with the bowl of the spoon. Place under a preheated hot conventional grill until the sugar melts and turns dark brown. Remove carefully from the grill and replace in the refrigerator for 15 minutes before serving.

(F) The custards freeze well for up to 1 month but bring them back to refrigerator temperature before adding the sugar and caramelizing.

Left to right: Buttered tagliatelle; Poussin with Stilton; Fruit brûlée

FRIDAY SUPPER

FRIED FISH IN MUSHROOM SAUCE

VICHY CARROTS

SAVOURY TOMATOES

The fish mixture can be prepared and shaped in advance up to the end of step 3, then chilled. Complete just before serving. The fish cakes may also be completely cooked and reheated for 2–3 minutes but they will not be as crisp.
The Vichy Carrots can be cooked in advance. Cover and reheat on Maximum (Full) for 2–3 minutes.
Crumbs for the Savoury Tomatoes can be prepared in advance, the tomatoes set in the crumbs (see step 3) and kept chilled until required. Allow an extra 30 seconds if the dish is to be reheated from cold.

FRIED FISH IN MUSHROOM SAUCE

PREPARATION TIME: *5 minutes*
COOKING TIME: *3 minutes, plus deep frying*
MICROWAVE SETTING: *Maximum (Full)*

100g (4oz) skinned and boned fresh or thawed haddock, cod or other white fish	*4 tablespoons milk*
	salt
	freshly ground black pepper
50g (2oz) button mushrooms, finely sliced	*6 tablespoons water*
15g (½oz) butter or margarine	*8 tablespoons gram or besam flour*
15g (½oz) flour	*oil for deep frying*

Gram or besam flour, as it is sometimes called, is available from Asian grocers. It is good for batters as it mixes easily with water and coats well.

1. Put the fish into a basin, slice and add the mushrooms. Cover with cling film and cook for 1½ minutes or until completely cooked. Leave to stand with the juices.
2. To make the sauce, put the butter or margarine into a small bowl and cook for 15 seconds or until melted. Stir in the flour and cook for a further 15 seconds. Measure and add the juices from the fish and make up to 5 tablespoons with the milk. Blend thoroughly, then cook for 1 minute until the sauce thickens. Beat vigorously.

Add salt and pepper to taste.
3. Flake the fish with a fork or sharp knife and add the sauce. Mix thoroughly and shape into two 5cm (2 inch) diameter cakes on a floured board. Chill until cool.
4. Combine the water and gram or besam flour in a shallow dish and add salt and pepper. The mixture should be the consistency of heavy cream. Put 1 fish cake into the mixture and spoon the batter over the top.
5. Heat about 5cm (2 inches) oil in a small saucepan and when sufficiently hot (185–190°C/360–375°F) add 1 coated fish cake, flipping it over carefully as soon as the underside is brown. Cook for 2–3 minutes, reducing the heat if necessary. Drain on a paper towel and keep warm.
6. Coat the second fish cake and fry similarly. Serve hot.

VICHY CARROTS

PREPARATION TIME: *5 minutes*
COOKING TIME: *about 6 minutes, plus standing*
MICROWAVE SETTING: *Maximum (Full)*

100g (4oz) carrots, peeled	*salt*
2 tablespoons water	*freshly ground black pepper*
1 teaspoon butter	
1 teaspoon sugar (optional)	*2 sprigs parsley*

1. Cut the carrots diagonally into thin slices.
2. Put the water, butter and sugar, if using, in a bowl or dish and sprinkle with salt.
3. Stir in the carrots, cover with cling film and cook for 3 minutes. Stir, then replace the cover and cook for a further 2 minutes or until the carrots are tender. Drain if necessary and top with the parsley sprigs.

SAVOURY TOMATOES

PREPARATION TIME: *about 5 minutes*
COOKING TIME: *about 4 minutes*
MICROWAVE SETTING: *Maximum (Full)*

25g (1oz) salted butter	*25g (1oz) fresh breadcrumbs*
½–1 teaspoon dried basil leaves	*1 large tomato*

1. Put the butter in a 450ml (¾ pint) oval dish. Cook for 30 seconds or until melted. Stir in the herbs and breadcrumbs and cook for 1 minute. Stir to mix thoroughly, then cook for 30 seconds and stir once more. Cook for a further 15 seconds or until the crumbs are golden.
2. Cut the tomato in half and arrange in the dish of crumbs cut side up and 2.5cm (1 inch) apart. Spoon some of the crumbs on top and press well down.
3. Cook, uncovered, for 45 seconds or until soft.

Savoury tomatoes; Fried fish in mushroom sauce; Vichy carrots

MENUS

FOR

TWO

Because of the speed of cooking smaller quantities of food in the microwave cooker, you might even be tempted to make a choice of dishes for one of the courses. Many of the dishes in the menus can be interchanged. There is no reason at all why you cannot have Ginger Pudding instead of Apple Brown Betty, serving the custard with the apple pudding. Have Kedgeree instead of Shepherd's Pie for the Homely Dinner or try the Espagnole Sauce with the Shepherd's Pie. Ceviche, which is a kind of pickled fish, is good in place of the Stuffed Mushrooms in the Good and Substantial dinner and Mushroom and Walnut Quiche can take the place of the Puffy Omelette.

There are any number of permutations and this will create different menus for several weeks. Reheating food for two is also speedy, so that your wait between courses is never very long even if you do vary the menu suggestions given. To save a long wait after the meal always make the coffee earlier on, strain it and then reheat when you're ready to serve.

SCOTS BRUNCH

KEDGEREE

OATIE CAKES

POTTED CHEESE

MELON AND GRAPEFRUIT BOATS WITH MELBA SAUCE

*Prepare the Potted Cheese up to 24 hours ahead and keep chilled.
Prepare, cover and chill the melon boats up to 24 hours ahead.
Prepare the Kedgeree and the egg garnish separately up to 24 hours
ahead. Just before serving, cover and reheat the Kedgeree for 2–3
minutes, stirring occasionally, then garnish with the eggs and parsley.
Prepare the Oatie Cakes up to 1 hour ahead and keep covered. Reheat
for 20–30 seconds just before serving.
Prepare the sauce ahead of time, but reduce the cornflour to
½ teaspoon. Warm briefly on Maximum (Full) for 20 seconds.*

KEDGEREE

PREPARATION TIME: *15–20 minutes*
COOKING TIME: *about 5 minutes, plus cooking rice*
MICROWAVE SETTING: *Maximum (Full)*

225 g (8 oz) smoked haddock fillet	*freshly ground black pepper*
25 g (1 oz) butter or margarine	*2 hard-boiled eggs*
1 tablespoon milk	*1 tablespoon fresh chopped parsley*
25 g (1 oz) prawns	*¼ teaspoon cayenne pepper*
175 g (6 oz) cooked long-grain rice	*lemon wedges, to garnish*

1. Put the fish, skin side down, on a plate, cover with cling film and pull back one corner to vent. Cook for 2 minutes or until the flesh is opaque. Remove the skin and bones and flake the flesh.
2. Put the butter and milk into a serving dish and cook for 1 minute or until the butter is melted. Stir then mix in the fish, prawns and rice and add pepper to taste.
3. Cook, uncovered, for 2–3 minutes, stirring occasionally, until hot. Cover and keep warm.
4. Separate the white and yolk of the eggs, chop the whites and sieve the yolks. Mix the sieved yolk, parsley and cayenne pepper together.
5. Uncover the fish, stir in the egg white and sprinkle with the egg yolk topping. Garnish with the lemon wedges.

OATIE CAKES

PREPARATION TIME: *15 minutes*
COOKING TIME: *4 minutes, plus standing*
MICROWAVE SETTING: *Maximum (Full)*

175 g (6 oz) plain wholewheat flour	*6 tablespoons porridge oats*
½ teaspoon salt	*1 teaspoon malt extract*
1 teaspoon baking powder	*1 egg (size 1), beaten*
75 g (3 oz) butter	*4 tablespoons plain unsweetened yogurt*
2 tablespoons dried milk granules	

1. Sift the flour, salt and baking powder into a mixing bowl. Rub in the butter until crumbs form, then stir in the dried milk granules and the porridge oats.
2. Mix the malt extract, beaten egg and yogurt together thoroughly in another bowl, then work this mixture into the dry ingredients until a soft, though manageable, dough is formed.
3. Shape the mixture into a round on a well-floured board and using well-floured hands, flatten until 1 cm (½ inch) deep. Place on a folded sheet of greaseproof paper. Using a sharp knife, mark into 4 wedges, pressing the knife in deeply but not cutting through completely. Cook for 4 minutes or until the cake is just dry on top. Stand for 4 minutes, then transfer to a board.
4. Cut into wedges and serve warm, split and generously buttered.

POTTED CHEESE

PREPARATION TIME: *10 minutes*
COOKING TIME: *30 seconds–1 minute*
MICROWAVE SETTING: *Medium Low (35%)*

1 medium orange	*½ small banana*
25 g (1 oz) unsalted butter	*¼ dessert apple*
25 g (1 oz) cream cheese	

1. Cut the orange in half. Using a grapefruit knife, remove the orange segments from 1 half and set aside. Scoop out the remaining pith, leaving the orange shell smooth and dry.
2. Put the butter in a basin and if necessary soften in the microwave for a few seconds.
3. Beat in the cheese. Peel and mash the banana, then add to the cheese mixture and beat thoroughly until smooth.
4. Peel, core and chop the apple finely and fold the apple into the cheese mixture with the orange segments. Pile into the reserved orange shell and serve at once. Garnish with orange slices cut from the remaining half. If the cheese has to be kept waiting, sprinkle the top with any remaining orange juice, then cover and keep chilled.

Melon and grapefruit boats with Melba sauce; Kedgeree; Potted cheese; Oatie cakes

MELON AND GRAPEFRUIT BOATS WITH MELBA SAUCE

PREPARATION TIME: *15–20 minutes, plus chilling*
COOKING TIME: *3 minutes*
MICROWAVE SETTING: *Maximum (Full)*

½ *Honeydew melon*	1 *tablespoon clear honey*
1 *medium grapefruit*	100 g (4 oz) *raspberries*
Sauce:	1 *teaspoon cornflour*
2 *tablespoons redcurrant jelly*	1 *tablespoon cold water*

1. Remove the seeds and cut the melon into 2 wedges.
2. Slide a sharp knife between the flesh and the peel but leave the melon on the peel. Slash into about 6 slices.
3. Cut the grapefruit in half, then remove the grapefruit segments from the membranes.
4. Arrange the grapefruit segments on top of the melon in an overlapping line. Chill until required.
5. To make the sauce, combine the redcurrant jelly and honey in a jug and cook for 30 seconds or until the jelly is melted.
6. Stir in the raspberries and cook for 2 minutes or until pulped. Press the mixture through a sieve into a bowl and discard the pips.
7. Blend the cornflour and water together, stir into the purée and cook for 1–1½ minutes until the mixture thickens. Stir thoroughly. Cover and leave to cool.
8. Spoon the sauce over the fruit when ready to serve.

BUSY BEE LUNCH

TRIPLE DECKER BURGERS

TOMATOES IN A BED OF RICE

APPLE DESSERT

Mix the burgers ahead of time if preferred but allow extra cooking time if they have been kept in the refrigerator.
The Apple Dessert can be prepared ahead of time and served cold or reheated in the microwave oven for 2 minutes, or can be cooked up to the end of step 1 before the meal and finished off after the main course has been eaten.
Tomato rice can be assembled ahead of time or while the burgers are cooking. Cook while the burgers are standing. It will be ready to serve when the burgers have had their standing time.

TRIPLE DECKER BURGERS

PREPARATION TIME: *about 6 minutes*
COOKING TIME: *about 5 minutes, plus standing*
MICROWAVE SETTING: *Maximum (Full)*

225 g (8 oz) raw minced lean beef	*2 large sausages*
salt	*50 g (2 oz) Cheddar cheese, finely chopped*
freshly ground black pepper	

1. Season the minced beef with the salt and pepper, work in the chopped cheese, then divide into 4 equal portions. Using floured hands, shape into burgers 7½ cm (3 inches) across.
2. Skin the sausages and shape each to a round the same diameter as the burgers. Place on top of two of the burgers.
3. Cover with the remaining 2 burgers and press down gently on the top to make the layers stick together. Put the burgers side by side on a plate or dish and cook for 5 minutes, give each burger a half turn, halfway through.
4. Drain and transfer to hot serving plates. Leave to stand, uncovered, for 3 minutes before serving with a mixed salad.

TOMATOES IN A BED OF RICE

PREPARATION TIME: *3 minutes*
COOKING TIME: *3 minutes*
MICROWAVE SETTING: *Maximum (Full)*

2 tomatoes	*1 tablespoon chopped mixed nuts*
225 g (8 oz) cold cooked rice (see page 87)	*salt*
4 tablespoons mayonnaise (see page 127)	*freshly ground black pepper*

1. Halve the tomatoes and arrange in the centre of a 15 cm (6 inch) round dish.
2. Mix the rice, mayonnaise and nuts together and season to taste with salt and pepper. Arrange in a border around the tomatoes. Cook, uncovered, for 3 minutes.

APPLE DESSERT

PREPARATION TIME: *4 minutes*
COOKING TIME: *3 minutes*
MICROWAVE SETTING: *Maximum (Full)*

350 g (12 oz) cooking apples	*150 ml (¼ pint) orange juice*
1 tablespoon custard powder	*1–2 tablespoons sugar*
	slice of kiwi fruit (optional), to decorate

1. Peel, core and quarter the apples into a small bowl. Three-quarters cover with cling film and cook for 3 minutes, until the apples are soft enough to mash. Mash with a fork or potato masher.
2. Blend the custard powder and orange juice together until smooth. Mix into the mashed apples and cook for 1 minute. Sweeten to taste with the sugar. Stir thoroughly and serve hot or cold with cream and decorated with the kiwi fruit, if liked.

Triple decker burgers; Tomatoes in a bed of rice; Apple dessert

GOOD AND SUBSTANTIAL

STUFFED MUSHROOMS
ROAST PORK
CREAMED GREENS
JUGGED LAYERED FRUIT SUET PUDDING

Prepare the mushrooms ahead of time and serve cold or reheat, uncovered, for 30 seconds – 1 minute before serving.
Assemble the Creamed Greens up to the end of step 2. Complete while the pork is standing.
Cook the pork just before the meal.
Prepare the pudding while the pork is roasting and set to cook while eating the main course but at step 4, cook for the full 3 minutes without turning. Prepare the sauce at step 5 ahead of time but cook just before serving.

STUFFED MUSHROOMS

PREPARATION TIME: *10 minutes*
COOKING TIME: *about 4 minutes*
MICROWAVE SETTING: *Maximum (Full)*

2 large open flat mushrooms, at least 7½cm (3 inches) in diameter	*4 tablespoons fresh brown breadcrumbs*
15g (½oz) butter	*1 teaspoon mixed dried herbs*
1 small onion, finely chopped	*¼ teaspoon Worcestershire sauce*
salt	*1 tablespoon sherry*
freshly ground black pepper	*½ beaten egg*
	15g (½oz) slivered flaked almonds

1. Wipe the mushrooms, remove and chop the stems. Set the caps aside.
2. Put the butter in a medium bowl and cook for 30 seconds or until melted. Add the chopped stems and the onion and cook for 2 minutes or until the onions are soft. Season to taste with salt and pepper.
3. Mix in the breadcrumbs, herbs, Worcestershire sauce and sherry. Bind with the beaten egg. Stir in the almonds.
4. Pile the mixture on to the dark side of the mushrooms and cook, uncovered, for 1 minute. Turn the dish and cook for a further minute. Serve hot or cold with lettuce and watercress.

ROAST PORK

PREPARATION TIME: *10 minutes*
COOKING TIME: *20 minutes, plus standing*
MICROWAVE SETTING: *Maximum (Full)*

1 × 1 kg (2 lb) joint boneless pork
1 teaspoon salt

Although pork crackling is tough when roasted in a microwave cooker and therefore should be discarded after cooking, a good skin is desirable because it encloses the juices, producing a more tender meat. Allow 9–10 minutes per 450g (1 lb), turning over halfway through and give a few minutes longer standing for larger joints.

1. Slash the skin diagonally at 2½cm (1 inch) intervals and rub the salt into the slits.
2. Put the joint on a rack in a shallow dish fat-side up and cover with a split roaster bag. Cook for 10 minutes.
3. Turn the joint over and turn the dish round. Cook for a further 10 minutes or until the internal temperature measures 80°C/175°F. The juices should run clear when the meat is pierced.
4. Transfer the joint to a heated serving dish and tent with foil or an upturned bowl. Leave to stand for 10 minutes before serving with buttered carrots.

CREAMED GREENS

PREPARATION TIME: *15 minutes*
COOKING TIME: *10 minutes, plus standing*
MICROWAVE SETTING: *Maximum (Full)*

225g (8oz) spring greens, washed and drained	*1 × 285ml (10 floz) ready-to-use can cream of leek soup*
	spring onion rings, to garnish

1. Trim away the coarse stalks from the greens and shred the leaves.
2. Put the leaves in an 18cm (7 inch) round dish.
3. Pour the soup over the greens, cover with cling film, pulling back one corner to vent, and cook for 5 minutes. Turn the dish, then cook for a further 5 minutes. Leave for 5 minutes before carefully removing the cling film. Garnish with the spring onion and serve hot.

Creamed greens; Jugged layered fruit suet pudding with gooseberry sauce; Stuffed mushrooms; Roast pork

JUGGED LAYERED FRUIT SUET PUDDING WITH GOOSEBERRY SAUCE

PREPARATION TIME: *20 minutes*
COOKING TIME: *about 5 minutes*
MICROWAVE SETTING: *Maximum (Full)*

Filling:	pinch of salt
1 × 300 g (10½ oz) can gooseberries in syrup	35 g (1¼ oz) shredded suet
	25 g (1 oz) soft brown sugar
25 g (1 oz) sultanas	
25 g (1 oz) currants	2½ tablespoons milk
25 g (1 oz) ground almonds	**Sauce:**
	1 teaspoon arrowroot
Pastry:	1 egg yolk
65 g (2½ oz) self-raising flour	1 tablespoon single cream
	1 tablespoon sugar

A 600 ml (1 pint) pudding basin could be used if you do not have a glass measuring jug of the right size.

1. To make the filling, drain the gooseberries and reserve the syrup. Mix together with the sultanas, currants and ground almonds.

2. To make the pastry, sift the flour and salt into a mixing bowl. Stir in the suet and sugar. Add sufficient milk to mix to a soft but not sticky dough.

3. Cut the dough into 6 equal pieces and grease a 600 ml (1 pint) glass measuring jug. Shape the pastry into circles the diameter of the jug and place one in the base. Cover with a layer of the sultana, currant and ground almond mixture and gooseberries. Repeat the layers, finishing with pastry. You will need about one-fifth of the filling between each layer.

4. Press the top of the pastry down, then cover the jug loosely with cling film and pull back one corner to vent. Cook for 1½ minutes, then turn the dish round and cook for a further 1½ minutes or until the pastry is just dry on top. Release the cling film for steam to escape but do not remove it completely. Leave for 5 minutes while preparing the sauce.

5. To make the sauce, pour a little of the reserved syrup into a small bowl or jug, stir in the arrowroot and make up to 150 ml (¼ pint) with the remaining syrup. Cook for 1 minute, stir, then cook for a further minute or until the sauce thickens slightly and clears.

6. Stir the egg yolk and cream together in a small bowl, add the sugar and 2 tablespoons of the hot sauce. Pour back into the sauce, stir thoroughly and cook for 30 seconds only. Further cooking will thin the sauce.

7. Turn the pudding out and serve with the sauce.

DAIRY DUO

PUFFY OMELETTE WITH SPINACH SAUCE

CARROT AND CELERY SALAD

GRILLED CHIPS

MOCHA MILK SHAKE

Prepare the salad ahead of time, add an extra tablespoon of French dressing just before serving.
Prepare the milk shake up to the end of step 3 ahead of time and keep chilled in the goblet. Liquidize again for a few seconds just before serving. Store the crushed flake chilled and the ice cream frozen. Complete the milk shakes just before serving.
Prepare the spinach sauce ahead of time and reheat while the omelette is browning.
Prepare the chips up to the end of step 2 before the omelette and brown under the grill while cooking the omelette.

PUFFY OMELETTE WITH SPINACH SAUCE

PREPARATION TIME: *10 minutes*
COOKING TIME: *6 minutes (omelette); 3 minutes (sauce), plus standing and browning*
MICROWAVE SETTING: *Maximum (Full); then Medium Low (35%)*

Sauce:	Omelette:
150g (5oz) chopped cooked spinach (fresh, frozen or canned), drained	*3 eggs, separated*
	3 tablespoons milk
	¼ teaspoon salt
1 tablespoon vegetable oil	*¼ teaspoon white pepper*
2 teaspoons cornflour	*15g (½oz) butter or*
5 tablespoons milk	*margarine*
salt	*tomato slice, to garnish*
freshly ground black pepper	

1. To make the sauce, put the spinach into a 1.2 litre (2 pint) bowl and stir in the vegetable oil. Sprinkle over the cornflour and stir to mix thoroughly. Add the milk and stir again until well mixed.
2. Cook, uncovered, for 1½ minutes, stir and cook for a further minute or until the sauce thickens. Season to taste with salt and pepper. Cover with cling film and set aside while preparing the omelette.
3. To make the omelette, place the egg yolks, milk, salt and pepper in a large bowl and beat together with a fork.
4. Whisk the egg whites in another bowl until stiff. Stir 1 tablespoon of the beaten whites into the yolk mixture, then fold in the remainder gently.
5. Put the butter in a 23cm (9 inch) round dish and cook on Maximum (Full) for 45 seconds or until melted. Swirl the butter round the dish to coat all over.
6. Pour the egg mixture into the buttered dish, reduce the setting and cook on Medium Low (35%) for 1 minute. Quickly open the oven door and give the dish a quarter turn. Repeat twice more, then cook for 2 minutes or until the mixture is only just set. Leave to stand for 1 minute.
7. Carefully slide the omelette on to a flameproof plate, and fold over. Brown under a preheated hot conventional grill. Reheat the sauce for 1 minute. Pour over the omelette and garnish with the tomato.

CARROT AND CELERY SALAD

PREPARATION TIME: *10 minutes*
COOKING TIME: *about 1 minute*
MICROWAVE SETTING: *Maximum (Full)*

1 medium carrot, peeled and coarsely grated	*2 spring onions, topped, tailed and finely sliced*
1 large centre celery stick, finely sliced	*2 tablespoons mayonnaise (see page 127)*
	watercress sprig, to garnish

1. Combine the prepared vegetables in a small bowl, cover with cling film and cook for 30 seconds. Remove the cover, stir and cook for a further 30 seconds. Then leave to stand, covered, until cool.
2. Chill until ready to serve, then stir in the mayonnaise and garnish with the watercress.

GRILLED CHIPS

PREPARATION TIME: *10 minutes*
COOKING TIME: *8 minutes, plus browning*
MICROWAVE SETTING: *Maximum (Full)*

450g (1 lb) potatoes
2 tablespoons oil
salt

1. Peel, rinse and dry the potatoes, then cut into 1 cm (½ inch) chips.
2. Place the chips in a dish, cover with cling film and cook for 4 minutes, stir and cook for a further 3 minutes or until tender. Drain, pat dry with kitchen paper and stir in the oil, tossing the chips to make sure that they are all well coated. Sprinkle with salt.
3. Transfer the chips to a flameproof dish and brown on all sides under a preheated conventional grill.

MOCHA MILK SHAKE

PREPARATION TIME: *about 5 minutes*
COOKING TIME: *about 45 seconds, plus cooling*
MICROWAVE SETTING: *Maximum (Full)*

300ml ($\frac{1}{2}$ pint) milk
2 teaspoons instant coffee
1 teaspoon cocoa powder
$\frac{1}{2}$–1 medium banana
2 tablespoons pineapple juice

2 scoops or 2 heaped tablespoons vanilla ice cream
1 tablespoon finely crushed chocolate flake

1. Chill the liquidizer goblet in the refrigerator.
2. Put 4 tablespoons of the milk in a small bowl or glass and stir in the coffee granules and cocoa powder. Cook for 45 seconds or until the milk is steaming, then stir to dissolve the coffee and cocoa and leave to cool.
3. Peel and cut the banana into chunks. Place in the liquidizer with the coffee mixture, the remaining milk, the pineapple juice and half the ice cream. Blend until smooth.
4. Divide the milk shake mixture between 2 chilled glasses or mugs. Add the remaining ice cream and sprinkle the tops with chocolate flake.

Mocha milk shake; Grilled chips; Puffy omelette with spinach sauce; Carrot and celery salad

```
 PERUVIAN PROMISE
```

CEVICHE

LA BERZA COLMADA CON SALSA CHILLI
(Stuffed Cabbage in Chilli Sauce)

MESCLADO CELESTIAL
(Heavenly Trifle)

LEMON SPRITZ DRINK

Prepare the Ceviche up to 24 hours ahead of time and the topping several hours beforehand. Assemble up to 2 hours ahead of time. Prepare the trifle up to 24 hours ahead of time and keep chilled. Prepare the Lemon Spritz Drink a few hours ahead of time up to the end of step 2. Complete at the moment of serving. Prepare the cabbage up to the end of step 2, then complete about 30 minutes before the meal.

CEVICHE

PREPARATION TIME: *20 minutes*
COOKING TIME: *2 minutes, plus marinating overnight*
MICROWAVE SETTING: *Maximum (Full)*

175 g (6 oz) fresh haddock fillet, skinned and cut into narrow strips	*1 tomato, peeled and cut into 8 segments*
1 × 175 g (6 oz) can crabmeat, drained	*juice of 2 limes*
	1 tablespoon salad oil
½ green pepper, finely sliced	*½ teaspoon dried marjoram*
1 onion, peeled and finely chopped	*½ teaspoon salt*
	¼ teaspoon freshly ground black pepper
1 canned chilli, finely chopped	*4 tablespoons sweetcorn kernels*

1. Combine the haddock, crab, pepper, onion, chilli, tomato, lime juice, oil, marjoram, salt and pepper in a bowl. Stir together thoroughly, then cover and chill overnight. Stir once or twice during marinating. When the dish is ready, the fish will be opaque.
2. Put 2 tablespoons of salted water in a roaster bag or casserole and add the sweetcorn. Close the bag with an elastic band, leaving a hole at the top for the steam to escape or partially cover the casserole. Cook for 2 minutes, shaking the bag or stirring halfway through. Drain and leave to cool.
3. Using a slotted spoon, transfer the fish mixture to cleaned scallop shells or individual dishes and top with the sweetcorn. Serve with brown bread.

LA BERZA COLMADA CON SALSA CHILLI
(Stuffed Cabbage in Chilli Sauce)

PREPARATION TIME: *about 20 minutes*
COOKING TIME: *about 23 minutes*
MICROWAVE SETTING: *Maximum (Full)*

1 small savoy cabbage, weighing about 1 kg (2¼ lb)	*300 ml (½ pint) water*
	Sauce:
1 medium onion, peeled and finely chopped	*5 tablespoons tomato purée*
1 egg	*¼ teaspoon hot chilli powder*
350 g (12 oz) lean minced raw beef	*¼ teaspoon Worcestershire sauce*
1 tablespoon easy-cook long-grain rice	*salt*
5 tablespoons beef stock	*freshly ground black pepper*
1 teaspoon fresh lemon juice	*1 tablespoon instant potato powder*
2 teaspoons salt	
½ teaspoon freshly ground black pepper	

1. Wash the cabbage and remove any damaged outer leaves. Trim the base and remove part of the centre core with a sharp knife. Pull the leaves open and scoop out the centre, reserving this part for use another time.
2. To make the filling, mix together the onion, egg, mince, rice, stock, lemon juice, salt and pepper and spoon into the hollow of the cabbage, pressing the mixture down firmly. Fold the outer leaves over the top of the filling or use a separate leaf to cover.
3. Pour the water into a large bowl and put in the cabbage. Cover with cling film, vent and cook for 20 minutes. Carefully transfer the cabbage to a serving dish (reserving the liquid) and tent with foil or an upturned bowl. Leave to stand while making the sauce.
4. To make the sauce, stir the tomato purée, chilli powder and seasoning into the liquid remaining in the bowl, then mix in the dried potato. Cook, uncovered, for 3 minutes or until the sauce boils and thickens. Stir vigorously. Hand the hot sauce separately.

Ceviche; Stuffed cabbage in chilli sauce

MESCLADO CELESTIAL (Heavenly Trifle)

PREPARATION TIME: *25–30 minutes, plus chilling*
COOKING TIME: *about 8½ minutes*
MICROWAVE SETTING: *Maximum (Full)*

25 g (1 oz) sugar	*4 tablespoons double or*
6 tablespoons water	*whipping cream*
2 eggs, separated	*1 teaspoon icing sugar*
pinch of ground mixed	*6 × 1 cm (½ inch) slices jam*
spice	*Swiss roll*
2 tablespoons sherry	*2 passion fruit*
few drops of vanilla	*15 g (½ oz) dessert*
essence	*chocolate*
2 drops vinegar	

1. Stir the sugar and water together in a 1.2 litre (2 pint) basin and cook for 1 minute or until the syrup boils. Stir once, then cook for a further 5 minutes, until the temperature reaches 107°C/225°F or when a little of the syrup dropped into cold water forms a fine thread. Leave to cool.
2. Beat the egg yolks, mixed spice, sherry and vanilla essence together in a small bowl. Stir into the syrup and cook for 1½ minutes, beating vigorously every 10 seconds until the mixture is thick and custard-like.
3. In a grease-free bowl and using grease-free beaters, whip the egg whites and vinegar together until soft peaks form.
4. In another bowl whip the cream and icing sugar until stiff peaks form. Fold the whipped cream into the beaten egg whites.
5. Put 3 of the Swiss roll slices in the base of a 13 cm (5 inch) diameter and 5 cm (2 inch) deep pie dish.
6. Halve the passion fruit and scoop the pulp over the cake. Cover with a layer of half the custard, then a layer of half the cream. Add the remaining cake, then the rest of the custard, finishing with the remaining cream. Chill for 30 minutes.
7. Fold a 20 cm (8 inch) square of greaseproof paper in half to form a triangle, with the longest side facing you. Fold the right hand point up to the top point. Then fold again, so that the point now in the middle of the left hand side touches the middle of the top edge. Now fold again to bring the right hand point over to the left hand. Open out to a cone and fold over the point at the top to secure.
8. Grate the chocolate into the paper cone, pushing the pieces towards the pointed end. Fold down the top to enclose. Put on the microwave oven shelf and switch on for 1 minute to melt the chocolate. Snip away a small piece of the paper at the end of the cone, then dribble the melted chocolate over the chilled dessert. Cover and chill for 15 minutes.

Variation:
Orange segments or fresh chopped pear can be substituted for the passion fruit.

LEMON SPRITZ

PREPARATION TIME: *about 10 minutes, plus chilling*
NO COOKING REQUIRED
MAKES 750 ml (1¼ PINTS)

225 g (8 oz) seedless	*175 ml (6 fl oz) soda water*
grapes, washed	*ice cubes, to chill*
1½ tablespoons fresh lemon	*fresh grapes, to decorate*
juice	
250 ml (8 fl oz) bottled	
ginger ale	

1. Blend the grapes in a liquidizer, then strain through a sieve into a jug or lipped bowl.
2. Stir in the lemon juice and ginger ale and chill for at least 2 hours. At the same time chill a serving jug and 2 wine glasses. (To frost the glasses dip the rims in lemon juice, then caster sugar and chill until set.)
3. Just before serving, pour the soda water into the lemon mixture. Pour into the glasses, add ice cubes and garnish with the grapes.

Lemon spritz; Heavenly trifle

ROMANTIC EVENING

MELON WITH PARMA HAM

COQUILLES ST JACQUES

ASPARAGUS TIPS

PANCAKES STUFFED WITH LOGANBERRIES

Prepare the melon with Parma ham ahead of time up to the end of step 6. Complete up to 30 minutes before the meal (if left for longer the lettuce leaves will wilt).

Pipe the potato around the scallop shells ahead of time, then cover. Infuse the milk a few hours ahead of time and keep covered. Cook and complete the scallops just before the meal up to the end of step 5, then brown under the grill after eating the main course.

Cook the asparagus ahead of time, drain after standing and cool under cold running water. Drain again, cover and chill. Reheat, covered, for 2–3 minutes, rearranging once, then melt the butter, while browning the Coquilles St Jacques.

Prepare the pancakes and stuffing separately ahead of time. Just before the meal assemble the pancakes on a suitable serving dish and when ready to eat, heat, then dust with icing sugar.

MELON WITH PARMA HAM

PREPARATION TIME: *10 minutes, plus chilling*
NO COOKING REQUIRED

1 ogen melon
4 wafer-thin slices Parma
ham
2 thin centre slices lemon,
cut into quarters

1. Wash and dry the melon thoroughly. Cut in half horizontally and discard the seeds.
2. Using a teaspoon or melon baller, scoop out smooth marble-sized pieces of melon, leaving a firm wall. Put the melon balls into a bowl, adding any juices left in the melon shell.
3. Slice the ham across the width into thin strips.
4. Using a slotted spoon, fill the reserved shells with the melon balls, mixing in a few of the ham strips.
5. Garnish with the remaining ham strips, and arrange the lemon quarters in the centre.
6. Moisten with 1 or 2 tablespoons of the reserved juices. Cover and chill in the refrigerator for 1–2 hours before serving.
7. To serve, set the melon halves on a bed of lettuce leaves to hold the melon firmly in position.

Melon with Parma ham

COQUILLES ST JACQUES

PREPARATION TIME: *10 minutes (excluding potatoes)*
COOKING TIME: *about 8 minutes, plus infusing*
MICROWAVE SETTING: *Maximum (Full)*

175g (6oz) creamed mashed potato	*¼ teaspoon pepper*
150ml (¼ pint) milk	*8 scallops, cleaned and de-bearded*
½ bay leaf	*25g (1oz) softened butter*
1 sprig parsley	*20g (¾oz) flour*
2 peppercorns, bruised	*2 teaspoons fresh white breadcrumbs*
1 slice onion	
4 thin slices celery	*2 teaspoons grated Parmesan cheese*
1 blade mace	
¼ teaspoon salt	

1. Using a star nozzle, pipe a border of potato around 2 clean scallop shells or individual flameproof dishes.
2. Combine the milk, bay leaf, parsley, peppercorns, onion, celery, mace, salt and pepper in a bowl or large jug and cook for 1½ minutes or until the milk is steaming. Cover and set aside for 15–30 minutes.
3. Place the scallops in a bowl and strain the milk over them. Cook for 2½ minutes or until the milk boils and the scallops are just tender. Do not overcook. Remove the scallops with a slotted spoon, cover and keep warm.
4. Mix the butter and flour together to a smooth paste in a small bowl and add teaspoons of the paste to the milk, beating thoroughly until the butter mixture is dissolved. Cook for 45 seconds, then stir and cook for a further 45 seconds or until the sauce thickens. Beat thoroughly.
5. Spoon a little of the sauce into each of the shells or dishes. Place half the scallops in each dish, then add the remaining sauce.
6. Mix the breadcrumbs and cheese together and sprinkle on top of the sauce. Brown lightly under a preheated conventional grill and serve hot.

ASPARAGUS TIPS

PREPARATION TIME: *10 minutes*
COOKING TIME: *about 6 minutes, plus standing*
MICROWAVE SETTING: *Maximum (Full)*

450g (1 lb) fresh asparagus spears or 225g (8oz) frozen asparagus	*50g (2oz) butter*
	salt
6 tablespoons water	*freshly ground black pepper*

The frozen asparagus is cooked as for freshly trimmed asparagus. It doesn't need to be thawed.

1. Rinse the fresh asparagus gently without damaging the tips. Remove and discard the thick inedible part of the stalk. You can usually identify this by bending the stalk end: the inedible part will remain rigid. Scrape or shave a layer of the stalk using a potato peeler.
2. To cook, arrange the asparagus spears in a rectangular or oval dish, the stalks towards the outside and overlapping the tips in the centre. Add the water to the dish, cover with cling film and cook for 3 minutes. Rearrange the asparagus, moving the outside pieces towards the centre, then re-cover and cook for a further 2–4 minutes or until the asparagus is just softening. Leave to stand for 5 minutes.
3. Put the butter, salt and pepper in a small dish and cook for 30 seconds or until melted. Serve the asparagus tips on heated plates and pour the butter over the tips, but not the stalks.

PANCAKES STUFFED WITH LOGANBERRIES

PREPARATION TIME: *5 minutes (excluding pancakes)*
COOKING TIME: *about 1½ minutes*
MICROWAVE SETTING: *Maximum (Full)*

1 teaspoon arrowroot	*100g (4oz) loganberries, picked over and cleaned*
2 tablespoons fresh orange juice	
	4 × 15cm (6 inch) pancakes, made from 150ml (¼ pint) milk, 1 egg, 50g (2oz) plain flour
3 tablespoons icing sugar, sifted	

Raspberries are just as good with the pancakes, when loganberries are not available.

1. Blend the arrowroot, orange juice and 1 tablespoon of the icing sugar in a bowl and cook for 30 seconds. Stir, then cook for a further 15 seconds or until the mixture is very thick.
2. Carefully mix in the loganberries (some of the juice will escape and mix into the sauce).
3. Divide the filling between the 4 pancakes and roll up.
4. Lift the pancakes carefully on to a suitable serving dish and cook for 30–45 seconds or until the pancakes are warm to the touch.
5. Dust with the remaining icing sugar and serve hot.

Coquilles St Jacques; Asparagus tips; Pancakes stuffed with raspberries

SLIMMING SUPPER

RASPBERRY AND TOMATO SOUP

MARINATED DICED BREAST OF CHICKEN

CHOPPED LEAF SPINACH

LEMON JELLY CUPS

Prepare the fruit soup up to 24 hours ahead of time.
Prepare the jelly cups a few hours ahead of time and keep cool but do not freeze.
The chicken must be marinated for a minimum of 2 hours but can be left overnight in the refrigerator if preferred. Cook it just before or during the first course. Cover and keep hot.
Cook the spinach before serving the first course, or cook ahead of serving time. Reheat the spinach when ready to eat.

RASPBERRY AND TOMATO SOUP

PREPARATION TIME: *about 4 minutes*
COOKING TIME: *about 8 minutes*
MICROWAVE SETTING: *Maximum (Full)*

150ml (¼ pint) water	175g (6oz) fresh or frozen raspberries
300ml (½ pint) tomato juice	salt or sugar (optional)
	chopped parsley, to garnish

Frozen raspberries do not need to be thawed but may need 2 extra minutes cooking. The sugar or salt are optional flavourings depending on whether you like a more savoury or sweet-tasting first course. The salt will make the tomato flavour more prominent and the sugar will bring out the taste of the raspberries.

1. Put the water, tomato juice and raspberries in a medium bowl, three-quarters cover with cling film and cook until boiling, about 6 minutes. Stir and cook for a further 2 minutes.
2. Strain through a nylon sieve, making sure that all the raspberry juice is extracted. Reheat for 1 minute, then add salt *or* sugar to taste, if liked. Serve hot or leave to cool, then chill until required. Garnish with chopped parsley.

Clockwise from bottom right: Raspberry and tomato soup; Chopped leaf spinach; Lemon jelly cups; Marinated diced breast of chicken

MARINATED DICED BREAST OF CHICKEN

PREPARATION TIME: *about 10 minutes*
COOKING TIME: *about 10 minutes, plus marinating*
MICROWAVE SETTING: *Maximum (Full)*

Marinade:	¼ teaspoon dried marjoram leaves
5 tablespoons dry white wine	½ garlic clove, crushed
1 tablespoon olive oil	½ teaspoon salt
4 tablespoons fresh orange juice	¼ teaspoon freshly ground black pepper
grated rind of ½ orange	225g (8oz) raw skinned chicken breast, cubed
¼ teaspoon fresh rosemary leaves	orange quarters, to garnish
¼ teaspoon dried thyme leaves	sprig of rosemary, to garnish

1. Combine the 10 marinade ingredients and stir in the chicken cubes. Cover and leave in the refrigerator for at least 2 hours, stirring 2 or 3 times during marinating.
2. Remove the chicken cubes, strain the marinade to remove the herbs, then mix the chicken and marinade in a 1.2 litre (2 pint) bowl. Three-quarters cover with cling film or a vented lid and cook for 4 minutes or until the chicken is tender, stirring once during cooking.
3. Using a slotted spoon, transfer the chicken cubes to a hot serving dish, cover and keep warm.
4. Uncover the marinade and cook for 6 minutes or until only about 2 tablespoons of the liquid remain. Pour over the chicken and serve hot or cold, garnished with orange quarters and rosemary.

CHOPPED LEAF SPINACH

PREPARATION TIME: *about 10 minutes*
COOKING TIME: *about 4½ minutes*
MICROWAVE SETTING: *Maximum (Full)*

450g (1lb) fresh spinach	pinch of ground nutmeg (optional)
salt	chopped almonds (optional), to garnish
freshly ground black pepper	

1. Wash the spinach in cold water and discard the thick stems. Drain thoroughly but do not dry.
2. Place the spinach in a roaster bag and seal with an elastic band (not a metal tag).
3. Cook for 4½ minutes or until the spinach leaves collapse and darken slightly. Using oven gloves, tilt the bag so that the excess liquid drains through the opening. Then remove the elastic band, turn out the spinach and chop with scissors or a sharp knife.
4. Season to taste with salt, pepper and nutmeg and serve hot or cold, garnished with chopped almonds.

LEMON JELLY CUPS

PREPARATION TIME: *about 10 minutes*
COOKING TIME: *about 30 seconds, plus setting*
MICROWAVE SETTING: *Maximum (Full)*

3 tablespoons evaporated milk	*1 teaspoon powdered gelatine*
2 well-shaped large lemons, washed and dried	*2–3 drops yellow food colouring*
3 tablespoons water	*sugar, to taste*
	angelica, to garnish

1. Put the milk into a 1.2 litre (2 pint) bowl and chill for 30 minutes.
2. Stand the lemons on the work surface and turn them to a position where they will sit firmly. Slice off a lid from the top of each. Scoop out the pulp and strain. Retain the lid, shells and juice.
3. Put the water in a small jug and heat for 20 seconds. Sprinkle the gelatine over the water, stir, then heat for 10 seconds or until the water is very hot. Remove the jug from the cooker and stir until fully dissolved.
4. Add 2 tablespoons of the reserved lemon juice, the yellow food colouring and sweeten to taste. Leave until cool but not set.
5. Using an electric beater, whisk the evaporated milk until frothy and mousse-like. Continue beating while pouring on the cooled gelatine in a thin stream from a height. Whisk continuously until the mixture is even.
6. Pour the mousse into the reserved lemon shells and place the lids on top. Decorate with pieces of angelica. If the lids do not fit closely, cover the top half of the lemons with cling film. Chill until set.

VEGETARIAN FARE

COLD CUCUMBER SOUP

STUFFED AUBERGINE

LYONNAISE POTATOES

CHOCOLATE BISCUIT LOG

Prepare the Chocolate Biscuit Log up to 1 or 2 days ahead of time if more convenient.
Prepare the soup ahead of time and keep chilled.
Prepare the stuffed aubergine ahead of time up to the end of step 4 and cover with cling film.
Prepare the Lyonnaise Potatoes just before the meal. Switch on the grill during or after the soup course and brown the potatoes. While they are browning, cover the aubergine and reheat for 3 minutes, then sprinkle with the cheese and complete under the grill.

COLD CUCUMBER SOUP

PREPARATION TIME: *about 15 minutes*
COOKING TIME: *about 5 minutes, plus cooling and chilling*
MICROWAVE SETTING: *Maximum (Full)*

1 small cucumber, washed, unpeeled and diced	$\frac{1}{4}$ teaspoon ground white pepper
200ml (7 fl oz) milk	1 small peeled shallot or $\frac{1}{4}$ medium onion
2 teaspoons flour	
15g ($\frac{1}{2}$oz) soft margarine	3 sprigs parsley
1 teaspoon salt	

This soup may also be served hot if preferred.

1. Purée half the cucumber and half the milk plus the other ingredients in the liquidizer. Pour into a 2.8 litre (5 pint) bowl.
2. Purée the remaining cucumber and milk and add to the bowl. Stir thoroughly. Three-quarters cover the bowl with cling film and cook for 2 minutes, then stir and cook for a further 3 minutes or until the soup thickens and a curd forms around the edges. Beat thoroughly. Leave until cool, then chill.

STUFFED AUBERGINE

PREPARATION TIME: *20 minutes*
COOKING TIME: *about 12 minutes, plus browning*
MICROWAVE SETTING: *Maximum (Full)*

1 × 350g (12 oz) aubergine	50g (2 oz) butter or margarine
1 small onion, finely chopped	40g (1$\frac{1}{2}$oz) fresh brown breadcrumbs
$\frac{1}{2}$ green pepper, seeded and finely chopped	salt
	freshly ground black pepper
225g (8 oz) tomatoes, skinned and finely chopped	100g (4 oz) Cheshire cheese, crumbled
50g (2 oz) mushrooms, chopped	chopped parsley, to garnish

The aubergine shells make an attractive serving dish but are not meant to be eaten.

1. Remove the stalk and cut the aubergine in half lengthways.
2. Scoop out the flesh, leaving a 5mm ($\frac{1}{4}$ inch) wall. Chop the flesh finely.
3. Combine the aubergine pulp in a bowl with the onion, pepper, tomatoes and mushrooms, then add the butter or margarine cut into 4 pieces. Three-quarters cover the bowl with cling film and cook for 10–12 minutes, stirring occasionally during cooking, until the pulp is tender.
4. Stir in the breadcrumbs and salt and pepper to taste. Pile the mixture into the reserved shells.
5. Transfer the shells to a shallow dish and cook for 2 minutes to reheat the mixture.
6. Sprinkle the cheese on top of the filling and brown under a preheated conventional grill. Serve hot, garnished with chopped parsley.

LYONNAISE POTATOES

PREPARATION TIME: *15 minutes*
COOKING TIME: *about 12 minutes, plus browning*
MICROWAVE SETTING: *Maximum (Full)*

25g (1 oz) butter	350g (12 oz) potatoes, peeled and washed
100g (4 oz) onions, peeled and finely sliced	1 teaspoon chopped fresh parsley
$\frac{1}{2}$ teaspoon salt	
$\frac{1}{4}$ teaspoon freshly ground black pepper	sprig of parsley, to garnish

A plastic dish is not suitable for cooking the potatoes if they are to be grilled. When using ovenglass pie plates, keep them well away from the flame or hot element of the grill.

1. Put the butter in a round-lipped pie dish measuring about 15 cm (6 inches) across the base. Cook for 30 seconds or until melted.
2. Add the onions and toss with tongs, then season with salt and pepper. Cook for 4 minutes, stirring once during cooking until the onions are golden brown.
3. Slice the potatoes and quickly shake dry in a clean cloth. Mix into the onions with the parsley, making sure that the potatoes are fully coated with the butter mixture. Cover the dish with cling film, pulling back one corner to vent and cook for 7 minutes or until the potatoes are tender and a top slice breaks easily when pressed with the tip of a fork through the cling film covering.
4. Carefully remove the cling film and brown the potatoes under a preheated conventional grill. Garnish with a sprig of parsley.

CHOCOLATE BISCUIT LOG

PREPARATION TIME: *10 minutes*
COOKING TIME: *$1\frac{1}{2}$ minutes, plus chilling*
MICROWAVE SETTING: *Maximum (Full)*

25 g (1 oz) plain dessert chocolate	*1 egg yolk, threads removed*
50 g (2 oz) unsalted butter	*1 teaspoon sherry*
4 tablespoons sifted icing sugar	*18 sponge finger biscuits*
	whipped cream, to serve

1. Put the chocolate in a small bowl and heat for about $1\frac{1}{2}$ minutes or until shiny on top and beginning to melt.
2. Stir in the butter until completely blended.
3. Add the icing sugar, mix thoroughly and cook for 10 seconds, just sufficient to warm the mixture.
4. Beat in the egg yolk, then mix in the sherry.
5. Break (but do not crush) about 8 sponge fingers into small pieces and, using a wooden spoon, stir into the chocolate mixture. Leave to cool slightly.
6. Place 3 sponge finger biscuits rough-side down on a large square of foil, pile the chocolate mixture on top. Use the remaining biscuits to cover the sides and top of the chocolate mixture, forming a log shape. Roll up the foil tightly and fold over the ends. Chill for 30 minutes, then unwrap and serve sliced, either plain or with whipped cream.

Lyonnaise potatoes; Cold cucumber soup; Stuffed aubergine; Chocolate biscuit log

HOMELY DINNER

CREAM OF ONION SOUP

SHEPHERD'S PIE

BRUSSELS SPROUTS IN
ROSEMARY MARINADE

APPLE AND COCONUT BROWN BETTY

Cook the soup ahead of time and pour into individual bowls. Cover with cling film, pulling back one corner to vent and reheat for 3–5 minutes while browning the Shepherd's Pie.

The Shepherd's Pie may be prepared up to the end of step 4 a few hours in advance, provided the flour and onion mixture is left to cool before the meat is added. Allow an extra 2 minutes cooking time. The sprouts can be prepared ahead of time. Reheat for about 3 minutes, covered, while eating the soup.

The Apple and Coconut Brown Betty can be prepared ahead of time up to the end of step 2. Either leave to cook while eating the main course but cook for a full 7 minutes without turning the dish, or cook ahead of time and reheat, uncovered, for about 3 minutes.

CREAM OF ONION SOUP

PREPARATION TIME: *15 minutes*
COOKING TIME: *18 minutes*
MICROWAVE SETTING: *Maximum (Full)*

350g (12oz) onions, peeled and finely sliced	*salt*
200ml (7floz) well-flavoured chicken stock	*freshly ground black pepper*
150ml (¼ pint) creamy milk	To garnish:
pinch of powdered bay leaf	*onion rings*
1 teaspoon cornflour	*parsley sprigs*
1 tablespoon cold water	*single cream*

1. Put the onions in a large bowl and add the chicken stock. Three-quarters cover with cling film and cook for 15 minutes until the onions are tender, stirring twice.
2. Uncover, stir in the milk and cook for 2 minutes or until boiling, then add the powdered bay leaf.
3. Blend the cornflour with the cold water. Stir in 1–2 tablespoons of the soup, then pour the mixture into the rest of the soup. Stir to mix well. Cook for ½–1 minute, then stir and cook for a further 30 seconds.
4. Purée the soup in the liquidizer, then add salt and pepper to taste. Pour into individual bowls and reheat if necessary. Garnish each bowl with onion rings, a sprig of parsley and a swirl of cream.

SHEPHERD'S PIE

PREPARATION TIME: *about 10 minutes (excluding potatoes)*
COOKING TIME: *about 10 minutes*
MICROWAVE SETTING: *Maximum (Full)*

½ onion, peeled and finely chopped	*225g (8oz) minced cooked beef*
1 tablespoon vegetable oil	*salt*
1½ tablespoons flour	*freshly ground black pepper*
½ beef stock cube, crumbled	*225g (8oz) cooked mashed potatoes*
150ml (¼ pint) boiling water	

1. Combine the onion and oil in an oval 600ml (1 pint) flameproof pie dish and cook for 2 minutes, stirring once during cooking, until the onion is soft.
2. Stir in the flour and cook for 2–2½ minutes, stirring every 30 seconds until the onion browns.
3. Dissolve the stock cube in the water and mix together thoroughly, then stir into the onion mixture. The flour will thicken naturally without further cooking.
4. Stir in the minced beef and season to taste with salt and pepper. Smooth the top with a palette knife.
5. Pile or pipe the mashed potatoes over the meat and ridge with a fork. Cook for 6 minutes or until a thermometer registers 80°C/175°F, giving the dish a quarter turn 3 times during cooking. Alternatively, brown under a preheated conventional grill if preferred.

BRUSSELS SPROUTS IN ROSEMARY MARINADE

PREPARATION TIME: *5–10 minutes*
COOKING TIME: *about 9 minutes*
MICROWAVE SETTING: *Maximum (Full)*

Marinade:	*½ small onion, cut into 4 slices*
8 tablespoons water	
2 teaspoons fresh lemon juice	*350g (12oz) fresh sprouts or 225g (8oz) frozen sprouts*
2 teaspoons rosemary leaves	*1 teaspoon butter*
¼ teaspoon salt	*1 teaspoon flour*
pinch of freshly ground black pepper	*sprig of rosemary, to garnish*

1. To prepare the marinade, combine the 6 ingredients in a medium bowl, cook for 2 minutes or until boiling, then cover and leave until cool. Strain into another bowl and reserve.
2. Wash and trim the fresh sprouts. The frozen sprouts

need no extra attention. Place the sprouts in a dish, add the strained marinade, cover with cling film, pulling back one corner to vent and cook for 6–7 minutes.
3. Carefully remove the cling film and take out the sprouts with a slotted spoon. Keep warm.
4. Cook the marinade uncovered for 30 seconds or until the mixture is boiling.
5. Blend the butter and flour together to a paste, then whisk into the boiling marinade in small portions. When the mixture is smooth, cook for 20–30 seconds, then stir vigorously.
6. Add the sprouts to the thickened sauce, toss and serve hot, garnished with rosemary.

APPLE AND COCONUT BROWN BETTY

PREPARATION TIME: *about 15 minutes*
COOKING TIME: *about 7 minutes*
MICROWAVE SETTING: *Maximum (Full)*

350g (12oz) cooking apples	*2 slices granary bread, crusts removed and cubed*
20g (¾oz) soft brown sugar	*1 tablespoon desiccated coconut*
¼ teaspoon ground cinnamon	*4 tablespoons clear honey*
pinch of salt	*1 tablespoon butter*

1. Peel, core and slice the apples. Mix the sugar, cinnamon and salt together and, starting with apples, layer in a 450ml (¾ pint) oval flameproof dish.
2. Spread the bread cubes over the apple and sprinkle with the desiccated coconut. Spoon the honey on top and cover with cling film.
3. Pull back one corner of the cling film to vent and cook for 3½ minutes. Turn the dish round and cook for a further 3½ minutes or until the apple is cooked.
4. Carefully remove the cling film and top the pudding with dabs of butter. Brown under a preheated conventional grill. Serve hot or cold with whipped cream or custard.

Clockwise from top: Cream of onion soup; Apple and coconut brown Betty; Shepherd's pie; Brussels sprouts in rosemary marinade

ARMCHAIR SUPPER

LIVER PÂTÉ

MUSHROOM AND WALNUT QUICHE

LETTUCE AND CUCUMBER SALAD

GINGER PUDDING WITH CUSTARD

Make up the liver pâté ahead of time and keep chilled.
Make the quiche ahead of time and keep chilled. Reheat on Defrost for about 5 minutes if serving hot.
Skewer the salad vegetables together ahead of time, cover and chill.
Prepare the French dressing ahead of time.
The custard can be prepared ahead of time, then covered with a damp disc of greaseproof paper. Reheat for 3 minutes on Medium Low (35%) during the pudding standing time.
Cook the pudding while eating the main course. It will not matter if it has its standing time in the microwave oven.

LIVER PÂTÉ

PREPARATION TIME: *10 minutes, plus chilling*
COOKING TIME: *4 minutes*
MICROWAVE SETTING: *Maximum (Full)*

100g (4oz) chicken livers, rinsed, trimmed and halved	*pinch of ground cloves*
3 tablespoons hot water	*pinch of ground allspice*
50g (2oz) butter at room temperature	*pinch of cayenne*
½ teaspoon salt	*pinch of freshly ground black pepper*
¼ teaspoon mustard powder	*1 teaspoon Madeira*
	cucumber twist, to garnish
	lettuce leaves, to garnish

1. Put the chicken livers in a large bowl with the water. Cover with cling film. Cook for 2 minutes or until just cooked and pinky brown inside. Leave to stand for 1 minute.
2. Transfer the chicken livers and liquid to a blender and liquidize. Add the butter and remaining ingredients. Blend until smooth.
3. Divide the mixture between 2 small ramekins. Cool rapidly and chill. Garnish with cucumber and lettuce and serve with toast or micro-dried crustless bread. To prepare this, cut the slices in half diagonally and place in a single layer in the microwave oven. Cook for 3 minutes or until the bread has dried out. The bread becomes even crisper after a standing time of 5–10 minutes.

MUSHROOM AND WALNUT QUICHE

PREPARATION TIME: *about 20 minutes*
COOKING TIME: *20–25 minutes*
MICROWAVE SETTING: *Maximum (Full); then Medium Low (35%)*

Pastry:	*75g (3oz) button mushrooms, sliced*
75g (3oz) plain flour	
pinch of salt	*15g (½oz) walnuts, chopped*
40g (1½oz) soft margarine	
1 tablespoon cold water	*1 × 170g (6floz) can evaporated milk*
Filling:	
15g (½oz) butter	*3 eggs*
1 small onion, peeled and finely chopped	*salt*
	freshly ground black pepper

1. To make the pastry, sift the flour and salt together and rub in the margarine until the mixture resembles heavy crumbs. Stir in the water and mix to form a dough.
2. Roll out the pastry to fit into a round shallow dish approximately 18cm (7 inches) across the top.
3. Place a piece of greaseproof paper in the pastry case, fill with dried beans and cook on Maximum (Full) for 2 minutes. Remove the paper and beans, give the dish a half-turn and cook for a further minute. (If using a conventional oven, bake blind at 200°C, 400°F, Gas Mark 6 for 10 minutes.)
4. To make the filling, combine the butter and onion in a bowl and cook for 1½ minutes. Stir, then cook for a further 1½ minutes or until the onion is soft. Drain and spread the onion in the flan case. Cover with the mushrooms and sprinkle the walnuts on top.
5. Put the milk in a jug and cook for 45 seconds or until warm. Beat in the eggs and season with salt and pepper.
6. Pour the egg mixture into the flan case, reduce the setting to Medium Low (35%) and cook for 10–12 minutes or until the custard is set round the edges and just a little wobbly in the centre. Give the dish a quarter turn every 2½ minutes during cooking. Leave to stand for 10 minutes, during which time the custard will begin to set. If it is still wobbly, cook for a few more minutes. The custard should set completely by the time it is cold.

LETTUCE AND CUCUMBER SALAD

PREPARATION TIME: *15 minutes*
NO COOKING REQUIRED

1 iceberg lettuce heart	*⅛ teaspoon salt*
¼ cucumber	*⅛ teaspoon pepper*
French dressing:	*⅛ teaspoon mustard powder*
3 tablespoons vegetable oil	
1 tablespoon white wine vinegar	

1. Cut the lettuce heart into 8 chunks and cut the cucumber into 18 thin slices.
2. Thread the lettuce and cucumber on to two 23 cm (9 inch) skewers, starting with a chunk of lettuce, then 3 cucumber slices and alternating lettuce and cucumber twice more. Finish with lettuce.
3. To make the marinade, mix all the ingredients together in a shallow dish and beat thoroughly.
4. Just before serving twirl the skewered salads in the dressing.

GINGER PUDDING WITH CUSTARD

PREPARATION TIME: *10 minutes (pudding); 5 minutes (sauce)*
COOKING TIME: *2 minutes, plus standing (pudding); 4 minutes (sauce)*
MICROWAVE SETTING: *Maximum (Full); then Medium Low (35%)*

Pudding:	25 g (1 oz) crystallized ginger, chopped
50 g (2 oz) butter	
50 g (2 oz) dark soft brown sugar	**Sauce:**
1 egg (size 1), beaten	25 g (1 oz) caster sugar
50 g (2 oz) self-raising flour	2 teaspoons cornflour
½ teaspoon ground ginger	200 ml (7 fl oz) milk
½ teaspoon dark treacle	¼ teaspoon vanilla essence
	1 egg yolk (threads removed)

1. Grease a 300 ml (½ pint) cereal bowl and place a 2½ cm (5 inch) circle of greaseproof paper or cling film in the base.
2. Beat the butter and sugar together in a mixing bowl until fluffy. Then gradually add alternate tablespoons of beaten egg and flour. Stir in the ginger and treacle. Lastly mix in all but a few pieces of the crystallized ginger.
3. Spoon the mixture into the prepared cereal bowl and smooth the top with a palette knife. Cook on Maximum (Full) for 1 minute. Give the dish a half turn, then cook for a further 1 minute or until the pudding is just dry on top. Cover with a plate and leave to stand for 3–5 minutes before turning out on to a warm dish.
4. While the pudding is standing, prepare the sauce. Combine the sugar, cornflour, milk and vanilla essence in a jug and blend thoroughly. Cook on Maximum (Full) for 1½ minutes, then stir and cook for a further 1½ minutes until the sauce thickens and a thick bracelet of curd appears round the edges.
5. Beat the egg yolk thoroughly, then add 2 tablespoons of the hot sauce and beat again. Pour into the sauce and stir thoroughly. Reduce the microwave setting to Medium Low (35%) and cook for a further minute. Stir before serving with the pudding. Decorate with the remaining pieces of ginger.

Clockwise from left: Liver pâté; Ginger pudding with custard; Lettuce and cucumber salad; Mushroom and walnut quiche

AUTUMN EVENING

CUCUMBER PISELLI

LAMB CHOPS IN ESPAGNOLE SAUCE

ROAST ONIONS

COFFEE AND WALNUT GÂTEAU WITH BRANDY SAUCE

Prepare the cucumber ahead of time and chill.
Cook the Roast Onions ahead of time. Reheat in a small serving dish for 2–3 minutes.
Cook the gâteau ahead of time and keep covered with cling film until required.
Cook the sauce ahead of time and chill until required.
Cook the lamb chops just before the meal but at step 6 cook covered and leave covered while reheating the onions.

CUCUMBER PISELLI

PREPARATION TIME: *about 10 minutes*
COOKING TIME: *about 7 minutes*
MICROWAVE SETTING: *Maximum (Full)*

$\frac{1}{2}$ *large cucumber, peeled*
100g (4oz) fresh or frozen peas
4 tablespoons salted water
1 sprig mint

3 tablespoons double cream
2 teaspoons chopped fresh parsley, to garnish
watercress, to garnish

1. Halve the cucumber crossways. Cut through the middle of each lengthways. Remove the seeds.
2. Place the 4 cucumber pieces, hollows uppermost, in a single layer in a small dish. Cover with cling film, vent and cook for 2 minutes or until tender. Drain thoroughly.
3. Put the peas, salted water and mint in a dish. Cover, vent and cook for 3 minutes, then drain. Purée the peas and mint with the cream, then spoon into the cucumber. Garnish with parsley and watercress. Serve warm.

Lamb chops in espagnole sauce with Roast onions; Cucumber piselli; Coffee and walnut gâteau with brandy sauce

LAMB CHOPS IN ESPAGNOLE SAUCE

PREPARATION TIME: *15 minutes*
COOKING TIME: *about 26 minutes*
MICROWAVE SETTING: *Maximum (Full); then Medium Low (35%)*

4 × 75 g (3 oz) lamb chops, 2.5 cm (1 inch) thick	*300 ml ($\frac{1}{2}$ pint) hot strong beef stock*
25 g (1 oz) butter	*$\frac{1}{4}$ teaspoon powdered bay leaf*
1 small onion, finely chopped	*2 parsley sprigs*
2 rashers back bacon, rinds removed and chopped	*5 thyme sprigs*
25 g (1 oz) flour	*$\frac{1}{4}$ teaspoon freshly ground black pepper*
	salt

1. Trim the chops and arrange in a shallow dish, placing the thick part of the chop towards the outside of the dish. Cook on Maximum (Full) for 2 minutes, then turn the dish and cook for a further 2 minutes. Cover and set aside.
2. Put the butter in a 1.2 litre (2 pint) bowl, add the onion and cook for 3 minutes. Stir in the bacon and cook for a further 2 minutes or until the onion is brown.
3. Stir in the flour and cook until brown, about 2 minutes.
4. Add the stock, bay leaf, parsley, 1 thyme sprig and pepper. Stir thoroughly, then three-quarters cover with cling film and cook for 3 minutes. Stir. Cook for a further 2 minutes, then add the juice from the chops.
5. Purée the sauce. Add salt to taste and reheat in the cooking bowl for 1 minute, then strain on to the chops.
6. Reduce the setting and cook, uncovered, on Medium Low (35%) for 5 minutes. Turn the dish, then cook for a further 5 minutes. Garnish with the remaining thyme.

ROAST ONIONS

PREPARATION TIME: *15 minutes*
COOKING TIME: *4 minutes, plus standing*
MICROWAVE SETTING: *Maximum (Full)*

1 tablespoon vegetable oil	*1 tablespoon soft dark brown sugar*
$\frac{1}{4}$ teaspoon salt	*$\frac{1}{4}$ teaspoon paprika*
225 g (8 oz) baby onions, peeled and left whole	

A browning dish is required for this recipe.

1. Preheat a browning dish to Maximum according to the manufacturer's directions. Quickly add the oil and salt, toss in the onions, then sprinkle with the sugar and paprika. Stir quickly, cover and cook for 2 minutes, then stir and cook for a further 2 minutes.
2. Remove the cover immediately after cooking and leave to stand for 2–3 minutes before serving.

COFFEE AND WALNUT GÂTEAU WITH BRANDY SAUCE

PREPARATION TIME: *10 minutes (cake); 5 minutes (sauce)*
COOKING TIME: *4 minutes, plus standing (cake); 8 minutes (sauce)*
MICROWAVE SETTING: *Maximum (Full); then Medium Low (35%)*

40 g (1$\frac{1}{2}$ oz) self-raising flour	**Sauce:**
15 g ($\frac{1}{2}$ oz) cornflour	*35 g (1$\frac{1}{4}$ oz) butter, softened*
$\frac{1}{2}$ teaspoon baking powder	*15 g ($\frac{1}{2}$ oz) flour*
50 g (2 oz) soft margarine	*9 tablespoons hot water*
50 g (2 oz) soft dark brown sugar	*1 egg yolk*
1 teaspoon coffee essence	*120 ml (4 fl oz) whipping cream*
1 egg	*2 teaspoons rum*
40 g (1$\frac{1}{2}$ oz) walnuts, finely chopped	*2 teaspoons brandy*
Filling:	*25 g (1 oz) icing sugar, sifted*
2 tablespoons apricot jam	*$\frac{1}{4}$ teaspoon vanilla essence*
1 × 300 g (11 oz) can mandarin segments, drained	*walnut half, to decorate*

1. Grease a 600 ml (1 pint), 12$\frac{1}{2}$ cm (5 inch) diameter soufflé dish and line the base and sides with greased greaseproof paper, so that the paper stands 2$\frac{1}{2}$ cm (1 inch) higher than the dish.
2. To make the cake, sift the flour, cornflour and baking powder together into a mixing bowl. Add the margarine, brown sugar, coffee essence, egg and walnuts and beat for 1 minute until the mixture is smooth. Spoon into the cake case and cook for 1 minute. Turn the dish and cook for a further minute, then leave to stand for 3–4 minutes. Carefully turn out the cake, then reverse again, so that the cake is the right way up. Leave to cool.
3. Split the cake horizontally into 3 pieces and sandwich with layers of jam and mandarin segments. Spread a border of jam round the top of the cake and decorate with a circle of mandarin segments and the walnut half. Transfer carefully to a serving plate.
4. To make the sauce, combine 15 g ($\frac{1}{2}$ oz) of the butter and the flour in a small bowl and beat until smooth.
5. Put the water into a medium bowl and cook for 2 minutes or until steaming. Whisk in the butter mixture a little at a time. Cook for 1 minute, stirring once.
6. Beat the egg yolk with 2 tablespoons of the sauce and gradually beat into the remaining sauce. Reduce the setting to Medium Low (35%) and cook for 1 minute, beating after 30 seconds and at the end until thickened.
7. Remove the bowl and beat in the remaining butter a little at a time. Leave to cool.
8. Half whip the cream, then add the rum, brandy, icing sugar and vanilla essence and beat until thick. Gradually beat the sauce into the cream. Serve with the gâteau.

MENUS

FOR

FOUR

Provided you have enough ideas, family meals need not be monotonous and you will find plenty of new recipes in this chapter. In keeping with the rest of the book each menu has a theme but you can mix and match to suit your whim. Some of the menus are designed to be easy on the food budget, whilst others verge on the exotic and upmarket.

Should you wish to extend any of the recipes to serve eight or more, you will be much more successful if you cook each batch separately, then put them together when reheating or serve in two separate dishes.

Family life is changing and eating together is becoming more and more of a rarity. Cook ahead and let each member help themselves, taking the prepared food direct from the refrigerator and reheating their own portions. The food will remain in good condition for all, whether they are eating at 6 p.m. or midnight.

```
┌──────────────────────────────────┐
│                                  │
│      WEEKEND BRUNCH              │
│                                  │
│      MIXED FRUIT COMPOTE         │
│                                  │
│    GAMMON AND HONEY STEAKS       │
│                                  │
│         SODA BREAD               │
│                                  │
│       BLACKBERRY JAM             │
│                                  │
└──────────────────────────────────┘
```

The Blackberry Jam can be prepared 1–2 weeks ahead and kept in a cool place.

Prepare the compote and the topping up to 2 days ahead of time but do not assemble. Keep chilled separately. Add the topping just before serving.

Trim, snip and arrange the gammon steaks in the dish, cover with greaseproof paper and overwrap with cling film. Keep chilled for up to 12 hours, but extend the cooking time due to the cooler starting temperature. You can prepare the sauce ahead of time in a jug or bowl, then complete the dish just before serving the compôte, reheating the steaks and sauce for 2 minutes if necessary.

The Soda Bread is best freshly cooked but can be refreshed on Maximum (Full) for 30–60 seconds.

MIXED FRUIT COMPOTE

PREPARATION TIME: *about 10 minutes*
COOKING TIME: *13 minutes, plus standing*
MICROWAVE SETTING: *Maximum (Full)*

3 oranges	Topping:
2 teaspoons lemon juice	25g (1oz) shelled
1 tablespoon sugar	almonds, slivered with a
200ml (7floz) water	sharp knife
225g (8oz) mixed dried	2 tablespoons rolled
apricots, peaches and	porridge oats
pears	

1. Squeeze the juice from one of the oranges and put into a 2 litre (3½ pint) bowl with the lemon juice and sugar. Add the water, then stir in the fruit.
2. Cover the bowl with cling film, pulling back one corner to vent and cook for 5 minutes.
3. Pull the cling film back just sufficiently to insert a wooden spoon, stir the fruit, then cook for a further 5 minutes. Without uncovering, leave to stand for at least 30 minutes.
4. Meanwhile prepare the topping. Mix the slivered almonds and oats together on a piece of greaseproof paper and cook for 2–3 minutes, stirring frequently until the almonds are just lightly browned. (Stirring is important, otherwise patches of burnt almonds and oats will appear. It is also important to keep checking the nuts as they can burn quite quickly.)
5. After the fruit has had its standing time, remove the cover and segment the remaining 2 oranges into the fruit, squeezing the surplus juice from the membranes. Stir, then cover and chill until required.
6. Sprinkle the topping over the fruit in individual bowls just before serving.

GAMMON AND HONEY STEAKS

PREPARATION TIME: *about 5 minutes*
COOKING TIME: *about 11 minutes*
MICROWAVE SETTING: *Maximum (Full)*

4 × 120g (4½oz) gammon steaks	1 teaspoon lemon juice
	pinch of ground cloves
5 tablespoons chicken stock	1 teaspoon cornflour
	To garnish:
2 tablespoons clear honey	lemon slices
	sprig of parsley

1. Trim away the excess fat from the gammon steaks, then snip through the edges with scissors to prevent them from curling up during cooking. Place the slices in a large shallow dish, cover with greaseproof paper and cook for 2 minutes.
2. Put the chicken stock, honey, lemon juice, cloves and cornflour into the cooking dish and stir together until well blended. Cook for 2 minutes or until thick, stirring once during cooking.
3. Replace the gammon in the dish, repositioning the slices so that the less cooked parts are towards the outside. Spoon over the sauce and cook for 4 minutes. Turn the steaks over and cook for a further 3 minutes or until the gammon is just tender. Cover and leave to stand for about 3 minutes before serving garnished with lemon slices and parsley.

SODA BREAD

PREPARATION TIME: *15 minutes*
COOKING TIME: *6 minutes, plus standing*
MICROWAVE SETTING: *Maximum (Full)*

100g (4oz) plain flour	1 tablespoon salad oil
200g (8oz) wholewheat flour	150ml (¼ pint) plain unsweetened yogurt
1 teaspoon bicarbonate of soda	150ml (¼ pint) water
1 teaspoon baking powder	1 teaspoon molasses (optional)
1 teaspoon salt	1 teaspoon milk (optional)

1. Mix together the flours, bicarbonate of soda, baking powder and salt in a bowl.
2. Add the oil, yogurt and water and mix to form a soft dough.
3. Shape the dough into a 15 cm (6 inch) round on a well-floured surface, then using a long-bladed knife, make 2 deep cuts crossways cutting almost through the dough.
4. Lift it carefully on to a paper towel and cook for just 5 minutes.
5. Mix together the molasses and milk, if using, then brush over the surface. Cook for a further minute.
6. Remove the bread, peel off the paper and leave to stand for 5 minutes, before slicing and serving.

BLACKBERRY JAM

PREPARATION TIME: *5 minutes*
COOKING TIME: *14 minutes*
MICROWAVE SETTING: *Medium Low (35%); then Maximum (Full)*

225 g (8 oz) frozen blackberries
225 g (8 oz) caster sugar

1. Mix the blackberries and sugar together in a 2.75 litre (5 pint) ovenglass mixing bowl. Three-quarters cover with cling film and cook on Medium Low (35%) for 6 minutes or until the blackberries are thawed and the sugar is beginning to dissolve. Stir thoroughly.
2. Raise the setting to Maximum (Full), uncover and cook for 3 minutes, stirring every minute, until all the sugar is dissolved.
3. Cook for a further 5 minutes without stirring until the jam is boiling rapidly. Stir with a long-handled wooden spoon as the jam tends to rise and foam up. Test for setting by dropping a teaspoon of the liquid on to a cold plate. Draw the tip of a spoon or finger through the syrup which should wrinkle slightly. Do not overcook as the jam continues to thicken as it cools.
4. Spoon the jam into an attractive dish or pot and seal in the usual way if the jam is to be kept for more than a few days.

Gammon and honey steaks: Soda bread with blackberry jam; Mixed fruit compote

FREEZE NOW, EAT LATER

SPLIT PEA SOUP

BEEF CARBONNADE

RATATOUILLE

RASPBERRY CHEESECAKE

As the title suggests, all these dishes may be prepared in advance and frozen. For maximum success it is advisable to transfer the dishes from the freezer to the refrigerator several hours before reheating.
Freeze the Beef Carbonnade for 3–4 months, thaw in the microwave oven and reheat thoroughly, stirring occasionally, allowing 10–20 minutes, then keep hot in a conventional oven.
Freeze the Split Pea Soup for up to 4 months, thaw in the microwave oven or in a saucepan on the hob.
Freeze the Ratatouille for 3–4 months. It reheats well in the microwave oven and can be thawed and reheated on Medium (50%) while the main course is being eaten. Stir once and allow an extra 2 minutes on Maximum (Full) before serving.
Freeze the Raspberry Cheesecake for up to 2 months. To hasten thawing, it may be heated on Low (10%) for a few minutes.

SPLIT PEA SOUP

PREPARATION TIME: *10 minutes, plus soaking*
COOKING TIME: *about 40 minutes*
MICROWAVE SETTING: *Maximum (Full)*

225 g (8 oz) green or yellow split peas	*1 celery stick, scraped and finely chopped*
1.2 litres (2 pints) boiling water	*15 g (½ oz) butter*
	½ teaspoon fennel seed
2 bacon rashers, rinded and chopped	*1 beef stock cube*
	salt
1 small onion, peeled and finely chopped	*freshly ground black pepper*
	single cream, to garnish

If the soup is left to stand after cooking, it will thicken, so add a little stock or water when reheating.

1. Wash and drain the split peas in a strainer. Put into a large 2.75 litre (5 pint) bowl with 600 ml (1 pint) boiling water. Stir once, then cover and leave to soak for 2 hours.
2. Meanwhile, combine the bacon, onion, celery and butter in a 1.2 litre (2 pint) basin. Cook for 5 minutes or until the onion is soft, stirring once.

3. Add the mixture to the split peas and liquid in the large bowl. Stir in the fennel seeds, crumble in the stock cube and add the remaining 600 ml (1 pint) boiling water.
4. Three-quarters cover with cling film and cook for 30 minutes, stirring occasionally until the peas are soft.
5. Liquidize the soup, return to the large bowl and reheat for 3–5 minutes. Add salt and pepper to taste.
6. Cool and freeze in the usual way if required. (F) Thaw and reheat in a saucepan on the hob or in the bowl in the microwave oven on Maximum (Full), breaking up the soup as it thaws. Allow about 8 minutes in a covered bowl for reheating after thawing. Stir once or twice during reheating. Swirl with cream before serving.

BEEF CARBONNADE

PREPARATION TIME: *15 minutes*
COOKING TIME: *30 minutes, plus tenderizing and standing*
MICROWAVE SETTING: *Maximum (Full)*

750 g (1½ lb) chuck steak, cut 1 cm (½ inch) cubes	*2 bay leaves*
	1 tablespoon dark brown sugar
1 teaspoon meat tenderizer	
2 tablespoons plain flour	*1 tablespoon vinegar*
2 tablespoons salad oil	*300 ml (½ pint) brown ale*
1 large onion, peeled and sliced into rings	*150 ml (¼ pint) beef stock*
	salt
1 garlic clove, peeled and crushed	*freshly ground black pepper*
	2 teaspoons cornflour
1 teaspoon chopped thyme	*2 tablespoons cold water*
1 tablespoon chopped fresh parsley	

If the reheated gravy is too thin, thicken with a little flour and butter, but traditionally this is not a thick gravy.

1. Put the cubed beef into a bowl and sprinkle with the meat tenderizer. Stir once, then cover and leave at room temperature for 30 minutes.
2. Combine the flour and oil in a large deep casserole and cook for 6 minutes or until the mixture is brown.
3. Add the beef, stir once and cook for 5 minutes.
4. Add the onion, garlic, herbs, sugar, vinegar, brown ale and beef stock with salt and pepper to taste. Cover and cook for 20 minutes, stirring occasionally.
5. Blend the cornflour and cold water together, stir into the stew and cook for 5 minutes until the sauce bubbles and thickens. Leave to stand for 5 minutes before serving.
6. Cool rapidly, then freeze in the usual way. (F)
7. To thaw and reheat, put the block of stew into the casserole in which it was cooked, add 2 tablespoons cold water and cook covered on Maximum (Full) for 5 minutes or until the meat softens around the outside. Break up the pieces, then re-cover and cook for 5 minutes. Repeat once or twice until fully thawed, then cook for 5 minutes or until bubbles appear round the edge. Stir once and cook until the bubbles re-appear round the edge, when the meat will be hot enough.

Ratatouille; Beef carbonnade; Split pea soup

RATATOUILLE

PREPARATION TIME: *15 minutes*
COOKING TIME: *22 minutes, plus standing*
MICROWAVE SETTING: *Maximum (Full)*

1 × 225 g (8 oz) aubergine	*225 g (8 oz) tomatoes,*
salt	*skinned and coarsely*
1 large onion, peeled and	*chopped*
finely chopped	*2 tablespoons tomato*
1 garlic clove, peeled and	*purée*
crushed	*1–3 tablespoons red wine*
1 tablespoon olive oil	*pinch of sugar*
1 red pepper, cored,	*freshly ground black*
seeded and cut into strips	*pepper*
1 green pepper, cored,	
seeded and cut into strips	

1. Top, tail and slice the unskinned aubergine. Put into a colander, sprinkle with salt and leave for 45 minutes. Drain and pat dry with paper towels.

2. After the aubergine has been standing for 30 minutes start to cook the remaining ingredients. Combine the onion, garlic and olive oil in a deep casserole and cook for about 6 minutes until the onion is soft but not brown. Stir occasionally during cooking.

3. Add the aubergine slices and the pepper strips, cover and cook for 6 minutes.

4. Stir in the tomatoes, tomato purée and 1 tablespoon wine, the pinch of sugar, pepper and salt to taste. Cook uncovered for 5 minutes or until most of the liquid has been absorbed, but if the mixture dries out too much, add the remaining wine. The vegetables should be tender.

5. Cover and cook for a further 5 minutes, then leave to stand for 10 minutes before serving.

6. To freeze, pack and store in the usual way. (F) Defrost and reheat the ratatouille in a covered container on Maximum (Full), gently stirring as soon as it is possible to separate the pieces. Leave to stand for 5 minutes, then continue reheating for about 8 minutes or until hot. Ratatouille may also be served cold: Ignore the reheating times and thaw overnight in the refrigerator.

RASPBERRY CHEESECAKE

PREPARATION TIME: *15 minutes*
COOKING TIME: *10 minutes, plus standing*
MICROWAVE SETTING: *Maximum (Full); then Medium Low (35%)*

Crumb crust:

50g (2oz) butter or margarine

100g (4oz) shortcake biscuits, finely crushed

25g (1oz) grated hazelnuts

Filling:

100g (4oz) cottage cheese

100g (4oz) full fat soft cheese

50g (2oz) sugar

1 egg, beaten

3 teaspoons fresh lemon juice

½ teaspoon vanilla flavouring

Topping:

1 tablespoon cornflour

1 × 275g (10oz) can raspberries in syrup

whipped cream, to decorate

Blackcurrants or redcurrants could be used in place of the raspberries for the topping.

1. To make the crumb crust, put the butter or margarine in a 15 cm (6 inch) diameter shallow plastic cake dish and

Raspberry cheesecake

cook on Maximum (Full) for 30 seconds or until the butter has melted. Stir in the biscuits and nuts and press evenly into the base of the dish. Cook for 1 minute.
2. Beat the cheeses, sugar, egg, lemon juice and vanilla flavouring thoroughly together in the liquidizer or mix by hand. Press through a sieve into a jug or bowl.
3. Cook the filling on Maximum (Full) for 30 seconds, whisk and cook for another 30 seconds. Whisk again, then cook for a further 30 seconds, or until thickened. Whisk and pour the mixture into the crumb-lined dish. Reduce the setting to Medium Low (35%) and cook for 4 minutes, giving the dish a quarter-turn every minute. Leave to stand for 15 minutes, then chill.
4. To make the topping, blend the cornflour and 2 tablespoons of the juice from the raspberries in a 1.2 litre (2 pint) bowl and stir in the raspberries and juice. Cook on Maximum (Full) for 3½ minutes, stirring once, until the mixture thickens to a dropping consistency.
5. Spread the topping over the chilled cheesecake and refrigerate or freeze. (F)
6. To thaw, preferably leave at room temperature but thawing can be hastened by giving an occasional 20 seconds on Medium Low (35%) or better still for 10 minutes on Low (10%). To unmould dip the base of the dish into hot water for a few seconds. Decorate with piped, whipped cream.

LOW FAT FARE

HOT SPICED GRAPEFRUIT

KIDNEY BEAN BOLOGNESE

TARRAGON POTATOES

FRUIT SALAD MERINGUE

Prepare the grapefruit in advance but cook just before your proposed serving time.
Cook the Kidney Bean Bolognese a few hours ahead of time and keep chilled. Reheat in a covered dish while eating the grapefruit.
Prepare and cook the Tarragon Potatoes just before the meal and keep hot in a conventional oven.
Cook the Fruit Salad Meringue up to 6 hours ahead of time and keep chilled. Serve cold or reheat just before serving but do not leave the kitchen while you are reheating the meringue as it requires watching.

HOT SPICED GRAPEFRUIT

PREPARATION TIME: *about 5 minutes*
COOKING TIME: *4 minutes*
MICROWAVE SETTING: *Maximum (Full)*

2 × 350–400g (12–14oz) grapefruit, rinsed and dried
1 tablespoon lime cordial
1 teaspoon ground nutmeg
twists of lime peel, to garnish

1. Halve the grapefruit in the usual way, and loosen the segments with a grapefruit knife. Sprinkle with the lime cordial and nutmeg.
2. Put into suitable individual dishes to make handling easier and cook for 2 minutes. Give each dish a half-turn and cook for a further 2 minutes. Serve hot, garnished with lime.

Hot spiced grapefruit

KIDNEY BEAN BOLOGNESE

PREPARATION TIME: *about 10 minutes*
COOKING TIME: *20 minutes*
MICROWAVE SETTING: *Maximum (Full)*

350g (12 oz) lean minced beef	*2 tablespoons plain flour*
1 back bacon rasher, rinded and finely chopped	*1 beef stock cube*
	300ml (½ pint) boiling water
1 small onion, peeled and finely chopped	*1 × 215g (7½ oz) can red kidney beans*
1 carrot, scraped and grated	*salt*
1 celery stick, finely chopped	*freshly ground black pepper*

1. Mix the beef, bacon, onion, carrot and celery in a 2 litre (3½ pint) bowl and cook for 5 minutes, stirring occasionally.
2. Stir in the flour. Crumble the meat stock cube into the water, blend well, then add to the meat mixture. Add the kidney beans and salt and pepper to taste. Three-quarters cover with cling film and cook for 15 minutes, stirring occasionally. Serve with potatoes, pasta or boiled rice.

TARRAGON POTATOES

PREPARATION TIME: *about 10 minutes*
COOKING TIME: *9 minutes, plus browning (optional)*
MICROWAVE SETTING: *Maximum (Full)*

450g (1 lb) potatoes	*1 small onion, peeled and minced*
150ml (¼ pint) skimmed chicken stock	*½ teaspoon dried tarragon*
1 small green pepper, cored, seeded and minced	*salt*
	freshly ground black pepper

1. Peel the potatoes, slice 3mm (⅛ inch) thick and cut into matchstick strips.
2. Combine all the ingredients, adding salt and pepper to taste, and spread evenly in a 20–23cm (8–9 inch) round dish (flameproof if possible), cover with cling film, pulling back one corner to vent and cook for 9 minutes or until the potatoes are tender.
3. Carefully remove the cling film, if necessary, transfer the potatoes to a dish suitable for placing under a preheated conventional grill and brown them.

FRUIT SALAD MERINGUE

PREPARATION TIME: *about 5 minutes, plus chilling*
COOKING TIME: *2½ minutes*
MICROWAVE SETTING: *Maximum (Full)*

2 × 285g (10 oz) cans fruit cocktail in fruit juice	*50g (2 oz) sifted icing sugar*
1 egg white	*4 glacé cherries, to decorate*

If you decide to serve this dessert hot, do not worry if the meringue seems to sink in the glasses when chilled. It will rise and puff up again as new. When hot the dessert is equally delicious and it may be a good choice to serve in the colder weather.

1. Put 4 wine glasses into the refrigerator to chill. Place the cans of fruit cocktail in the refrigerator for 30 minutes, then open the cans and divide the fruit and juices between the glasses.
2. Beat the egg white until stiff, then beat in the sugar until the mixture regains its stiffness.
3. Top the fruit with the meringue which should be 8mm (¾ inch) below the rim of the glass.
4. Cook the glasses together for 1½ minutes. Give each glass a half-turn, then cook for a further minute or until the meringue puffs up above the glasses. Decorate with the cherries and serve directly, chill in the refrigerator if preferred, or reheat, allowing about 30 seconds per glass on Maximum (Full) just before serving.

Clockwise from bottom: Kidney bean bolognese with pasta serving suggestion; Tarragon potatoes; Fruit salad meringue

CHEAP AND CHEERFUL

CHICKEN SOUP

LIVER RAGOÛT

BAVARIAN CABBAGE

ORANGE BREAD AND BUTTER PUDDING

Cook the Bavarian Cabbage without adding the soured cream up to 24 hours ahead. Reheat while browning the Liver Ragoût, or reheat up to 1 hour before serving time. Stir in the cream, cover the dish with foil and keep warm in a low conventional oven.

Prepare the ingredients for the Chicken Soup and cook in the microwave oven or in a saucepan just before the meal or cook up to 3 hours ahead and reheat on Maximum (Full) in a covered tureen for 5–8 minutes before serving. Remember to stir thoroughly before serving. Assemble the Liver Ragoût up to 1 hour ahead of time and cook while serving and eating the first course.

Prepare the Orange Bread and Butter Pudding up to the end of step 3 ahead of time, then cook while eating the main course or serve cold.

CHICKEN SOUP

PREPARATION TIME: *about 20 minutes*
COOKING TIME: *50–60 minutes*
MICROWAVE SETTING: *Maximum (Full)*

1 chicken carcass	1 bay leaf
giblets, excluding liver (optional)	1 chicken stock cube, crumbled (optional)
1.2 litres (2 pints) water	175 g (6 oz) leftover cold chicken, shredded
salt	
freshly ground black pepper	2 tablespoons frozen peas
½ onion	2–3 small boiled potatoes, quartered
½ carrot	1 cooked carrot, sliced

1. To make stock from one carcass, cut up the bones and, if using the giblets, halve the pieces except for the gizzard. This is to prevent popping during cooking.
2. Put the bones and giblets into a 2 litre (3½ pint) bowl, cover with the water and add salt, pepper, a piece of onion and a piece of carrot. Three-quarters cover with cling film and cook for 35–45 minutes.
3. Put the chicken stock, bay leaf and crumbled stock cube, if using, into a large 2.75 litre (5 pint) bowl and cook 8 minutes. Strain the stock into another bowl, cool

rapidly, then chill until the fat solidifies. Remove the fat and use as required. If not used immediately, boil up the stock once in every 24 hours to prevent rancidity; 900 ml (1½ pints) stock takes about 8 minutes.
4. Add the remaining ingredients. Three-quarters cover with cling film and cook for 8 minutes or until the chicken is thoroughly reheated. Serve hot.

LIVER RAGOÛT

PREPARATION TIME: *about 15 minutes*
COOKING TIME: *about 15 minutes, plus browning*
MICROWAVE SETTING: *Maximum (Full)*

450 g (1 lb) ox liver, rinsed, trimmed and thinly sliced	6 streaky bacon rashers, rinded and cut into thin strips
salt	
freshly ground black pepper	1 beef stock cube, crumbled
1 medium onion, peeled and thinly sliced	300 ml (½ pint) hot water
450 g (1 lb) potatoes, peeled and thinly sliced	2 tablespoons tomato ketchup
	sprig of sage

1. Layer the liver in a deep flameproof dish, sprinkling each layer lightly with salt and pepper.
2. Spread the onion over the liver, cover with the potatoes and top with the bacon strips.
3. Dissolve the beef stock cube in the hot water, then stir in the tomato ketchup. Pour into the casserole, cover with a lid and cook for 15 minutes or until the liver is just pink inside and the potatoes are soft.
4. For a crispy browned finish, brown under a preheated conventional grill. Garnish with the sage and serve hot.

BAVARIAN CABBAGE

PREPARATION TIME: *15 minutes*
COOKING TIME: *15 minutes*
MICROWAVE SETTING: *Maximum (Full)*

450 g (1 lb) red cabbage, shredded	2 tablespoons soured cream
2 red dessert apples, cored and chopped	salt
8 tablespoons water	freshly ground black pepper
1 teaspoon fresh lemon juice	

1. Mix the cabbage, apples, water and lemon juice in a large dish. Three-quarters cover with cling film and cook for 15 minutes, stirring about 3 times through the gap.
2. Carefully remove the cling film, stir in the soured cream and add salt and pepper to taste.

Clockwise from top left: Chicken soup; Orange bread and butter pudding; Bavarian cabbage; Liver ragoût

ORANGE BREAD AND BUTTER PUDDING

PREPARATION TIME: *10 minutes*
COOKING TIME: *about 11½ minutes, plus browning*
MICROWAVE SETTING: *Maximum (Full); then Medium Low (35%)*

3 slices bread from a large cut loaf, buttered	*1 tablespoon mixed chopped peel*
300ml (½ pint) milk	*3 tablespoons demerara sugar*
2 tablespoons sultanas	
1 tablespoon currants	*2 eggs*
2 tablespoons grated orange rind	*orange quarters, to garnish*

1. Cut each slice of bread into 4 triangles and arrange 10 of these around the base and sides of a 2 litre (1½ pint) pie dish, buttered side against the dish. Place the extra 2 triangles buttered side up in the centre of the dish. The crusts should form a border around the edges of the dish.

2. Combine the milk, sultanas, currants, grated orange rind and chopped peel and 1 tablespoon of the sugar in a bowl or jug and without covering, cook for 2½ minutes or until the milk is hot but not boiling.

3. Beat the eggs in a separate small bowl. Add 2 tablespoons of the hot milk mixture, stir thoroughly, then pour into the milk mixture. Stir, then pour into the pie dish.

4. Reduce the setting to Medium Low (35%) and cook for 7 minutes. Turn the dish round, sprinkle the remaining sugar over the pudding and cook for a further 2 minutes or until the custard is just set. The 2 triangles of bread placed in the base of the dish may rise to the top during cooking and the custard may not be quite set in the middle, but do not give additional cooking time which might cause curdling.

5. For a more attractive finish, brown the pudding under a preheated conventional grill at a distance of 15–21 cm (6–8 inches). Serve hot or cold, garnished with the orange quarters.

MEAL IN ONE

SOUP AND CHICKEN COMBO

BAKED APPLES

The Soup and Chicken Combo is just as delicious if it has been prepared ahead of time and frozen. Freeze for up to 6 months. Otherwise prepare a few hours ahead and keep chilled. Reheat in the microwave oven or in a saucepan on the hob according to the recipe instructions.

For an ordinary family meal Baked Apples may be prepared ahead of time and reheated on Maximum (Full), allowing approximately 30 seconds per apple but because of the likelihood of collapse, it is probably better to prepare the apples just before the meal, part cook during the meal and complete cooking after the chicken and soup have been served. If when reheating one or more apples cook more quickly than the others, remove it while cooking the rest.

SOUP AND CHICKEN COMBO

PREPARATION TIME: *about 20 minutes*
COOKING TIME: *1–1½ hours, plus chilling and reheating*
MICROWAVE SETTING: *Maximum (Full); then Medium (50%) or Medium Low (35%)*

1 × 1.5 kg (3½ lb) oven-ready chicken, cut into sixteen pieces (well washed giblets, except the liver, may be included)	*2 tablespoons pearl barley*
	1½ teaspoons salt
	½ teaspoon celery salt
	¼ teaspoon freshly ground black pepper
350 g (12 oz) onions, peeled and finely sliced	*2 bay leaves*
1 large carrot, scraped and grated	*600 ml (1 pint) boiling water*
	chopped parsley, to garnish

This is a very versatile dish. The soup can be served thick without the chicken pieces, which can be kept for another dish. The soup can be served as a first course, followed by the chicken which can be reheated separately and served with rice or other vegetables, or the dish can be served as a meal in one.

1. Combine all the ingredients in a large 2.5 litre (4½ pint) deep casserole. Cover with the lid and cook on Maximum (Full) for 15 minutes, repositioning the chicken pieces once during cooking.
2. Reduce the setting to Medium (50%) and cook for 45 minutes or Medium Low (35%) and cook for 1 hour. Reposition the chicken pieces once during cooking.

3. Take out the chicken pieces and giblets with a slotted spoon, remove the skin and bones and discard the giblets (this is easier if you wait until the chicken is cool enough to handle).
4. Cool rapidly, then cover and keep chilled.
5. Cool the soup in the casserole, then chill until the fat solidifies on top. Remove the fat.
6. Stir the chicken pieces into the soup and reheat on Maximum (Full) for 10–15 minutes, stirring occasionally. (The soup thickens considerably during chilling time. Add extra stock if necessary before reheating.) (F) Serve straightaway garnished with chopped parsley.

BAKED APPLES

PREPARATION TIME: *5 minutes*
COOKING TIME: *10 minutes, plus standing*
MICROWAVE SETTING: *Maximum (Full)*

4 tablespoons raisins	*4 × 225 g (8 oz) cooking apples*
75 g (3 oz) soft dark brown sugar	
	whipped cream, to serve
6 tablespoons water	*lime peel, to decorate*

1. Combine the raisins, sugar and water in a large shallow dish.
2. Rinse, dry and core the apples and score them round the waist with a stainless steel knife. Pare away a sliver of peel from around the core area at either end.
3. Put the apples in the dish, placing them as near to the corners as possible and cook, uncovered, for 5 minutes. Turn the apples over and cook for a further 5 minutes, then cover with cling film or foil and leave for 10 minutes or until the apples are tender (the skins of baked apples when cooked in the microwave remain tough).
4. Scoop the filling from the dish into the centres of the apples and serve at once with a spoonful of cream, studded with pieces of lime peel.

Baked apple; Soup and chicken combo

SUNSHINE LUNCH

ASPIC TOMATOES

CHICKEN À LA KING

PILAU RICE

PINEAPPLE UPSIDE-DOWN PUDDING

Pre-cook and freeze the Pilau Rice if preferred for up to 2 months. Thaw uncovered in the microwave oven while eating the first course, allowing about 4 minutes on Maximum (Full). Stir before serving. Cook the Chicken à la King in advance and keep chilled or freeze. Store frozen for up to 2 months. Reheat before serving the Aspic Tomatoes; or cook freshly just before the meal. Cover with foil and keep hot in a low conventional oven.
The Pineapple Upside-Down Pudding can be prepared in advance up to the end of step 2, then completed and put in the oven to cook just before eating the main course. Alternatively, it can be completely cooked ahead of time and frozen for up to 3 months. Preferably defrost at room temperature but it may be thawed and reheated on Maximum (Full) for 1 minute, followed by Medium Low (35%) for 8–10 minutes. This pudding can be cooked several hours ahead and then refreshed. Place on the serving dish pineapple-side up and allow 3–4 minutes on Maximum (Full), giving the dish a quarter-turn every minute.

ASPIC TOMATOES

PREPARATION TIME: *15 minutes*
COOKING TIME: *45 seconds, plus standing*
MICROWAVE SETTING: *Maximum (Full)*

4 firm medium tomatoes	*⅛ teaspoon freshly ground black pepper*
4 tablespoons tomato juice	
1 teaspoon powdered gelatine	*Worcestershire sauce*
	50g (2oz) shelled cooked prawns
pinch of salt	
pinch of sugar	

1. Remove a slice from the top of each tomato and set aside. Scoop the seeds and pulp into a strainer over a small bowl and press the pulp through. Turn the tomato shells upside down and place in the strainer to drain.
2. Put the tomato juice in a jug and cook for 45 seconds or until nearly boiling. Sprinkle the powdered gelatine over the surface and stir until dissolved. Leave for 5 minutes, then pour from a height into the tomato mixture.
3. Stir in the salt, sugar, pepper, a few drops of Worcestershire sauce and the prawns and chill until just beginning to set.

4. Spoon the jellied tomato into the shells and top with the reserved lids. Chill until set. Serve on a bed of shredded crisp lettuce, watercress and chicory leaves.

CHICKEN À LA KING

PREPARATION TIME: *15 minutes*
COOKING TIME: *16 minutes*
MICROWAVE SETTING: *Maximum (Full)*

4 boneless chicken breasts, total weight 500g (1¼lb)	*¼ green pepper, cored seeded and finely diced*
salt	*40g (1½oz) flour*
freshly ground black pepper	*450ml (¾ pint) milk*
	½ chicken stock cube
50g (2oz) butter or margarine	*100g (4oz) button mushrooms, sliced*
¼ red pepper, cored, seeded and finely diced	*1 tablespoon sherry*
	2 tablespoons double cream

The sauce may thicken during standing and cooling. If reheating add a few extra spoonfuls of milk or stock.

1. Skin the chicken, sprinkle with salt and pepper, then cut into bite-sized chunks, cover and set aside.
2. Put the butter in a deep casserole or bowl and cook for 1 minute or until melted. Stir the diced peppers into the butter and cook for 2 minutes.
3. Mix in the flour, then stir in the milk and crumble in the stock cube. Cook for 4 minutes, stirring once.
4. Add the mushrooms, the reserved chicken and the sherry, three-quarters cover with a lid or cling film and cook for 9 minutes, stirring at least 3 times. (F)
5. Add salt and pepper to taste, stir in the cream and serve.

PILAU RICE

PREPARATION TIME: *10 minutes*
COOKING TIME: *16 minutes, plus standing*
MICROWAVE SETTING: *Maximum (Full)*

175g (6oz) easy-cook long-grain rice	*½ teaspoon salt*
	¼ teaspoon ground cardamom
40g (1½oz) butter	*½ teaspoon ground turmeric*
1 garlic clove, peeled and crushed (optional)	*¼ teaspoon ground coriander*
25g (1oz) flaked almonds	
450ml (¾ pint) nearly boiling water	*2 tablespoons sweetcorn kernels*
¼ chicken stock cube, crumbled	*2 tablespoons frozen peas*
	2 tablespoons sultanas
pinch of ground ginger	

1. Rinse the rice in a strainer under hot running water and

shake dry. Rest the strainer on a pad of paper towels to prevent dripping and absorb any residual liquid.

2. Put the butter in a 1.5 litre (2½ pint) deep casserole or bowl and cook for 1 minute or until melted. Stir in the garlic if using, add the rice and almonds and cook for 3 minutes, stirring once during cooking.

3. Add all the remaining ingredients, making sure that the stock cube is dissolved in the hot water. (Although the water can be boiled in the microwave, it is simpler and quicker to boil it in a kettle.) Stir thoroughly, then cook without covering for 12 minutes until the rice is tender and most of the liquid has been absorbed. Immediately cover and stand for 10 minutes before serving. (F)

PINEAPPLE UPSIDE-DOWN PUDDING

PREPARATION TIME: *about 5 minutes*
COOKING TIME: *about 9 minutes, plus standing*
MICROWAVE SETTING: *Maximum (Full)*

50g (2oz) butter	*75g (3oz) caster sugar*
100g (4oz) soft dark brown sugar	*2 large eggs*
1 × 432g (15¼oz) can pineapple rings in natural juice	*125g (5oz) self-raising flour*
	¼ teaspoon baking powder
about 3 glacé cherries, halved	*1 teaspoon lemon juice*
	2 tablespoons milk
100g (4oz) soft margarine	*whipping cream, whipped, to decorate*

1. Put the butter and sugar into a 23cm (9 inch) round cake dish and cook for 45 seconds, stirring once during cooking until the sugar is melted. Swirl the mixture round the base of the dish.

2. Drain the pineapple rings, reserving 150ml (¼ pint) juice, and arrange the rings on the base of the dish, placing one whole ring in the centre and 5 half rings around the outside. Place the remaining 5 half rings curved-side up against the side of the dish. Put the cherries shiny-side down in the middle of the rings.

3. Put the margarine, caster sugar, eggs, flour, baking powder, lemon juice and milk all together in a mixing bowl and beat for 30–60 seconds until smooth.

4. Pour the cake mixture into the prepared dish and cook, uncovered, for 8 minutes, giving the dish a half-turn half-way through cooking. Test by inserting a round-bladed knife into the centre of the sponge mixture; when withdrawn the blade should be clean. Leave to stand for 2 minutes. (F)

5. Pour the reserved pineapple juice evenly and slowly over the surface of the cake mixture until the liquid is absorbed. Leave in the dish for about 4 minutes before turning out on to a hot serving dish. Decorate with piped cream.

Pineapple upside-down pudding; Aspic tomatoes; Chicken à la king and Pilau rice

WINTER WARMER

TOMATO AND ORANGE SOUP

STEAK AND KIDNEY PUDDING

BRAISED CELERY WITH WALNUTS

HOT PEARS IN RED WINE

Prepare the Tomato and Orange Soup a few hours ahead of time and chill or cook ahead and freeze for up to 3 months. Thaw and reheat either in the microwave or in a saucepan on the hob. Keep hot in a saucepan on the hob.

You can cook the Braised Celery ahead of time. Reheat while the Steak and Kidney Pudding is standing.

The steak and kidney filling can be prepared ahead of time up to the end of step 3, but in this case allow an extra 3 minutes cooking time at step 8.

The Hot Pears in Red Wine can be cooked ahead of time and served cold or reheated, uncovered, on Medium Low (35%) while eating the main course. Alternatively the syrup may be cooked ahead of time, adding 2 tablespoons water after step 3. Peel and heat the pears covered with cling film for 4 minutes before serving.

TOMATO AND ORANGE SOUP

PREPARATION TIME: *10 minutes*
COOKING TIME: *10 minutes*
MICROWAVE SETTING: *Maximum (Full)*

2 cans tomatoes, 1 × 225 g (8 oz) and 1 × 400 g (14 oz)	juice and grated rind of 1 small orange
300 ml (½ pint) tomato juice	½ teaspoon dried basil
1 beef stock cube, crumbled	salt
	freshly ground black pepper
	strips of orange peel, to garnish

1. Drain the canned tomatoes and purée in the liquidizer, then strain into a large 2.75 litre (5 pint) bowl, adding the tomato liquid.
2. Stir in the tomato juice, stock cube, orange juice and grated rind and the basil and add salt and pepper to taste.
3. Three-quarters cover the top of the bowl with cling film and cook for 10 minutes without stirring. (F)
4. Pour the soup into a hot tureen and garnish with the strips of orange.

Clockwise from left: Steak and kidney pudding; Tomato and orange soup; Braised celery with walnuts; Hot pears in red wine

STEAK AND KIDNEY PUDDING

PREPARATION TIME: *10 minutes using the food processor;*
20 minutes preparing by hand
COOKING TIME: *51 minutes, plus standing*
MICROWAVE SETTING: *Maximum (Full); then Medium Low*
(35%)

Filling:	450g (1 lb) chuck steak,
25g (1 oz) butter or	wiped, trimmed and finely
margarine	chopped or minced
25g (1 oz) flour	2 medium onions, peeled
1 beef stock cube,	and grated or puréed
crumbled	Pastry:
1 teaspoon salt	225g (8 oz) plain flour
1/4 teaspoon freshly ground	2 teaspoons baking
black pepper	powder
200ml (1/3 pint) hot water	1 teaspoon salt
225g (8 oz) ox kidney,	100g (4 oz) shredded suet
rinsed, trimmed and	8–10 tablespoons cold
chopped	water
	sprig of fresh parsley, to
	garnish

Steak and kidney pudding is made more quickly in the
microwave than in a conventional oven but the texture of
the filling will be firmer than the traditional recipe.

1. Put the butter or margarine in a 2 litre (3½ pint) bowl
and cook on Maximum (Full) for 1 minute or until it has
just melted.
2. Stir in the flour, then add all the remaining filling
ingredients. Stir thoroughly, then three-quarters cover
with cling film and cook on Maximum (Full) for 20
minutes, stirring every 5 minutes. Reduce the setting to
Medium Low (35%) and cook for a further 15 minutes,
stirring once during cooking.
3. Meanwhile prepare the suet pastry. Sift the flour,
baking powder and salt into a mixing bowl, then stir in
the suet. Gently mix in sufficient cold water to form a soft
but manageable dough.
4. Gather the dough into a ball with the hands and shape
on a lightly floured work surface. Cut out one-quarter of
the dough, cover with cling film and set aside.
5. Roll or press the remaining pastry into a circle and fit
into a well-greased 1 litre (2 pint) pudding basin,
coaxing the pastry so that it reaches about 2 cm (1 inch)
above the rim of the basin. (If the filling is not yet cooked
cover the basin and pastry with cling film until needed.)
6. Spoon the filling into the basin, shape the reserved
pastry quarter into a lid and lightly place on top of the
meat. Damp the edges of the protruding pastry and fold
over the lid to form a seal.
7. Slit the pastry lid with a sharp knife, then cover the
basin loosely with cling film so that there is plenty of
room for the pudding to rise. Cook on Medium Low
(35%) for 15 minutes, giving the dish a quarter-turn at 4-
minute intervals. Release the cling film at one corner and
leave the pudding to stand for 10 minutes before turning
out on to a hot dish. Garnish with the parsley.

BRAISED CELERY WITH WALNUTS

PREPARATION TIME: *10 minutes*
COOKING TIME: *10 minutes*
MICROWAVE SETTING: *Maximum (Full)*

6 tablespoons well-	pinch of celery seeds
flavoured chicken stock	1 tablespoon chopped
salt	walnuts
freshly ground black	1 small head of celery,
pepper	trimmed and cut into 5 cm
	(2 inch) slices

1. Place the chicken stock in a 1.2 litre (2 pint) pudding
basin. Stir in the salt, pepper and celery seeds, then add
the walnuts and celery.
2. Cover with cling film, vented at one corner. Cook for 5
minutes. Give the bowl a shake to toss the celery, then
cook for another 5 minutes or until just tender.
3. Turn into a serving dish and serve hot.

HOT PEARS IN RED WINE

PREPARATION TIME: *about 10 minutes*
COOKING TIME: *13 minutes*
MICROWAVE SETTING: *Maximum (Full)*

100g (4 oz) caster sugar	few drops of red food
150ml (1/4 pint) red wine	colouring
4 tablespoons water	4 large dessert pears, each
pinch of ground mixed	weighing about 200g
spice	(7 oz)
25g (1 oz) butter at room	
temperature	

1. Combine the sugar, wine, water and spice in a 1.2 litre
(2 pint) basin and cook for 2 minutes. Stir until the sugar
is completely dissolved. Continue cooking for about 8
minutes without stirring, until about 6 tablespoons of
thick syrup remain.
2. Stir in the butter and food colouring which will thicken
the syrup further.
3. While the syrup is cooking, peel the pears but leave the
stalks.
4. When the syrup is cooked, put the pears into the basin
but do not spoon the syrup over them as it will just roll off
again. Cover with cling film and cook for 3 minutes until
the pears are hot but still firm.
5. Transfer the pears to a serving dish, standing them
upright, spoon the syrup over the top and serve at once,
or serve cold.

SUNDAY LUNCH

TOMATO OR FRUIT JUICE†
ROAST BEEF
YORKSHIRE PUDDING
ROAST POTATOES
BUTTERED PARSNIPS
RHUBARB AND GINGER CRUMBLE

Prepare and cook the Rhubarb and Ginger Crumble several hours ahead of time, then reheat in the microwave oven on Medium (50%) allowing 7–8 minutes while eating the main course. Or prepare and cook the rhubarb and prepare the crumble topping separately, then assemble and cook in the microwave oven while eating the main course. Brown under a conventional grill just before serving.
Prepare the Yorkshire Pudding batter before the roast beef. Then heat the greased patty tins, fill and set to bake about 25 minutes before ready to eat or cook in advance and freeze for 1–2 months.. While the roast beef, Yorkshire pudding and roast potatoes are roasting in the conventional oven, cook the parsnips. While the parsnips are cooking, prepare the crumble mixture.
Put the roast beef in to cook about 45 minutes before the meal and while it is cooking in the microwave, prepare the potatoes. Put the beef into the pre-set conventional oven while the potatoes are cooking in the microwave, then put the cooked potatoes into the conventional oven.
†Pour out the tomato or fruit juice.

ROAST BEEF

PREPARATION TIME: *5 minutes*
COOKING TIME: *30–50 minutes*
MICROWAVE SETTING: *Maximum (Full); then Medium Low (35%) if second method is followed*
CONVENTIONAL OVEN: *220°C, 425°F, Gas Mark 7*

1 × 1.5 kg (3 lb) rolled joint
of topside beef, about
10–13 cm (4–5 inches) in
diameter

The joint is cooked partly in the microwave and partly in the conventional oven, but may be cooked entirely in the microwave oven, covered with a split roaster bag.

1. Rest the joint on a rack in a glass roasting dish and cook on Maximum (Full) for 10 minutes.
2. Spoon away the surplus fat, turn the joint over and transfer to a preheated conventional oven for 30 minutes. Or reduce the microwave setting to Medium Low (35%) for 20 minutes for rare meat or 40 minutes for medium-cooked meat. Serve with horseradish sauce.

YORKSHIRE PUDDING

PREPARATION TIME: *about 10 minutes, plus standing*
COOKING TIME: *20–25 minutes*
OVEN: *220°C, 425°F, Gas Mark 7*

125 g (4 oz) plain flour	*2 eggs*
salt	*275 ml (½ pint) milk*
freshly ground black pepper	*25 g (1 oz) cooking fat*

Yorkshire Pudding is not suitable for microwave cooking but it can be frozen and reheated in the microwave oven on Maximum (Full) for a few seconds.

1. Put the flour, salt and pepper into a mixing bowl. Make a well in the centre, then beat in the eggs one at a time. When these are incorporated, gradually mix in the milk and beat for 4–5 minutes with a wooden spoon. Leave to stand for 30 minutes.
2. Use two 9-hole patty tins or one 15-hole patty tin. Put a little cooking fat into each hole and place on the top shelf of the preheated oven until the fat is very hot.
3. Quickly half-fill each patty tin with the batter, then bake for 20–25 minutes until the puddings are well risen and brown. (F) Serve with roast beef and roast potatoes.

ROAST POTATOES

PREPARATION TIME: *about 10 minutes*
COOKING TIME: *about 45 minutes*
MICROWAVE SETTING: *Maximum (Full)*
CONVENTIONAL OVEN: *225°C, 425°F, Gas Mark 7*

1 kg (2 lb) potatoes
8 tablespoons water
salt
3 tablespoons cooking oil

The potatoes are par-cooked in the microwave oven, then roasted in the conventional oven. They can be roasted alongside the joint in which case the rack should be removed from the meat dish. The potatoes can also be browned in the browning dish or under the grill.

1. Scrub and peel the potatoes and cut into suitable sizes for roasting. Put into a roaster bag with the water and seal loosely with an elastic band, leaving a gap in the top for the steam to escape. Cook for 15 minutes, shaking the bag to reposition the potatoes half way through cooking. Leave for 5 minutes, then remove the potatoes from the bag and drain thoroughly.
2. Salt the potatoes and place them in a roasting dish with the oil, turning them over, so that they are fully coated. Put into a preheated conventional oven and roast for about 30 minutes.

Tomato juice; Roast beef with Yorkshire pudding and Roast potatoes; Buttered parsnips

BUTTERED PARSNIPS

PREPARATION TIME: *about 10 minutes*
COOKING TIME: *about 12 minutes*
MICROWAVE SETTING: *Maximum (Full)*

450g (1 lb) parsnips,
peeled and cut into chunks
8 tablespoons water

½ teaspoon salt
¼ lemon
1 teaspoon butter
parsley, to garnish

1. If the parsnips are old, remove the white stem from the centre. Put them in a roaster bag or casserole with the water, salt, piece of lemon and butter. Seal the bag with an elastic band, leaving an aperture for the steam to escape or cover the casserole, pulling it aside slightly, so that there is a vent.
2. Cook for 12 minutes, shaking the bag or stirring the parsnips once or twice during cooking. To keep the parsnips hot, drain just before serving. They may be reheated in the microwave oven, allowing about 4 minutes on Maximum (Full) in a covered dish. Serve garnished with parsley.

Rhubarb and ginger crumble

RHUBARB AND GINGER CRUMBLE

PREPARATION TIME: *15 minutes*
COOKING TIME: *14 minutes, plus standing and browning*
MICROWAVE SETTING: *Maximum (Full)*

500 g (1¼ lb) fresh rhubarb, trimmed and cut into chunks or 450 g (1 lb) thawed rhubarb chunks
2 tablespoons water
½ jar ginger in syrup
50 g (2 oz) chopped almonds

75 g (3 oz) butter or margarine
150 g (6 oz) flour
100 g (4 oz) demerara sugar
orange quarters, to decorate

1. Put the rhubarb into a deep 1.2 litre (2 pint) oval pie dish and the water. Three-quarters cover with cling film and cook for 5 minutes. Stir so that the harder pieces are moved towards the centre.
2. Add 2 tablespoons of the ginger syrup, 4 pieces of the ginger, sliced finely, and 25 g (1 oz) of the chopped almonds and stir to mix. Three-quarters cover with cling film and cook for 2 minutes.
3. Rub the butter or margarine into the flour until the mixture resembles fine crumbs. Stir in the remaining almonds and the demerara sugar.
4. Spoon the crumble mixture evenly over the rhubarb, pressing the topping down lightly. Cook for 6–7 minutes until the crumble is set and a round-bladed knife inserted through the topping only comes out clean.
5. Leave to stand for 5 minutes, then brown at a distance of 15 cm (6 inches) beneath a conventional preheated grill. Decorate with orange quarters.

SEAFOOD SALAD

ARTICHAUTS AU BEURRE

SEAFOOD SALAD PLATTER

PIQUANT MOUSSELINE SAUCE

BUTTERSCOTCH FLAN

Cook the artichokes just before the meal and the butter just before serving. Provided the artichokes are kept covered they will keep hot for about 10 minutes. Alternatively, cook the artichokes ahead of time and reheat in a covered dish to which has been added a tablespoon of water. Allow about 7 minutes reheating time for 4 artichokes, then heat the butter just before serving.
Seafood should be cooked as freshly as possible which should be just before the meal.
The Piquant Mousseline Sauce however can be prepared ahead of time to the end of step 3 and frozen without the beaten egg white for up to 1 month. Thaw on Medium Low (35%), beating frequently, then add the beaten egg white. This can be done up to 1 hour before serving time.
Prepare the Butterscotch Flan ahead of time if it is to be served cold. If you wish to serve it hot, prepare in advance up to the end of step 3.

ARTICHAUTS AU BEURRE

PREPARATION TIME: *10 minutes*
COOKING TIME: *21 minutes, plus standing*
MICROWAVE SETTING: *Maximum (Full)*

4 globe artichokes	*100g (4oz) butter*
150ml (¼ pint) water	*freshly ground black*
½ teaspoon salt	*pepper*
2 teaspoons lemon juice or vinegar	

The recipe given is for large artichokes. Smaller ones will take less time to cook.
Artichokes may also be served cold with vinaigrette, mayonnaise or Piquant mousseline sauce (page 76), omitting the chopped pimentos.

1. Cut off the long stems from the artichokes, then open out the leaves with the fingers and wash under cold running water (if the artichokes are gritty, soak them upside down in lightly salted water for 30 minutes before cooking).
2. Put the water and lemon juice or vinegar into a 2.5 litre (4½ pint) deep casserole and arrange the artichokes in a

single layer, the tips of the leaves towards one another or towards the centre and the stems towards the outside of the dish. Cover tightly and cook for 15 minutes.
3. Uncover carefully and turn the artichokes over, so that the parts that have previously been underneath are now on the top. Re-cover and cook for 5 minutes, then leave to stand for 5 minutes.
4. Test to see if an outside leaf will easily pull away from an artichoke, then continue cooking if necessary.
5. Drain the artichokes upside down in a colander, then transfer to hot serving plates.
6. To make the butter sauce, put the butter into a suitable serving jug and cook for 1 minute or until just melted. There may be a little unmelted butter still in the jug but this will melt when stirred with a fork. Add salt and pepper to taste and serve with the artichokes.

Artichaut au beurre

SEAFOOD SALAD PLATTER

PREPARATION TIME: *about 20 minutes*
COOKING TIME: *8 minutes*
MICROWAVE SETTING: *Maximum (Full)*

12 thawed scallops, total weight about 225g (8oz)	24 fresh raw mussels, total weight 450g (1 lb)
12 shelled raw scampi, total weight 200g (7oz)	crabmeat from 1 large crab
7g (¼oz) butter	50g (2oz) shelled cooked prawns
2 tablespoons sherry	coriander sprigs, to garnish
about 300ml (½ pint) dry white wine	4 lemon wedges
2 slices onion	1 tablespoon plain flour
freshly ground black pepper	1 tablespoon cold water

Scampi is usually purchased frozen, so it can be kept in the freezer until required. Scallops may be purchased either fresh or frozen but mussels in their shells are purchased fresh and should not be kept waiting. If you are going to buy cooked crab and prepare it yourself, allow an extra 45 minutes. The crabmeat will keep in the refrigerator for up to 24 hours.

For this dish, either buy a dressed crab from the fishmonger or to deal with it yourself, first twist off the legs and reserve them to use as garnish. Crack the claws and remove the meat with a fork or pick. Discard the 'deadmen's fingers' which will be found in the underhalf of the shell and also remove the sac that will be found behind the head in the upper half, and if you wish separate the light from the dark meat.

To thaw raw scampi, arrange in a single layer in a dish, cover with vented cling film and cook on Medium Low (35%) for 4 minutes per lb. In this recipe 1–1½ minutes will be sufficient.

1. Rinse the scallops in cold water, removing any black parts or beard that may be attached but leaving the white and orange parts. Put on a small shallow dish with the scampi. Dot the scallops with butter and spoon the sherry over the scampi.
2. Cover with cling film, pulling back one corner to vent and cook for 1½–2 minutes or until the scampi are opaque (take care not to overcook or the scallops will become tough).
3. Put 3 scallops and 3 scampi on each of 4 dinner plates. Pour the juices into a measuring jug and add enough white wine to make it up to 300ml (½ pint). Pour the wine mixture into a 2 litre (3½ pint) bowl and add the onion and a shake of pepper.
4. Scrub the mussels under cold water, removing the beards and then wash the mussels in 3 or 4 changes of cold water. Discard any mussels that do not close when tapped.
5. Cook the bowl of wine mixture for 2 minutes or until boiling, then cook for a further 2 minutes. Add the

mussels in their shells and cook for 4 minutes, shaking the bowl stirring the mussels occasionally. Remove any cooked mussels as soon as they are ready (when the shells open to reveal a gap the size of your little finger). Discard any that do not open. As the mussels are cooked, drain them and put on to the dinner plates, allowing 6 per person.
6. Divide the crabmeat and the prawns between the servings and garnish with the coriander and lemon wedges. Serve cold with a sauce made from the mussel liquor, mayonnaise or a piquant sauce.
7. To make a sauce from the mussel liquor, strain it into a clean bowl. Blend the flour and water together, then stir into the liquor in the bowl. Cook for 2½ minutes until the mixture boils and thickens. Leave to cool.

PIQUANT MOUSSELINE SAUCE

PREPARATION TIME: *10 minutes*
COOKING TIME: *2 minutes*
MICROWAVE SETTING: *Maximum (Full)*

75g (3oz) unsalted butter	salt
3 tablespoons double cream	freshly ground black pepper
1 egg yolk	2 canned pimientos, well drained and finely chopped
1 teaspoon lemon juice	
1 teaspoon Worcestershire sauce	1 egg white

1. Put the butter in a 900ml (1½ pint) basin and cook for 1 minute or until melted.
2. Stir in the cream, then the egg yolk, the lemon juice, Worcestershire sauce and salt and pepper to taste. Cook for 1–2 minutes, beating every 15 seconds until the sauce thickens.
3. Stir the chopped pimientos into the sauce and chill until cool. (F)
4. Using clean beaters in a grease-free bowl, beat the egg white until soft peaks form, then fold into the cooled sauce. Serve this sauce cold with the seafood platter or other fish. If it is to be served hot, reheat it on Maximum (Full) for 30 seconds to 1 minute, beating every 15 seconds.

BUTTERSCOTCH FLAN

PREPARATION TIME: *about 20 minutes, plus standing*
COOKING TIME: *about 9 minutes (microwave oven); about 35 minutes (conventional oven)*
MICROWAVE SETTING: *Maximum (Full); then Medium Low (35%)*
CONVENTIONAL OVEN: *200°C, 400°F, Gas Mark 6; then 190°C, 375°F, Gas Mark 5*

Seafood salad platter; Piquant mousseline sauce; Butterscotch flan

Pastry case:

150g (6 oz) plain flour, sifted

pinch of salt

75g (3 oz) butter or hard margarine

1 × 50g (2 oz) piece of banana

1 tablespoon cold water

Filling:

75g (3 oz) unsalted butter

100g (4 oz) dark soft brown sugar

½ teaspoon vanilla essence

50g (2 oz) cornflour

100ml (3½ fl oz) single cream

2 egg yolks from size 2 eggs

Topping:

2 egg whites from size 2 eggs

75g (3 oz) caster sugar

1. Mix the flour and salt in a large bowl and rub in the butter.

2. Mash the banana with the water, stir into the mixture, then knead lightly (the pastry can be made successfully in the food processor). Roll out the dough and fit into a 21 cm (8½ inch) greased flan dish.

3. Leave to stand at room temperature for 10–15 minutes only, then line with greaseproof paper and baking beans and bake blind in a conventional oven for 15 minutes. Remove the paper and beans, reduce the oven temperature and bake for a further 5–10 minutes until the pastry is cooked through.

4. While the pastry is baking, make the filling. Put the butter in a 1.2 litre (2 pint) basin and heat in the microwave oven on Maximum (Full) for 1 minute or until melted. Add the sugar, stirring until it is dissolved, then cook for 1 minute or until the mixture is bubbling. At this stage the sugar will appear to separate from the butter.

5. Combine the vanilla essence, cornflour, cream and egg yolks thoroughly, pour into the sugar mixture, reduce the setting to Medium Low (35%) and cook for 7 minutes, stirring frequently until the filling is thickened and creamy. Pour into the baked pastry shell.

6. To make the topping, beat the egg whites with grease-free beaters in a clean bowl and whisk in just under half of the sugar, beating until the mixture regains its stiffness. Sprinkle the remaining sugar over the surface and fold into the meringue.

7. Spread the meringue over the flan, lifting peaks with a fork or knife and make sure that the meringue is spread right to the edges of the pastry. Return the flan, still in its dish, to the conventional oven and bake at the lower temperature for 10–15 minutes until the meringue topping is light brown. Serve warm or cold.

COOK AHEAD SUPPER

MIXED CHOPPED VEGETABLE SOUP

MEAT LOAF RING

HERBY CARROTS IN ORANGE JUICE

JAM SPONGE PUDDING

Prepare the soup up to 48 hours ahead and refrigerate. Alternatively freeze for up to 3 months. Reheat and keep hot in a saucepan on the hob.

The Meat Loaf Ring may be prepared, overwrapped and frozen if preferred up to the end of step 3 but do not use frozen meat or sausages if you are going to freeze uncooked. Store frozen for up to 1 month. To thaw and cook, uncover and allow 20 minutes on Medium Low (35%) followed by 8 minutes on Maximum (Full). The meat loaf can also be cooked ahead of time and reheated from cold but it will be less juicy. Reheat on Maximum (Full), allowing about 5 minutes, giving the dish a quarter-turn every minute. The meat loaf may be reheated in the cooking dish or on the serving dish.

Prepare Herby Carrots ahead of time and serve cold with cold meat loaf or heat if you prefer, allowing 5–6 minutes on Maximum (Full). The mixture for the sponge pudding can be prepared and put into the basin a few hours ahead of time to be cooked just before serving the main course. The pudding can have its standing time while the main course is being eaten. The pudding also reheats well after turning out. Allow 2–3 minutes on Maximum (Full) and add extra blackberry jam for the topping.

MIXED CHOPPED VEGETABLE SOUP

PREPARATION TIME: *15 minutes*
COOKING TIME: *30 minutes*
MICROWAVE SETTING: *Maximum (Full)*

350g (12oz) prepared vegetables including 1 celery stick, 50g (2oz) piece of swede, onion , carrot, 50g (2oz) mushrooms and 2 runner beans	*pinch of ground ginger*
	pinch of cinnamon
	½ teaspoon dried basil
	1 tablespoon tomato purée
	salt
	freshly ground black pepper
25g (1oz) butter	*1 teaspoon cornflour*
750ml (1¼ pints) hot beef stock	*150ml (¼ pint) cold water*
1 tablespoon lemon juice	

If you prefer a smoother vegetable soup, purée it in the liquidizer or food processor, then reheat on Maximum (Full) for 4–5 minutes, stirring once during reheating. The soup improves and the vegetables soften further if the soup is chilled for 24 hours before serving. It can also be frozen either in one container or in individual servings.

1. Finely chop the celery, swede, onion and carrot. Put into a 2.75 litre (5 pint) bowl with the butter. Three-quarters cover with cling film and cook for 10 minutes, stirring 2 or 3 times during cooking.
2. While the other vegetables are cooking, wipe and slice the mushrooms, string and finely slice the beans.
3. Add the mushrooms, beans and the remaining ingredients (except cornflour and cold water) to the bowl, then three-quarters cover and cook for 15 minutes, stirring occasionally through the gap. Add salt and pepper to taste.
4. Blend the cornflour with the cold water, stir into the soup and cook uncovered for 5 minutes, stirring once during cooking. (F) Serve piping hot.

MEAT LOAF RING

PREPARATION TIME: *15 minutes*
COOKING TIME: *10 minutes, plus standing*
MICROWAVE SETTING: *Maximum (Full)*

225g (8oz) pork or beef sausage meat or sausages	*1 tablespoon mixed dried herbs*
450g (1lb) lean minced beef	*1 egg*
	salt
1 medium onion, peeled and grated	*freshly ground black pepper*
50g (2oz) fresh breadcrumbs	**To garnish:**
	cucumber slices
2 tablespoons bottled chilli sauce	*watercress sprigs*

1. With damp hands divide the sausage meat into 8 balls.
2. Combine all the other ingredients together, mixing thoroughly and adding salt and pepper to taste.
3. Put half the beef mixture into the base of a 900ml (1½ pint) plastic ring mould and arrange the sausage balls in a circle on top. Spoon the remaining beef mixture into the ring mould and smooth the top with a damp palette knife. (F)
4. Cook, uncovered, for 10 minutes, giving the dish a quarter-turn 3 times during cooking. Test with a thermometer (it should be 75°C/167°F) or cut through where a sausage is placed and judge by the colour of the sausage.
5. Leave to stand for 5 minutes, then turn the meat loaf out on to a wire tray over a deep plate, so that any surplus fat can escape. Garnish with a ring of cucumber slices and fill the centre with watercress sprigs. Serve hot or cold.

Herby carrots in orange juice; Mixed chopped vegetable soup; Meat loaf ring

HERBY CARROTS IN ORANGE JUICE

PREPARATION TIME: *about 10 minutes*
COOKING TIME: *about 14 minutes*
MICROWAVE SETTING: *Maximum (Full)*

450 g (1 lb) young carrots	*½ teaspoon salt*
6 tablespoons pure unsweetened orange juice	*pinch of pepper*
	⅛ teaspoon sugar
2 tablespoons water	*1 teaspoon lemon juice*
2 tablespoons chopped fresh parsley	*1 teaspoon salad oil*
	sprig of mint, to garnish
1 teaspoon chopped fresh mint	

1. Trim and scrape the carrots, then slice diagonally. Combine all the remaining ingredients except the salad oil in a 2 litre (3½ pint) bowl and stir in the carrots. Cover and cook for 10 minutes or until the carrots are tender.
2. Remove the carrots with a slotted spoon, replace the bowl of liquid in the microwave oven and cook for 4 minutes or until only 3 tablespoons liquid remains.
3. Stir in the salad oil and mix in the carrots, then transfer to a serving dish, cover and leave to cool. Chill until required. Garnish with mint before serving.

Jam sponge pudding

JAM SPONGE PUDDING

PREPARATION TIME: *about 8 minutes*
COOKING TIME: *about 4 minutes, plus standing*
MICROWAVE SETTING: *Maximum (Full)*

4 tablespoons blackberry jam	*50g (2oz) caster sugar*
100g (4oz) butter	*2 large eggs*
50g (2oz) golden syrup	*100g (4oz) self-raising flour*

1. Grease a 900ml (1½ pint) pudding basin and spread the jam in the base.
2. Put the butter and syrup in a glass mixing bowl and cook for 1 minute or until the butter has melted. If the butter is on one side of the bowl and the syrup on the other, melting may be uneven. To avoid this, stir once during cooking.
3. Stir in the sugar and mix thoroughly.
4. Beat in 1 egg and about 1 tablespoon of the flour, then beat in the remaining egg. Fold in the remaining flour.
5. Spoon the pudding mixture over the jam, smoothing the top and cook for 2 minutes. Turn the basin round and cook for a further 2 minutes. Leave to stand for 4–5 minutes before turning out. (The pudding should be eaten hot but take care that the jam has cooled a little to avoid burning the mouth.)

GLYNDEBOURNE GLORY

COURGETTE SOUP

CURRIED CHAUDFROID OF CHICKEN SUPRÊME

RICE AND PEPPER SALAD

TRUFFLE TRIANGLE TORTE

All the dishes may be prepared ahead of time and this is important if you are going to serve this menu for a picnic.
The Rice and Pepper Salad travels well and will keep for up to 24 hours provided that the peppers are not near damp salad items such as lettuce. They will keep better if only the tops are covered during refrigeration.
The Courgette Soup can be chilled then poured into a vacuum flask or be reheated and then put into the flask.
The chaudfroid of chicken should be prepared no more than a few hours ahead of time and it is essential that it is kept cold.
The Truffle Triangle Torte may be prepared in advance and if very firm you will require a sharp knife to slice it.

COURGETTE SOUP

PREPARATION TIME: *10 minutes*
COOKING TIME: *about 21 minutes*
MICROWAVE SETTING: *Maximum (Full); then Medium Low (35%)*

350g (12oz) firm courgettes	*sprig of rosemary*
2 medium tomatoes, skinned and quartered	*salt*
	freshly ground black pepper
450ml (¾ pint) milk	*2 tablespoons single cream*
½ teaspoon chopped chives	

1. Rinse, top and tail, then cut the courgettes into chunks and put into a 2 litre (3½ pint) bowl. Cover with cling film, pulling back one corner to vent and cook on Maximum (Full) for 3½ minutes or until the courgettes are just tender (do not overcook or they will become spongy).
2. Liquidize the courgettes with the tomatoes and milk, pour back into the bowl and add the chives and rosemary. Cook, uncovered, on Maximum (Full) for 4 minutes, stirring once during cooking, then reduce the setting to Medium Low (35%) and cook for a further 10 minutes, stirring once during cooking.
3. Add salt and pepper to taste, then pass through a strainer to remove the tomato pips and herbs and reheat on Maximum (Full) for 3–4 minutes.
4. Pour the hot soup into individual soup cups and add a swirl of cream.

CURRIED CHAUDFROID OF CHICKEN SUPRÊME

PREPARATION TIME: *15 minutes, plus setting*
COOKING TIME: *10 minutes*
MICROWAVE SETTING: *Maximum (Full); then Medium Low (35%)*

4 boneless chicken breasts, each weighing about 150g (5oz), skinned	*300ml (½ pint) mayonnaise*
	2 teaspoons curry powder
salt	*4 tablespoons double cream*
freshly ground black pepper	**To garnish:**
	cucumber
7 tablespoons cold water	*tomato skins*
2 teaspoons powdered gelatine	

1. Sprinkle the chicken with salt and pepper.
2. Arrange the chicken pieces in a single layer in a shallow dish. Cover with greased greaseproof paper, tucking it under the dish to hold it in place, and cook on Maximum (Full) for 3 minutes. Leave to stand for 1 minute, then carefully lift up the paper and reposition, putting the white cooked parts towards the centre.
3. Reduce the setting to Medium Low (35%), replace the greaseproof paper and cook for 6–8 minutes or until the chicken is no longer pink inside. Remove the chicken from the dish, cool rapidly and chill. Reserve the juices.
4. Put the water in a jug and cook on Maximum (Full) for 1 minute until nearly boiling. Sprinkle the gelatine over the surface and stir until it is dissolved and the water is clear. Leave until cool but not set.
5. Strain the chicken juices into a bowl, add the mayonnaise, curry powder, cream and liquid gelatine. Stir well but do not beat or tiny air bubbles will appear.
6. Put the chilled chicken pieces round side uppermost on a wire tray over a dish and coat with the chaudfroid sauce. Decorate with leaves and flowers cut from the cucumber and tomato skins. Chill until served.

RICE AND PEPPER SALAD

PREPARATION TIME: *15 minutes*
COOKING TIME: *15 minutes*
MICROWAVE SETTING: *Maximum (Full)*

1 orange (4 tablespoons fresh orange juice)	*1 hard-boiled egg*
	15g (½oz) butter
50g (2oz) pudding rice	*¼ teaspoon paprika*
2 large red peppers	*salt*
1 yellow pepper	*freshly ground black pepper*
1 tomato	
1 × 5cm (2 inch) piece cucumber, unpeeled	*cucumber slices (optional), to garnish*

1. Squeeze the orange juice and make up to 300ml (½ pint) with cold water. Pour into a 2 litre (3½ pint) bowl and stir in the rice. Cook, uncovered, for 15 minutes or until the rice is tender and the liquid is absorbed. (If the liquid evaporates before the rice is cooked, add a few tablespoons of boiling water.)
2. While the rice is cooking halve the red peppers lengthways and remove the cores and seeds. Core, seed and dice the yellow pepper, skin and coarsely chop the tomato and dice the cucumber. Separate the egg white from the yolk, chopping the white and sieving the yolk.
3. When the rice is cooked, drain if necessary and stir in the butter, the paprika and salt and pepper to taste. Mix in the chopped and diced vegetables and egg white and press the mixture into the halved red peppers. Cover with the sieved egg yolk, pressing it well down. Garnish with cucumber slices, if liked.

TRUFFLE TRIANGLE TORTE

PREPARATION TIME: *about 10 minutes*
COOKING TIME: *about 11 minutes, plus cooling*
MICROWAVE SETTING: *Maximum (Full); then Medium Low (35%)*

50g (2oz) cooking chocolate drops	*25g (1oz) chopped walnuts*
50g (2oz) sugar	**Topping:**
50g (2oz) butter or margarine	*5 tablespoons double cream*
1 large egg	*75g (3oz) cooking chocolate drops*
½ teaspoon vanilla essence	
100g (4oz) plain flour	*4 tablespoons flaked almonds*
2 tablespoons rum	
½ teaspoon baking powder	*whipped cream or ice cream, to serve*
2 tablespoons mincemeat	

1. Put the cooking chocolate drops, sugar and butter or margarine in a large bowl and cook on Maximum (Full) for 2 minutes, stirring once during cooking.
2. Thoroughly mix in the egg, vanilla essence, flour, rum and baking powder, then cook for 2–2½ minutes or until the mixture is just dry on top.
3. Stir in the mincemeat and chopped walnuts, mixing to a heavy paste. Put on to a tray or dish and shape into a 15cm (6 inch) triangle.
4. To make the topping, put the cream into a bowl and cook on Medium Low (35%) for 2 minutes or until boiling. Stir in the chocolate until melted. Set aside for 5 minutes.
5. Spread the almonds on a piece of greaseproof paper and cook for 3 minutes, stirring 2 or 3 times during cooking until beginning to brown. Leave until cool.
6. Pour the cooled icing over the cake and sprinkle with the browned almonds. Chill until cool.

Curried chaudfroid of chicken suprême; Rice and pepper salad; Truffle triangle torte

MEXICAN MEAL

GUACAMOLE

MEXICAN CORNED BEEF STEW

BABY CORN COBS

TORTA CON BANANAS ASCADAS

The pastry case for the torta can be baked and stored in the freezer for a few weeks or in an airtight container for a few days. Prepare the filling up to 12 hours ahead. Fill the pastry and chill until required.
Prepare the Guacamole up to 12 hours in advance and sprinkle with lemon juice. Cover and keep chilled. Mix in the lemon juice just before serving.
Prepare the Mexican Corned Beef Stew up to the end of step 3. Then complete the cooking up to the end of step 4 during the first course and reheat the taco shells and fill in between the courses.
Cook the baby corns before the meal and reheat for 3 minutes while filling the taco shells.

GUACAMOLE

PREPARATION TIME: *about 10 minutes*
COOKING TIME: *2 minutes*
MICROWAVE SETTING: *Maximum (Full)*

150ml ($\frac{1}{4}$ pint) water	pinch of ground coriander
1 medium tomato	pinch of chilli powder
2 teaspoons fresh lemon juice	1 × 175g (6oz) ripe avocado
1 teaspoon olive oil	salt
1 slice of onion	freshly ground black pepper
shake of garlic salt	

1. Put the water into a bowl and cook for 1$\frac{3}{4}$ minutes or until boiling. Lower the tomato into the boiling water and cook for 15 seconds. Carefully pour away the boiling water and refill the bowl containing the tomato with cold water, then remove the tomato, peel, quarter it and remove the seeds.
2. Put the tomato, lemon juice, olive oil, onion, garlic salt and spices in the liquidizer and process for 20 seconds.
3. Halve the avocado, remove the stone, then peel the avocado halves, cut into slices, add to the liquidizer or food processor and blend until puréed. Add salt and pepper to taste.
4. Spoon the guacamole into a dish and serve as a dip with corn chips, potato crisps or fingers of dry toast.

MEXICAN CORNED BEEF STEW

PREPARATION TIME: *10 minutes*
COOKING TIME: *13 minutes, plus standing*
MICROWAVE SETTING: *Maximum (Full)*

1 medium onion, peeled and finely chopped	1 canned chilli, finely chopped
1 tablespoon vegetable oil	100g (4oz) Cheddar cheese, diced
3–4 teaspoons chilli sauce	8 taco shells
1 × 225g (8oz) can baked beans in tomato sauce	To garnish:
1 × 225g (8oz) can tomatoes	onion rings
	strips of green pepper
1 × 340g (12oz) can corned beef, coarsely chopped	orange wedges

1. Combine the onion and oil in a 2 litre (3$\frac{1}{2}$ pint) bowl and cook for 6 minutes, stirring once or twice during cooking, until the onions are just beginning to brown.
2. Stir in the chilli sauce according to taste, remembering that some varieties are hotter than others, and half the baked beans. Mash with a potato masher or fork.
3. Pour in the tomatoes and their juice and crush the tomatoes lightly. Add the corned beef, then stir in the remaining beans and the chopped chilli.
4. Cook, uncovered, for 7 minutes or until the mixture is hot, stirring once during cooking.
5. Stir the cheese into the hot beef mixture, cover and leave to stand for 2 minutes.
6. While the meat is standing, spread the taco shells on the microwave oven shelf or turntable and heat for about 4 minutes; they will become hot and slightly crisp.
7. Fill the taco shells with the beef mixture and garnish with the rings of raw onion, green pepper and orange.

BABY CORN COBS

PREPARATION TIME: *1 minute*
COOKING TIME: *6 minutes, plus standing*
MICROWAVE SETTING: *Maximum (Full)*

12 baby corns, total weight 175g (6oz)	freshly ground black pepper
6 tablespoons water	butter
salt	tomato, chives and onion rings, to garnish

1. Rinse the corns and put into a round shallow dish. Add the water, cover with cling film and cook for 6 minutes. Leave to stand for 3 minutes before uncovering.
2. Drain and sprinkle with salt and pepper. Serve topped with butter and garnished with tomato, chives and an onion ring.

Guacamole; Torta con bananas ascadas; Baby corn cobs; Mexican corned beef stew

TORTA CON BANANAS ASCADAS

PREPARATION TIME: *5 minutes*
COOKING TIME: *about 5½ minutes*
MICROWAVE SETTING: *Maximum (Full)*

15 g (½ oz) butter	*1 teaspoon Tia Maria*
4 large bananas	*1 × 16 cm (6¼ inch) ready*
100 g (4 oz) caster sugar	*baked shortcrust pastry*
pinch of salt	*case*
juice of 1 lime (2 tablespoons)	*3–4 digestive biscuits, crushed*
⅛ teaspoon ground nutmeg	

1. Put the butter into a 2 litre (3½ pint) bowl and cook for about 30 seconds or until melted.
2. Peel the bananas, cut into chunks and mash into the butter.
3. Stir in the sugar and salt and mix thoroughly. Cook for 3 minutes or until the mixture bubbles round the edges. Stir, then cook for a further 2 minutes or until the mixture thickens noticeably. Leave to cool.
4. Whip the lime juice, nutmeg and Tia Maria into the cooled banana mixture and pour into the prepared pastry case. Sprinkle with the crushed digestive biscuits.

recommended by the manufacturer (about 5 minutes), adding the oil 30 seconds before the end of this time.
3. Quickly add the Kofta balls and toss so that they are brown on all sides. Cook for $2\frac{1}{2}$ minutes. Serve at once, garnished with lettuce and red pepper rings.

INDIAN INFLUENCE

KOFTA MEATBALLS

CHICKEN CURRY

TARKA DHAL

GARLIC RICE

GULABJAMUN

Cook the dhal 48 hours ahead and keep chilled. Add 1–2 extra tablespoons water, cover and reheat on Maximum (Full) for about 5 minutes, stirring once just before serving.
Chicken Curry is greatly improved if cooked and kept chilled 24 hours ahead of time. Reheat in a covered casserole on Maximum (Full) for 10–15 minutes before the meal and keep hot in a low conventional oven.
The Kofta Meatballs may be mixed as at step 1 and refrigerated a few hours ahead of time. Cook to coincide with your proposed serving time or cook up to 12 hours ahead and reheat in a serving dish on Maximum (Full) for about $2\frac{1}{2}$ minutes, repositioning the meatballs once during reheating.
Garlic Rice may be cooked a few hours ahead of time and reheated or cooked and frozen if preferred. If freezing add a little more liquid to the cooked rice and store for up to 3 months. Defrost on Maximum (Full) for about 5 minutes, breaking up the lumps as soon as possible. Reheat on Maximum (Full) for about 4 minutes. This can be done while eating the first course.
Prepare the Gulabjamun up to 12 hours ahead of time and serve cold.

KOFTA MEATBALLS

PREPARATION TIME: *10 minutes*
COOKING TIME: *$2\frac{1}{2}$ minutes*
MICROWAVE SETTING: *Maximum (Full)*

350g (12oz) minced raw lamb	*$\frac{1}{8}$ teaspoon cayenne pepper*
$\frac{1}{2}$ teaspoon salt	*$1\frac{1}{2}$ tablespoons gram or besam flour*
$\frac{1}{2}$ teaspoon freshly ground black pepper	*5 teaspoons plain unsweetened yogurt*
$\frac{3}{4}$ teaspoon ground cumin	*1 tablespoon vegetable oil*
$\frac{3}{4}$ teaspoon ground coriander	*lettuce and red pepper rings, to garnish*
$\frac{1}{8}$ teaspoon nutmeg	
$\frac{1}{8}$ teaspoon ground mixed spice	

1. Mix all the ingredients except the oil and form into 12 small balls.
2. Meanwhile preheat a browning dish to the maximum

CHICKEN CURRY

PREPARATION TIME: *about 15 minutes*
COOKING TIME: *40 minutes, plus standing*
MICROWAVE SETTING: *Maximum (Full); then Medium Low (35%)*

2 large onions, peeled and finely chopped	*1 teaspoon salt*
1 garlic clove, peeled and crushed	*$\frac{1}{4}$ teaspoon freshly ground black pepper*
2 tablespoons vegetable oil	*$\frac{1}{4}$ teaspoon ground cinnamon*
1 teaspoon ground cumin	*$\frac{1}{4}$ teaspoon grated nutmeg*
1 teaspoon ground coriander	*pinch of chilli powder*
$\frac{1}{4}$ teaspoon ground ginger	*1 × 225g (8oz) can tomatoes*
1 teaspoon ground turmeric	*1.25kg ($2\frac{1}{2}$lb) chicken pieces, skinned*
1 teaspoon ground cardamom	*6 bay leaves*

This is a mild curry, if you prefer a slightly hotter one, increase the quantities of the spices accordingly.

1. Combine the onion, garlic and oil in a casserole and cook for 8 minutes on Maximum (Full) stirring occasionally until the onions are soft and just beginning to colour.
2. Stir in the cumin, coriander, ginger, turmeric, cardamom, salt, pepper, cinnamon, nutmeg and chilli powder and cook for 2 minutes or until the mixture thickens. Stir once during cooking.
3. Add the tomatoes and their juice and coarsely break up the tomatoes with a fork. Add the chicken pieces and 4 bay leaves, and turn the chicken over, so that it is basted with the sauce. Cover and cook for 10 minutes.
4. Reposition and turn the chicken pieces over. Cover again and cook on Medium Low (35%) for 15 minutes.
5. Remove all the chicken bones and the bay leaves, then cover and raise the setting to Maximum (Full). Cook for 5 minutes, then leave to stand for 5–10 minutes before serving, garnished with the remaining bay leaves.

TARKA DHAL

PREPARATION TIME: *10 minutes*
COOKING TIME: *about 22 minutes, plus soaking*
MICROWAVE SETTING: *Maximum (Full)*

Clockwise from right: Kofta meatballs; Tarka dhal; Chicken curry with Garlic rice

100g (4oz) red lentils
1 teaspoon ground cumin
5 peppercorns
1 tablespoon vegetable oil
1 medium onion, peeled and finely chopped
1 garlic clove, peeled and crushed

450ml ($\frac{3}{4}$ pint) hot water
$\frac{1}{2}$ teaspoon turmeric
salt
freshly ground black pepper
lime quarters and onion rings, to garnish

1. Pick over and wash the lentils in a colander under cold running water, then place in a bowl, cover with cold water and leave for 1 hour to soak. Drain.
2. While the lentils are soaking, mix the cumin, peppercorns and vegetable oil together in a 2 litre (3$\frac{1}{2}$ pint) bowl and cook for 1 minute.
3. Stir in the onion and garlic and cook for 5 minutes or until the onion is a light golden colour, stirring once.
4. Add the hot water and bring back to the boil, 1–4 minutes.
5. Stir in the lentils and turmeric, then three-quarters cover the bowl with cling film and cook for 15 minutes, stirring occasionally, until the lentils are cooked. Add salt and pepper to taste. Transfer to a serving dish and garnish with lime quarters and onion rings.

GARLIC RICE

PREPARATION TIME: *5 minutes*
COOKING TIME: *13 minutes, plus standing*
MICROWAVE SETTING: *Maximum (Full)*

225g (8oz) easy-cook long-grain rice, rinsed and drained
1 teaspoon salt
750ml (1$\frac{1}{4}$ pints) boiling water

1 teaspoon vegetable oil
1 garlic clove, peeled and crushed
15g ($\frac{1}{2}$oz) butter

1. Put the rice, salt and boiling water in a large 2.75 litre (5 pint) bowl, stir once, then cover with cling film, pulling back one corner to vent. Cook for 12 minutes then completely cover and leave for 10 minutes. Drain if necessary and fork up the rice. (F)
2. Stir the oil and garlic together in a small bowl and cook for 1 minute until the garlic is soft but not brown. Stir the butter into the oil and garlic until it is melted, then stir the entire mixture into the cooked rice. Serve straightaway.

GULABJAMUN (Deep-fried dough balls in rose syrup)

PREPARATION TIME: *10 minutes*
COOKING TIME: *12 minutes, plus frying*
MICROWAVE SETTING: *Maximum (Full)*

18 tablespoons dried skimmed milk with vegetable fat

4½ tablespoons self-raising flour

4½–6 tablespoons milk

oil for deep frying

Syrup:

350g (12oz) sugar

300ml (½ pint) boiling water

2 tablespoons rose water or ¼ teaspoon rose-flavoured food essence

1. Sift the powdered milk and flour into a mixing bowl and mix to a stiff dough with the fresh milk.
2. Using floured hands, form the dough into a sausage shape 2½cm (1 inch) thick and cut into 12 lengths. Shape into balls.
3. Heat the oil in a conventional deep fryer to 180°C/370°F and fry the Gulabjamun making sure they are completely submerged, reducing the heat as soon as the outside has browned. Drain the balls on paper towels.
4. To make the syrup, combine the sugar and water in a large 2.75 litre (5 pint) bowl and cook for 2 minutes. Stir to dissolve the sugar, then cook for 2 minutes or until boiling. Stir once, then cook for 8 minutes without stirring until a thin syrup is formed. Carefully stir in the rose water or flavouring.
5. Put the Gulabjamun into the hot syrup, spooning the syrup over to baste, then leave to soak for 15 minutes. Serve warm or cold.

Gulabjamun

CARIBBEAN MEAL

ACKEE AND SALT FISH STUFFED PANCAKES

CURRIED MUTTON

RICE IN COCONUT MILK

MANGO MOUSSE

Curried Mutton is even better if cooked and frozen up to 1 month ahead of time. Transfer to the refrigerator a few hours before your proposed serving time and reheat on Maximum (Full) in a covered casserole, stirring frequently. Allow about 7 minutes for reheating once the dish is thawed. The Curried Mutton may be thawed and reheated just before the meal, to be kept hot in a conventional oven. Cook the pancakes and freeze or refrigerate, interleaved with greaseproof paper. If frozen, store for up to 3 months. Thaw before filling. The filling can be prepared a few hours ahead of time up to the end of step 6 but the ackees do not keep well. Complete just before your proposed serving time.

The Rice in Coconut Milk may be frozen for up to 3 months, then thawed and reheated while eating the pancakes.

The Mango Mousse keeps very well for several days so may be prepared up to the end of step 5 ahead of time and kept chilled. Decorate a few hours before serving and chill again.

ACKEE AND SALT FISH STUFFED PANCAKES

PREPARATION TIME: *about 15 minutes*
COOKING TIME: *about 22 minutes, plus soaking overnight*
MICROWAVE SETTING: *Maximum (Full)*

175g (6oz) salted cod fillet (not smoked)	*freshly ground black pepper*
50g (2oz) butter	*175g (6oz) drained ackees*
1 onion, finely sliced	*4 × 18cm (7 inch)*
100g (4oz) fresh tomatoes, skinned and chopped	*pancakes (made from 150ml (¼ pint) batter)*
	tomato slices, to garnish

Ackees (a Jamaican fruit) and salt fish are obtainable from West Indian shops. If it is not possible to buy a small quantity of fish, any surplus can be tightly wrapped in cling film and kept chilled for several weeks. Ackees are only obtainable in 550ml (19 fl oz) cans and their bland flavour makes them suitable for adding to all kinds of stews and casseroles.

1. Put the salt fish into a 2 litre (3½ pint) bowl, cover with cold water and leave overnight. Strain and discard the liquid.
2. To cook, cover the fish with cold water. Cover with cling film, pulling back one corner at either side, then cook until boiling point is reached, about 4 minutes. Carefully drain, leaving the cling film in position and refill with cold water. Bring to the boil again, about 3½ minutes, and repeat twice more.
3. Carefully put the fish in a colander and cool under gently running cold water. Drain, remove the skin and bones, flake the fish and set aside.
4. Put the butter and onion in a bowl and cook for 30 seconds, then stir and cook for a further 30 seconds or until the onion is slightly soft.
5. Stir in the flaked fish and cook for 1½ minutes. Stir, then cook for a further 1½ minutes.
6. Add the tomatoes with pepper to taste and cook for 2 minutes.
7. Add the ackees to the fish mixture. Cook for 1 minute, then stir and cook for a further 30 seconds or until the ackees are hot.
8. Divide the mixture between the 4 pancakes and roll up. Arrange on a serving dish and cook for 30 seconds to reheat. Garnish with tomato slices.

Ackee and salt fish stuffed pancakes

CURRIED MUTTON

PREPARATION TIME: *about 15 minutes*
COOKING TIME: *about 48 minutes, plus standing overnight*
MICROWAVE SETTING: *Maximum (Full); then Medium Low (35%)*

750g (1½lb) mutton, trimmed and cut into 5cm (2 inch) cubes	*2 large onions, thinly sliced*
	2 tablespoons freshly grated coconut
2 teaspoons meat tenderizing powder	*½ teaspoon ground allspice*
2 teaspoons paprika	*300ml (½ pint) beef stock*
2 teaspoons curry powder	*1 teaspoon tamarind concentrate*
1 garlic clove, peeled and crushed	*2 bay leaves*
25g (1 oz) butter	*3 shakes Tabasco sauce*

1. Mix the mutton, meat tenderizer, 1 teaspoon paprika, 1 teaspoon curry powder and garlic in a large bowl. Stir thoroughly, cover and keep chilled overnight.
2. Put the butter into a 2.75 litre (5 pint) bowl and cook on Maximum (Full) for 30–60 seconds or until melted. Stir in the onions and cook for 4 minutes or until they are tender.
3. Stir in the grated coconut, 1 teaspoon curry powder, 1 teaspoon paprika and the allspice and cook for 3 minutes.
4. Mix the beef stock and tamarind concentrate together, then stir into the onion mixture, adding the bay leaves and the Tabasco sauce.
5. Fold in the seasoned mutton, cover with cling film and cook for 20 minutes, stirring once during that time. Reduce the setting to Medium Low (35%) and cook for 20 minutes, stirring twice during cooking until the meat is tender. Serve in a border of Rice in Coconut Milk.

RICE IN COCONUT MILK

PREPARATION TIME: *about 10 minutes*
COOKING TIME: *about 22 minutes, plus standing*
MICROWAVE SETTING: *Maximum (Full)*

1 small coconut
225g (8oz) easy-cook long-grain rice
1 teaspoon salt

1. Pierce the coconut in 2 places and drain the milk into a bowl.
2. Break open the coconut and remove the flesh. Grate finely, adding the reserved coconut milk and water to make up to 600ml (1 pint). Stir, cover and leave to stand for 10 minutes.
3. Strain the liquid through a piece of muslin into a 2 litre (3½ pint) bowl and squeeze out all the juice. Measure to

make sure that 600ml (1 pint) juice is left, then cook until the liquid boils, about 4 minutes. (The residual coconut pulp can be used up in soups or stews).
4. Rinse the rice in a strainer under cold running water and drain thoroughly, then mix into the bowl with the boiling coconut milk. Stir in the salt and cook, uncovered, for 18 minutes or until nearly all the liquid is absorbed. Stir once, immediately cover and leave for 10 minutes. (F)
5. Arrange the hot rice in a border around a hot dish and fill the centre with curried mutton.

MANGO MOUSSE

PREPARATION TIME: *about 12 minutes, plus chilling*
COOKING TIME: *about 1 minute*
MICROWAVE SETTING: *Maximum (Full)*

1 × 150g (6oz) can evaporated milk	*1 × 470g (1.06lb) can sweetened mango pulp*
4 tablespoons water	*1 tablespoon sugar (optional)*
2 teaspoons powdered gelatine	*whipped cream or grated dark chocolate, to decorate*

A squeeze of fresh lime juice sprinkled over the mousse at the time of serving greatly enhances the flavour.

1. Chill the can of milk in the freezer for 30 minutes.
2. During the last 15 minutes, put the water in a jug and heat for 45 seconds or until boiling. Sprinkle the gelatine over the surface and stir into the water, then cook for 15 seconds until the mixture clears. Stir, then leave for 10–15 minutes to cool down.
3. In a 2 litre (3½ pint) bowl, using an electric whisk, beat the evaporated milk until it is thick.
4. Fold the mango pulp into the whisked milk, then pour the dissolved gelatine in from a height, and mix thoroughly (to achieve greatest volume, fold rather than stir in the dissolved gelatine).
5. Add sugar if needed, then pour into a serving dish and chill until set.
6. Decorate with whipped cream or grated chocolate.

Curried mutton and Rice in coconut milk served with a pineapple juice drink; Mango mousse

sauce is hot but not boiling (overheating will cause the soup to curdle).

4. Peel the avocados, remove the stones and cut into chunks. Sprinkle with the lemon juice, then purée in the liquidizer with the sauce (this can be done in 2 batches if the liquidizer goblet is not big enough).

5. Add salt and pepper to taste, then cover the soup and chill for several hours.

SOLE BEURRE BRUN

PREPARATION TIME: *15 minutes*
COOKING TIME: *about 12½ minutes*
MICROWAVE SETTING: *Maximum (Full)*

4 × 350g (12oz) Dover sole, weighing about 225g (8oz) each after trimming	*2 tablespoons water*
	4 tablespoons white wine vinegar
salt	*1 tablespoon capers*
freshly ground black pepper	*100g (4oz) butter*
	To garnish:
	sprig of parsley
	lemon wedge

1. Skin the sole on both sides, cut off the head and fins and rub the inside neck end with salt to remove the gut. Rinse in cold water, dry, then sprinkle with salt and pepper.

2. Cook the fish singly in a shallow dish. Place one fish in the dish, adding 2 tablespoons water, then cover with a lid or cling film and cook for 1½–2 minutes. Transfer the fish to a warm serving dish.

3. Without adding extra water, cook the remaining 3 fish one at a time. They will take less time than the first fish, about 1½ minutes each. Remove these fish to the serving dish. Cover to prevent drying out and keep warm in a low conventional oven.

4. Stir the vinegar and capers into the juices remaining in the dish and cook for 5 minutes or until the liquid is reduced to 1 tablespoon.

5. Heat a small browning dish to the maximum recommended by the manufacturer. Add the butter and cook for 30–60 seconds, stirring once during cooking (the butter foams up considerably, so do not allow it to boil over).

6. Pour the lightly browned butter into the liquid in the dish, stir thoroughly, then serve from a jug or spoon the juices directly over the fish. Garnish with parsley and lemon.

MANGE-TOUT

PREPARATION TIME: *about 5 minutes*
COOKING TIME: *9 minutes, plus standing*
MICROWAVE SETTING: *Maximum (Full)*

SPECIAL FISH SUPPER

ICED AVOCADO SOUP

SOLE BEURRE BRUN

MANGE-TOUT

LEMON MERINGUE PIE

Prepared the Iced Avocado Soup a few hours ahead of time and keep chilled.
Prepare the Lemon Meringue Pie a few hours ahead of time and keep chilled. The Lemon Meringue Pie may be reheated on Maximum (Full) while clearing away the main course but it does require some attention. During reheating the meringue will puff up again and if it rises too much, it will come over the sides of the pie.
Prepare the sole and the beurre brun just before the meal and keep the fish warm in a single layer on a serving dish, tented with foil in a low conventional oven. Reheat the beurre brun in the microwave on Maximum (Full) for 30 seconds to 1 minute before serving.
Cook the Mange-tout while the main course is being eaten.

ICED AVOCADO SOUP

PREPARATION TIME: *5 minutes*
COOKING TIME: *8½ minutes*
MICROWAVE SETTING: *Maximum (Full)*

25g (1oz) butter	*3 tablespoons double cream*
1 small onion, peeled and finely chopped	*2 ripe avocados*
15g (½oz) plain flour	*2 teaspoons fresh lemon juice*
450ml (¾ pint) chicken stock	*salt*
300ml (½ pint) milk	*freshly ground black pepper*
1 egg yolk	

If you wish to serve this rich soup for any special occasion buy an extra avocado. Slice it finely into crescents and float on top of the soup before serving.

1. Put the butter into a 2 litre (3½ pint) bowl and stir in the onion. Cook for 1 minute, then stir and cook for a further 2 minutes.

2. Mix in the flour, then add the chicken stock and milk and cook, uncovered, for 5 minutes, stirring twice during cooking. (The liquid will be very thin at this stage.)

3. Beat the egg yolk and cream together and strain into the liquid in the bowl. Cook for 15 seconds until the

*350g (12oz) fresh or
frozen mange-tout*
4 tablespoons water
salt

Sole beurre brun with Mange-tout; Iced avocado soup; Lemon
meringue pie

1. Top, tail and pull away the strings from fresh mange-tout.
2. Put the water in a shallow dish, stir in the salt to taste, then add the mange-tout.
3. Cover the dish with a lid or vented cling flim and cook for 4 minutes. Stir, then re-cover and cook for 5 minutes. Leave fresh mange-tout to stand for 5 minutes before draining. Frozen mange-tout may be drained immediately.

LEMON MERINGUE PIE

PREPARATION TIME: *8 minutes*
COOKING TIME: *12 minutes, plus browning*
MICROWAVE SETTING: *Maximum (Full)*

Crumb base:
50g (2oz) butter
*6 digestive biscuits,
crushed*
25g (1oz) caster sugar
Filling:
225g (8oz) caster sugar
4 tablespoons cornflour
pinch of salt
250ml (8floz) cold water
3 egg yolks

*120ml (4floz) fresh lemon
juice*
*2 teaspoons grated lemon
rind*
40g (1½oz) butter
Meringue topping:
3 egg whites
pinch of cream of tartar
100g (4oz) caster sugar
½ teaspoon vanilla essence

1. First prepare the crumb base. Put the butter in a 20cm (8 inch) round pie dish and cook for 1 minute or until melted. Stir in the biscuits and sugar, mixing thoroughly, and press the crust firmly into the base of the dish.
2. To make the filling, mix the sugar, cornflour and salt together in a small bowl.
3. Put the water into a 2 litre (3½ pint) bowl and cook for 3 minutes or until it is boiling. Immediately toss in the sugar mixture and beat vigorously until a smooth sauce is obtained. Cook for 3 minutes, stirring frequently.
4. Beat the egg yolks and lemon juice together and blend with a few spoonfuls of hot sauce.
5. Pour the cornflour mixture into the sauce, mixing thoroughly. Cook for 1 minute, then stir in the lemon rind and butter. Leave to cool for a few moments, then pour the filling into the crumb base.
6. To make the meringue topping, using clean beaters and a grease-free bowl whisk the egg whites and cream of tartar together until stiff. Add less than half the sugar in several batches, whisking in between each addition. Add the vanilla essence and whisk until the mixture is stiff once more. Fold in the remaining sugar.
7. Spoon the meringue evenly over the lemon filling, making sure that the meringue reaches the edge of the dish. Cook for 4 minutes, giving the dish a quarter-turn after each minute. If the meringue topping cracks during cooking and a wide chasm appears, close the gap by spreading the meringue gently back into position with a palette knife.
8. Brown the meringue briefly at a distance under a preheated conventional grill. Serve hot or cold.

PASTA DINNER

TOMATOES STUFFED WITH MUSHROOM PÂTÉ

LASAGNE AL FORNO

COURGETTE STICKS

CARAMEL ORANGES

Caramel Oranges can be prepared ahead of time and kept chilled for a few days.
The filling for the Stuffed Tomatoes, without the addition of the soured cream, can be made ahead of time and can be frozen after step 3. Store for up to 2 months. Thaw on Maximum (Full), stirring frequently before adding the soured cream. The filled tomato shells can be refrigerated for up to 24 hours.
Prepare the sauces for the Lasagne in advance and freeze if you prefer. Cook the Lasagne leaves, assemble the dish and bake to coincide with your proposed serving time. The Lasagne may be assembled with the cold sauces but it is then best to reheat on Medium Low (35%) for about 20 minutes. Either freeze the sauces separately or the completed dish and store for up to 3 months.
Prepare the Courgette Sticks several hours in advance and set to cook for the minimum time while eating the starter.

TOMATOES STUFFED WITH MUSHROOM PÂTÉ

PREPARATION TIME: *about 6 minutes*
COOKING TIME: *about 4 minutes*
MICROWAVE SETTING: *Maximum (Full)*

4 firm medium tomatoes, rinsed and dried	*2 teaspoons chopped fresh parsley*
salt	*$\frac{1}{4}$ teaspoon dried basil*
50 g (2 oz) button mushrooms, finely chopped	*$\frac{1}{4}$ teaspoon pepper*
	1 teaspoon cornflour
15 g ($\frac{1}{2}$ oz) butter	*2 teaspoons medium sherry*
4 spring onions, trimmed and finely chopped	*4 tablespoons soured cream*

1. Slice the caps from the tomatoes and set aside. Scoop the pulp and seeds from the tomato shells and reserve for use in another recipe. Sprinkle the inside of the shells with salt, then turn upside down to drain.
2. Place the mushrooms, butter and spring onions in a medium bowl and cook for 1½ minutes. Stir, then cook for a further 1½ minutes or until the mushrooms are soft.

3. Mix in the parsley, basil, ¼ teaspoon salt, the pepper and the cornflour mixed with the sherry. Cook for 30 seconds, stir and cook for a further 15 seconds or until thick. (F)
4. Stir in the soured cream. Cover and leave to cool.
5. Fill the tomato shells with the mushroom stuffing and top with the reserved caps. Arrange on a bed of lettuce leaves and serve cold.

LASAGNE AL FORNO

PREPARATION TIME: *12 minutes*
COOKING TIME: *24 minutes, plus browning*

Meat sauce:	Cheese sauce:
175 g (6 oz) lean minced beef	*35 g (1¼ oz) butter or margarine*
1 small onion, peeled and minced	*35 g (1¼ oz) flour*
2 tablespoons flour	*600 ml (1 pint) milk*
1 × 400 g (14 oz) can tomatoes	*75 g (3 oz) grated Cheddar cheese*
1 beef stock cube, crumbled	*6–8 sheets lasagne, cooked, drained and separated*
1 teaspoon mixed dried herbs	**Topping:**
salt	*25 g (1 oz) grated Cheddar cheese*
freshly ground black pepper	*sprig of parsley*

If it is more convenient, the lasagne may be baked in the conventional oven on 180°C/350°F/Gas Mark 4 for 30–40 minutes and the cheese should be sprinkled on before baking. To cook lasagne in the microwave oven, bring a casserole three-quarters filled with water to the boil, stirring in 1 teaspoon salt and 1 teaspoon vegetable oil. Add 1–2 leaves of lasagne, then return the casserole to the microwave oven for about 1 minute until the water comes back to the boil. Add a further 2 leaves of lasagne and then repeat as necessary. Cook for about 5 minutes, then cover with a lid and leave to stand for 5 minutes before draining.

1. To make the meat sauce, combine the beef and onion in a 2 litre (3½ pint) bowl and cook for 4 minutes, stirring once during cooking.
2. Stir in the flour, the tomatoes with their juice, the beef stock cube, dried herbs and salt and pepper to taste. Cook uncovered for 8 minutes, stirring occasionally until the sauce is thick. (F)
3. To make the cheese sauce, put the butter or margarine in a 2 litre (3½ pint) bowl and cook for 30 seconds or until melted. Stir in the flour and cook for 20 seconds or until the mixture puffs up, then add the milk. Stir with a wire whisk and cook for 2½ minutes.
4. Stir thoroughly and cook for a further 2½–3½ minutes, stir again, then mix in the cheese and stir once more. If not using immediately, cover with cling film. (F)

5. To assemble the dish, spread one-third of the meat sauce into the base of a deep round 23 cm (9 inch) flameproof dish and cover with a single layer of lasagne leaves, followed by a layer of cheese sauce. Repeat the layers, making sure that each thickness of pasta is separated from the next one by one of the sauces. Top the lasagne with a layer of cheese sauce and cook for 6 minutes or until the lasagne is hot throughout. Sprinkle with the remaining 25 g (1 oz) cheese and brown under the grill. Garnish with the parsley and serve hot.

COURGETTE STICKS

PREPARATION TIME: *about 10 minutes*
COOKING TIME: *5 minutes, plus standing*
MICROWAVE SETTING: *Maximum (Full)*

350 g (12 oz) courgettes	*salt*
15 g (½ oz) butter	*freshly ground black*
pinch of nutmeg	*pepper*

1. Wash, top and tail the courgettes and cut into medium matchsticks.
2. Put the prepared courgettes into a 900 ml (1½ pint) pie dish. Dot with butter and sprinkle with a little nutmeg.
3. Cover with cling film, pulling back one corner to vent and cook for 3–5 minutes or until just tender. Leave to stand for 5 minutes before uncovering, then sprinkle with salt and pepper to taste.

Lasagne al forno; Caramel oranges; Courgette sticks; Tomatoes stuffed with mushroom pâté

CARAMEL ORANGES

PREPARATION TIME: *about 10 minutes*
COOKING TIME: *20 minutes*
MICROWAVE SETTING: *Maximum (Full)*

175 g (6 oz) caster sugar
150 ml (¼ pint) water
4 oranges
1 tablespoon Curaçao

1. Stir the sugar and water together in a 2 litre (3½ pint) bowl and cook for 2 minutes. Stir until the sugar is completely dissolved, then cook for 1 minute or until the syrup begins to bubble. Cook for a further 5 minutes without stirring until a thick syrup is formed.
2. Peel the oranges, removing all the pith, then pare the zest and cut it into julienne strips.
3. Remove the bowl of syrup with oven gloves and place on a heatproof surface. Soak the oranges in the syrup for 5 minutes, then take them out and place on a serving dish. Meanwhile put the orange strips in a jug, cover with cold water and cook for 4 minutes. Drain.
4. Put the strips into the syrup, return the bowl to the oven and cook for 5 minutes, then remove the strips with a slotted spoon and place on top of the oranges.
5. Cook the syrup for a further 3 minutes or until a caramel colour, then add 2 tablespoons warm water and shake the bowl very gently until all the water is incorporated. Stir in the liqueur.
6. Slice the oranges, then reassemble and hold in position with a cocktail stick. Pour over the syrup and serve.

WHOLEWHEAT SUPPER

WHOLEWHEAT PIZZA

WALNUT, APPLE AND KOHLRABI SALAD

LIME JELLY MOUSSE

The Walnut, Apple and Kohlrabi Salad may be prepared up to 1 day ahead of time and kept chilled.
The Lime Jelly Mousse may be prepared up to 1–2 days in advance but the longer the refrigeration time, the firmer it will become. Decorate just before serving.
Cook the pizza topping in advance, then reheat just before step 9, allowing about 3 minutes on Maximum (Full). Prepare the pizza dough and synchronize cooking time with your proposed serving time, then complete just before the meal. Freezing the topped pizza is not recommended as when reheated, even in the browning dish, it tends to be soft and chewy.

WHOLEWHEAT PIZZA

PREPARATION TIME: *about 15 minutes*
COOKING TIME: *about 27 minutes*
MICROWAVE SETTING: *Maximum (Full)*

Dough:

150–200ml (5–7fl oz) water	1 teaspoon dried marjoram
¼ teaspoon sugar	1 × 396g (14oz) can tomatoes
225g (8oz) wholewheat flour	salt
½ teaspoon salt	freshly ground black pepper
1 teaspoon quick active yeast	225g (8oz) Cheddar cheese, grated
1 tablespoon vegetable oil	8 bacon rashers, pre-cooked and cut into thin strips or 2 cans anchovy fillets, drained and halved lengthways
Topping:	
25g (1oz) butter or margarine	
1 medium onion, skinned and finely chopped	16 pitted black olives, halved
2 teaspoons cornflour	

Quick active yeast is always mixed with the flour and never with the water. For this recipe, you can substitute 4 teaspoons dried yeast which should be dissolved in the warm water and left for 10 minutes to froth up.

1. To make the dough, put 150ml (¼ pint) cold water in a jug and cook for 1 minute or until warm to the touch. Stir in the sugar.
2. Put the flour into a 2 litre (3½ pint) bowl, stir in the salt and cook for 1 minute or until the flour is warm.
3. Mix the yeast into the flour, then stir in the sweetened warm water, mixing to a soft dough and adding more warm water if necessary.
4. Knead the dough lightly and shape into a ball. Replace in the bowl and cover with cling film.
5. Put about 450ml (¾ pint) water into a jug and bring to the boil. Push the jug towards the back of the oven, then put in the bowl of dough beside it. Close the door but do not switch on the oven. Leave for 20 minutes or until the dough rises (wholewheat dough does not rise very much).
6. Divide the dough in half, shape each into a round to fit into a large browning dish. Brush the tops with oil.
7. Put the butter or margarine in a 2 litre (3½ pint) bowl, and cook for 30 seconds or until melted. Stir in the onion and cook for a further 5 minutes, stirring occasionally.
8. Add the cornflour, marjoram, the contents of the can of tomatoes and salt and pepper to taste and cook for 6 minutes, stirring occasionally.
9. Brush the browning dish with oil and preheat for 5 minutes or according to the manufacturer's instructions. Immediately press in one piece of dough, then turn it over and cook for 1 minute. Cover with half the topping, then add the cheese. Arrange the bacon or anchovies on top and fill the centre with olives. Cook for 2 minutes.
10. Reheat the browning dish for 2–3 minutes, depending on how cool it has become, add an extra teaspoon of oil, then cook the remaining pizza.

WALNUT, APPLE AND KOHLRABI SALAD

PREPARATION TIME: *10 minutes*
COOKING TIME: *4 minutes*
MICROWAVE SETTING: *Maximum (Full)*

50g (2oz) shelled walnuts	1 teaspoon Dijon mustard
450g (1lb) kohlrabi	1 green dessert apple, rinsed and dried
150ml (¼ pint) mayonnaise	

Celeriac can be used instead of kohlrabi. Brush with lemon juice before blanching and mix with the mayonnaise immediately it has been grated, otherwise the celeriac will discolour.

1. Put the walnuts in a jug or small bowl, cover with cold water and cook for 2 minutes or until boiling. Drain, then re-cover with cold water. Bring back to the boil (about 1 minute). Cool the walnuts in a colander under cold running water and drain until dry.
2. Peel the kohlrabi, cut in half and put the pieces into the microwave oven. Cook for 1 minute until the kohlrabi is

hot but still firm. Put into a colander, cool under cold running water and pat dry with paper towels.
3. Coarsely chop the walnuts, coarsely grate the kohlrabi and mix both with the mayonnaise flavoured with Dijon mustard.
4. Core and dice the apple, add to the mixture and stir thoroughly so that the apple is entirely coated with the mayonnaise.

LIME JELLY MOUSSE

PREPARATION TIME: *about 10 minutes*
COOKING TIME: *3 minutes, plus setting*
MICROWAVE SETTING: *Maximum (Full)*

1 × 135g (4¾oz) packet lime jelly	*100g (4oz) full fat soft cheese*
grated rind and juice of 1 lime	*2 egg whites*
	1 bar flake chocolate (optional)

1. Put the jelly into a measuring jug and add water to make up to 450ml (¾ pint). Cook for 3 minutes or until the water is nearly boiling. Stir to dissolve the jelly thoroughly, then leave until cool but not set.
2. In a large bowl, beat the grated rind, lime juice and cheese together, then add the dissolved jelly, beating thoroughly. Leave in a cool place until the mixture is just beginning to set.
3. Using clean beaters and a grease-free bowl, stiffly whisk the egg whites. Stir one generous spoonful of the beaten whites into the jelly mixture, then fold in the remainder.
4. Spoon the mousse into individual ramekins or glasses and chill until set. Decorate with crushed flake chocolate if liked.

Clockwise from right: Walnut, apple and kohlrabi salad; Wholewheat pizza; Lime jelly mousse

MENUS
FOR
SIX

The flexibility afforded by using the microwave and conventional cookers together will speed the service of food in this section. Of course cooking and reheating dishes for six is necessarily longer, but once heated, most can be kept hot in the conventional oven. It often saves time to cook the starter to coincide with serving time rather than cooking ahead, and reheating. The main course, previously cooked, can be reheated while the first course is being consumed. Alternatively, you may find it better to reheat the main course prior to the meal and keep it hot in the conventional oven, whilst using the microwave oven to reheat or cook vegetables which may suffer if kept waiting too long in the hot dry atmosphere of an ordinary oven. Recipes that are new or unfamiliar should be practised before introducing them into the menu and you could cook just plain vegetables to accompany the main courses. Do not exclude the menus for six from your repertoire if there are only four people dining, since the ease and success of reheating prepared dishes in the microwave mean that you will have a ready meal for two in perfect condition to serve the next day.

ROMAN RELISH

MINESTRONE

VITELLO ROMANO

RUNNER BEANS WITH DILL BUTTER

CAULIFLOWER FLORETS

ZABAGLIONE

Prepare the Minestrone up to 24 hours in advance, add a little extra water or stock and reheat in the saucepan on the hob.

Beat the veal ahead of time and leave at room temperature for half an hour before cooking, keeping it covered, of course. Cook the veal at the last possible moment.

Cook the beans just before the meal, adding the dill butter just before serving. The butter can be prepared up to 2 months in advance because it is freezable. Slice while still frozen with a warm knife. Cover the beans and keep them hot in the conventional oven.

Cook the cauliflower florets while serving the first course.

The Zabaglione is delicious served cold and may be refrigerated for up to 24 hours. If you prefer to serve it hot, it is so good that it is worth keeping your guests waiting while you prepare it. Get all the ingredients out ahead of time, putting the wine in a jug and straining the egg yolks into the basin.

This should cut your preparation down to about 4 minutes and the cooking time will remain at 3½ minutes.

MINESTRONE

PREPARATION TIME: *about 10 minutes*
COOKING TIME: *20 minutes, plus standing*
MICROWAVE SETTING: *Maximum (Full)*

1 × 285g (10oz) can condensed consommé	*1 × 225g (8oz) can tomatoes*
450ml (¾ pint) boiling water	*1 small garlic clove, peeled and crushed*
1 × 150g (5.29oz) can baked beans in tomato sauce	*1 stick celery, scraped and finely sliced*
1 medium carrot, peeled and finely diced	*1 small onion, peeled and finely chopped*
1 medium leek, trimmed, cut into 5cm (2 inch) lengths and shredded	*25g (1oz) ham, diced (optional)*
	salt
50g (2oz) quick cook macaroni	*freshly ground black pepper*
	about 2 tablespoons grated Parmesan cheese

1. Combine the consommé, water, beans, carrot, leek, macaroni, tomatoes, garlic, celery, onion, ham, salt, pepper and 2 teaspoons of the Parmesan in a large 2.75 litre (5 pint) bowl, three-quarters cover with cling film and cook for 20 minutes, stirring through the gap twice during cooking. Leave to stand for 5 minutes before carefully removing the cling film.

2. Serve the soup hot, allowing about 200ml (⅓ pint) per person. Sprinkle over the remaining Parmesan.

VITELLO ROMANO
(Veal with cashew nuts in lemon sauce)

PREPARATION TIME: *about 10 minutes*
COOKING TIME: *about 13½ minutes*
MICROWAVE SETTING: *Maximum (Full); then Medium Low (35%)*

6 veal escalopes, each weighing 100g (4oz)	*1 tablespoon fresh lemon juice*
salt	*3 tablespoons water*
freshly ground black pepper	*5 tablespoons cashew nuts*
3 tablespoons plain flour	*150ml (¼ pint) double cream*
35g (1¼oz) butter	**To garnish:**
	strips of lemon and tomato
	sprig of coriander

1. Beat the escalopes to a 3mm (⅛ inch) thickness and sprinkle lightly with salt and pepper. Dip the escalopes in the flour, shaking off any surplus. Retain all the surplus flour.

2. Put the butter in a large shallow dish, cover with cling film and cook for 3 minutes or until it is foamy.

3. Quickly remove the cover and add 2 of the veal escalopes. Cook on Maximum (Full) for 1 minute, then turn the escalopes over and cook for a further 30 seconds. Remove the escalopes from the dish.

4. Reheat the butter for 20 seconds, then cook 2 further escalopes and repeat to cook the remaining 2 escalopes. Transfer the veal to a hot dish and keep covered while cooking the sauce.

5. To make the sauce, stir the lemon juice and water with 1 tablespoon of the reserved flour into the juices remaining in the dish and cook for 30 seconds. Stir.

6. Leave half the cashew nuts whole and chop the remainder. Stir into the mixture in the dish and cook for a further ½–1 minute until the sauce is bubbling.

7. Mix in the double cream and any remaining veal juices. Reduce the setting to Medium Low (35%) and season to taste with salt and pepper. Replace the veal in the sauce, spooning the sauce over to coat the veal. Cover and cook for 4 minutes. Either serve from the dish or transfer to a hot serving dish and garnish with lemon, tomato and coriander.

Vitello Romano; Minestrone

RUNNER BEANS WITH DILL BUTTER

PREPARATION TIME: *about 10 minutes, plus chilling*
COOKING TIME: *about 8 minutes, plus standing*
MICROWAVE SETTING: *Medium Low (35%); then Maximum (Full)*

40g (1½ oz) butter	*6 tablespoons water*
salt	*350g (12oz) runner*
freshly ground black	*beans, trimmed and sliced*
pepper	*diagonally*
1½ teaspoons dill weed	

1. First prepare the dill butter. Put the butter in a small bowl and soften on Medium Low (35%) for 20 seconds if necessary. Add salt, pepper and the dill weed and blend together.
2. Shape the butter into a sausage about 2½cm (1 inch) in diameter and roll up in greaseproof paper. Twist the ends of the paper Christmas cracker fashion and refrigerate for 1–2 hours or freeze. (F)
3. Put the water in a casserole or bowl and stir in ½ teaspoon salt. Add the beans, then cover and vent. Raise the setting and cook on Maximum (Full) for 8 minutes, then leave to stand for 4 minutes before draining.
4. While the beans are standing, slice the butter into pats and serve one with each portion of beans.

CAULIFLOWER FLORETS

PREPARATION TIME: *about 5 minutes*
COOKING TIME: *about 10 minutes*
MICROWAVE SETTING: *Maximum (Full)*

8 tablespoons water
½ teaspoon salt
1 × 750g (1½ lb)
cauliflower, trimmed and
cut into florets or 450g
(1 lb) cauliflower florets

If the cauliflower is to be reheated, refresh under cold running water when the cauliflower stems are still firm. Drain, replace in the serving dish, cover and reheat for about 5 minutes before serving. The reheating time is sufficient to complete cooking.

1. Put the water into a casserole or large bowl and stir in the salt. Add the cauliflower, cover with a lid or vented cling film and cook for 5 minutes.
2. Stir to reposition the cauliflower, and cook for a further 5 minutes or until the cauliflower is just tender. Drain, cover and serve within 10 minutes.

ZABAGLIONE

PREPARATION TIME: *about 6 minutes*
COOKING TIME: *about 3½ minutes*
MICROWAVE SETTING: *Maximum (Full)*

6 egg yolks (size 1)	*langues de chats biscuits,*
5 tablespoons caster sugar	*to serve*
175ml (6 fl oz) Marsala or	
medium sherry	

1. Beat the egg yolks, then strain into a 1.2 litre (2 pint) basin.
2. Stir in the sugar and, using an electric beater, whisk until thick and creamy.
3. Put the wine in a jug and cook for 3 minutes or until starting to boil. Pour on to the egg mixture, beating vigorously.
4. Cook for 30 seconds, beating thoroughly after about 15 seconds, when the mixture round the sides is seen to puff up. Beat thoroughly after cooking and continue beating for a few moments.
5. Pour into 6 wine goblets and serve at once with langues de chats biscuits

Cauliflower florets; Runner beans with dill butter; Zabaglione

HOT AND SPICY

SARDINES WITH CAPER SAUCE

SPICY GREEN LENTILS WITH PORK, BACON AND FRANKFURTERS

SPECKLED BROWN RICE WITH PINE NUTS

TOFFEE PEACHES

Prepare the caper sauce a few hours ahead of time.
Spicy Green Lentils with Pork, Bacon and Frankfurters can be cooked up to the end of step 3 and then frozen for up to 2 months. Transfer to the refrigerator a few hours in advance to hasten thawing, then heat on Maximum (Full), stirring occasionally for about 5 minutes until the pork is thoroughly hot, then complete the recipe from step 4. Cook the bacon rashers for garnish after the dish is reheated. Spicy Green Lentils keep their heat provided the dish is covered, so that you can start reheating about 20 minutes before serving the meal. Alternatively reheat and keep the dish hot in the conventional oven, making sure that it is covered.
Speckled Brown Rice with Pine Nuts may be prepared 12 hours ahead or may be frozen for up to 2 months. Thaw slowly in the refrigerator or in the microwave oven when convenient before the meal. Then reheat, adding a tablespoon of water, for about 5 minutes on Maximum (Full) while eating the main course. If preferred, cover and keep warm in a cool conventional oven.
Prepare the sardines up to the end of step 3 a few hours in advance. Cover and keep chilled. Cook the sardines just before the meal, allowing an extra 30 seconds because the starting temperature will have been lower. Give the sauce a stir before serving. Although the sauce is cold, it is better to serve the sardines on hot plates.
Prepare the Toffee Peaches about 1 hour before the meal.

SARDINES WITH CAPER SAUCE

PREPARATION TIME: *20 minutes*
COOKING TIME: *2–4 minutes*
MICROWAVE SETTING: *Maximum (Full)*

Sauce:	freshly ground black
4 tablespoons soured	pepper
cream	12 sardines, fresh or
1½ teaspoons chopped	thawed
capers	2 teaspoons lemon juice
½ teaspoon grated lemon	lemon slices and parsley
rind	sprigs, to garnish
salt	6 chives, chopped

1. To make the sauce, put the soured cream into a cold bowl and mix until smooth. Stir in the capers, lemon rind and salt and pepper to taste.

2. To prepare the sardines, remove the head, then pull out the sac behind the head to detach the bone. Rinse in cold water and dry the fish on paper towels.
3. Arrange 6 sardines in a single layer in a shallow dish, sprinkle with the lemon juice and with salt and pepper.
4. Cook without covering for 2 minutes or until the flesh is opaque. Do not overcook. Cook the remaining 6 in the same way. Serve on warm plates, garnished with lemon and parsley. Pour over the sauce and sprinkle with chives.

SPICY GREEN LENTILS WITH PORK, BACON AND FRANKFURTERS

PREPARATION TIME: *about 20 minutes, plus soaking overnight*
COOKING TIME: *about 35 minutes*
MICROWAVE SETTING: *Maximum (Full)*

100g (4oz) green lentils	1 teaspoon coriander seeds
1 medium onion, peeled	1 teaspoon ground
and finely chopped	turmeric
1 tablespoon vegetable oil	¼ teaspoon freshly ground
3–5 bacon rashers, rinded	black pepper
500g (1¼ lb) pork fillet,	450ml (¾ pint) water or
trimmed and cut into thin	stock
strips	2 frankfurters, cut into 1 cm
1 teaspoon fenugreek	(½ inch) slices
seeds	sprig of coriander, to
	garnish

1. Put the lentils into a bowl, cover with cold water, then cover and leave to soak overnight. Drain.
2. Put the onion and oil in a large deep dish and cook for about 3 minutes or until the onions are golden. Stir once during cooking.
3. Cut 3 bacon rashers into thin strips and stir into the onion mixture with the pork and the spices. Cook, uncovered, for 1½ minutes. Stir and cook for a further 1½ minutes. Add the pepper, the water or stock and stir in the drained lentils. Three-quarters cover with cling film and cook for 20 minutes, stirring about twice during cooking. (F)
4. Stir in the sliced frankfurters and cook for a further 6–9 minutes or until the lentils are pulpy and the mixture is thick.
5. For added colour, cook the extra 2 bacon rashers separately on a paper towel and place over the lentils just before serving. Garnish with coriander.

SPECKLED BROWN RICE WITH PINE NUTS

PREPARATION TIME: *20 minutes*
COOKING TIME: *41 minutes, plus standing*
MICROWAVE SETTING: *Maximum (Full)*

Spicy green lentils with pork, bacon and frankfurters; Sardines with caper sauce; Speckled brown rice with pine nuts

40g (1½oz) butter	*25g (1oz) pine nuts*
1 onion, peeled and finely chopped	*2 tomatoes, peeled and chopped*
1 small red pepper, cored seeded and finely chopped	*900ml (1½ pints) hot water*
	1–1½ teaspoons salt
1 garlic clove, peeled and crushed	*½ teaspoon freshly ground black pepper*
175g (6oz) brown rice	

1. Put the butter in a 1.75 litre (3 pint) casserole and cook for about 1 minute or until melted.

2. Stir in the onion, red pepper, garlic and rice and cook for 5 minutes, stirring once during cooking, until the rice grains are golden and the onions translucent.

3. Add the pine nuts, tomatoes, hot water, salt and pepper. Stir well. Cover and cook for 35 minutes, stirring once during cooking.

4. Stir once at the end of the cooking period, cover immediately and leave to stand for 10 minutes for the rice to absorb all the liquid fully. (F)

Toffee peaches

TOFFEE PEACHES

PREPARATION TIME: *10 minutes, plus chilling*
COOKING TIME: *about 5½ minutes*
MICROWAVE SETTING: *Maximum (Full)*

6 fresh peaches	*25 g (1 oz) pistachio nuts,*
450 g (1 lb) creamy toffees	*skinned and chopped, to*
2 tablespoons water	*decorate*
½ teaspoon salt	

1. Rinse, dry and halve the peaches. Remove the stones. Place skin-side up on non-stick silicone paper.
2. Put the toffees, water and salt in a 1.2 litre (2 pint) basin and cook for 2 minutes. Stir, then cook for a further 3 minutes. Stir until the toffee is smooth. If necessary cook for a further 30 seconds. Stand the basin in a bowl a quarter filled with boiling water to prevent the toffee from setting.
3. Spoon the toffee mixture over as many of the peach halves as possible and leave to cool slightly. Using a palette knife, transfer the peach halves, glossy-side up, to a serving dish. Scrape the excess toffee from the non-stick paper, replace in the bowl and cook for about 30 seconds or until melted once more. Coat the remaining peach halves. Chill the toffee peaches for 30 minutes before serving but do not freeze.
4. Decorate the serving dish with a border of chopped pistachio nuts.

SHELLFISH EXTRAVAGANZA

HOT VERMICELLI COCKTAIL

LOBSTER THERMIDOR

4C FLASH-COOKED SALAD

COLD LEMON SOUFFLÉ

Prepare the Hot Vermicelli Cocktail up to the end of step 4. Reheat as in step 5 on Maximum (Full) for 3 minutes just before serving, then garnish with the lemon slice or king prawn.

The Lobster Thermidor can be partially prepared in advance. Cut up the lobster meat, cover and keep chilled a few hours ahead of time. Cook the onions and butter together and stir in the wine and mustard but omit the lobster meat. Cover and set aside.

Prepare the white sauce without adding the lobster mixture. Add this just before the meal and cook for about 5 minutes (cooking is longer than in the recipe because the onion mixture will have cooled down). Combine this mixture with the sauce, then reheat on Maximum (Full) for 2–3 minutes, stirring once. Then continue with step 6 and keep the lobster hot in the conventional oven.

The salad can be cooked several hours in advance.

The Lemon Soufflé is best cooked about 12 hours in advance. Although freezing is possible, the soufflé tends to be lumpy when thawed.

HOT VERMICELLI COCKTAIL

PREPARATION TIME: *about 15 minutes*
COOKING TIME: *about 11 minutes, plus standing and reheating*
MICROWAVE SETTING: *Maximum (Full)*

90 g (3½ oz) vermicelli	*⅛ teaspoon dried marjoram*
1 tablespoon oil	*freshly ground black pepper*
salt	
1 small onion, peeled and finely chopped	*1 teaspoon lemon juice*
½ garlic clove, peeled and crushed	*225 g (8 oz) shelled prawns*
225 g (8 oz) fresh tomatoes, peeled and chopped	*6 tablespoons whipped cream*
	lemon slices and king prawns, to garnish

1. Put the vermicelli into a bowl, cover with boiling water and add 1 teaspoon of the oil and 1 teaspoon salt. Mix thoroughly. Three-quarters cover with cling film and cook for 5 minutes. Stand for 2 minutes, then drain.

2. Combine the onion and garlic with the remaining oil and cook for 2–2½ minutes or until the onion is soft.

3. Add the tomatoes to the onion mixture with the marjoram and cook for a further 4 minutes, stirring once during cooking. Add salt and pepper to taste. Stir in the lemon juice.

4. Mix the cooked vermicelli with the tomato sauce and leave until cool.

5. Mix in the prawns and whipped cream and spoon into individual wine glasses. These must not be made of crystal.

6. Place the glasses in a circle on the microwave shelf and heat on Maximum (Full) for 3 minutes. Decorate with a slit lemon slice and king prawn over the edge of the glass and place the glass on a saucer. Serve immediately with hot buttered toast if wished.

Hot vermicelli cocktail

LOBSTER THERMIDOR

PREPARATION TIME: *about 15 minutes*
COOKING TIME: *about 12 minutes, plus grilling*
MICROWAVE SETTING: *Maximum (Full); then Medium Low (35%)*

500g (1¼ lb) lobster meat or the meat from 3 medium lobsters	1½ teaspoons freshly made mustard
100g (4oz) butter	40g (1½oz) flour
1 medium onion, peeled and finely chopped	450ml (¾ pint) milk
5 tablespoons dry white wine	9 tablespoons grated Gruyère cheese
	3 tablespoons grated Parmesan cheese
	2 egg yolks

1. Cut the larger chunks of lobster meat into cubes and mix with the smaller pieces.
2. Put 65g (2½oz) of the butter into a 2 litre (3½ pint) bowl and cook for 1 minute or until melted. Stir in the onion and cook for a further 2 minutes or until soft.
3. Stir in the wine, mustard and lobster meat and cook for 3 minutes, stirring once.
4. In another large bowl put the remaining 35g (1½oz) butter and cook for 30 seconds or until the butter is melted. (Because of the residual heat on the oven shelf, the butter will melt quickly.)
5. Stir in the flour and cook for 45 seconds, then gradually stir in the milk. Cook for 2 minutes, then stir and cook for a further 2–3 minutes, stirring every minute until the sauce thickens. Beat in half of the cheeses and the egg yolks, then mix into the lobster. If the mixture is insufficiently hot, reduce the setting to Medium Low (35%) and cook for 1–2 minutes.
6. Divide the mixture between 6 lobster halves, scallop shells or individual dishes, sprinkle with the remaining cheese and brown under a preheated conventional grill.

4C FLASH-COOKED SALAD

PREPARATION TIME: *about 15 minutes*
COOKING TIME: *about 4 minutes, plus cooling*
MICROWAVE SETTING: *Maximum (Full)*

1 cucumber, washed and cut into 3mm (⅛ inch) slices	6 tablespoons medium red wine
6 celery sticks, scraped and finely sliced	4 tablespoons salad oil
100g (4oz) cauliflower florets, broken into sprigs	1 teaspoon freshly ground black pepper
100g (4oz) carrots, scraped and cut into matchsticks	½ teaspoon salt
	1 teaspoon sugar

1. Combine all the ingredients in a 2.75 litre (5 pint) bowl. Cover with cling film and cook for 2 minutes, stir thoroughly, then re-cover and cook for a further 2 minutes. Stir once more.
2. Leave to cool, but do not chill, then spoon the mixture into a suitable bowl.

COLD LEMON SOUFFLÉ

PREPARATION TIME: *about 15 minutes*
COOKING TIME: *about 4 minutes, plus cooling*
MICROWAVE SETTING: *Maximum (Full)*

grated rind and juice of 2 large lemons (6 tablespoons juice)	1 tablespoon powdered gelatine
100g (4oz) caster sugar	300ml (½ pint) double or whipping cream, half whipped
4 large eggs, separated	
6 tablespoons water	

The soufflé can also be served from a large dish with or without the greaseproof paper collar and suitable decorations are mimosa balls, lemon jelly slices or rosettes of whipped cream.

1. Combine the lemon rind, juice and sugar in a 1.2 litre (2 pint) basin and cook for 1½ minutes. Stir until the sugar has dissolved, then cook for a further 30 seconds or until boiling.
2. Remove the basin, leave to stand for 2 minutes, then beat the egg yolks and strain into the syrup. Beat vigorously.
3. Put the water in a small jug or cup and cook for about 1½ minutes or until boiling. Sprinkle the gelatine over the surface and stir thoroughly. Cook for 30 seconds, then stir until the gelatine has completely dissolved and the liquid is clear.
4. Pour the gelatine from a height into the hot lemon syrup and beat vigorously.
5. Leave the mixture until cool but not set, then fold in the cream.
6. Using grease-free beaters and a clean bowl, beat the egg whites until stiff peaks form. Stir a generous tablespoon of the beaten egg whites into the lemon mixture, then fold in the remainder.
7. Tie a collar of double thickness greaseproof paper around 6 individual ramekin dishes or 1 large and pour in the soufflé mixture, filling soufflé dish to about 1 cm (½ inch) above the rim of the dish. Chill until set, then with the aid of a warm round-bladed knife, remove the greaseproof collars. The finished soufflé will then have the appearance of a baked soufflé.

Lobster thermidor; 4C flash-cooked salad; Cold lemon soufflé

```
┌─────────────────────────────────────┐
│                                       │
│      CHRISTMAS COOKING                │
│                                       │
│   TURKEY WITH CHESTNUT STUFFING       │
│        BREAD SAUCE                     │
│       ROAST POTATOES                   │
│      BRUSSELS SPROUTS                  │
│     CHRISTMAS PUDDING                  │
│       BRANDY BUTTER                    │
│     CHOCOLATE TRUFFLES                 │
│                                       │
└─────────────────────────────────────┘
```

Prepare the Chocolate Truffles 1–2 weeks ahead and keep chilled or freeze for up to 2 months.
Prepare the Christmas Pudding up to 2 weeks ahead. To reheat, remove the wrappings, place the pudding on a suitable dish and allow 3–5 minutes on Maximum (Full) or 8–9 minutes on Medium Low (35%). Take care if reheating on full power as the dried fruit becomes very hot. If reheating just a portion allow 20–30 seconds only on Maximum (Full).
Prepare the Brandy Butter a few hours ahead and keep chilled. Cook the sprouts ahead of time and reheat, covered, adding 1–2 tablespoons water, on Maximum (Full) for about 4 minutes.
Make the Bread Sauce in advance. Add 1–2 tablespoons milk, stir thoroughly and reheat for 1 minute just before the dinner.
Cook the Roast Potatoes and Turkey freshly. The Stuffing may be prepared several hours in advance but it is advisable to stuff the turkey just before cooking.

TURKEY WITH CHESTNUT STUFFING

PREPARATION TIME: *about 20 minutes*
COOKING TIME: *about 90 minutes, plus standing*
MICROWAVE SETTING: *Maximum (Full); then Medium Low (35%)*

2 bacon rashers, rinded and diced	*1 egg, beaten*
25 g (1 oz) butter or margarine	*1 × 3½ kg (8 lb) fresh or thawed oven-ready turkey, weight excluding giblets*
225 g (8 oz) unsweetened chestnut purée made from fresh or canned chestnuts	*1 tablespoon vegetable oil*
75 g (3 oz) fresh white breadcrumbs	*1 teaspoon paprika*
	1 tablespoon cornflour
1 teaspoon chopped fresh parsley	*2–3 tablespoons cold water*
grated rind of 1 lemon	*watercress sprigs, to garnish*
salt	*bacon rolls (optional), to serve*
freshly ground black pepper	

To thaw frozen turkey, allow about 10 minutes per 450 g (1 lb) on Medium Low (35%), following each microwave time with an equivalent rest period. Turn the bird over and reposition after each heating period. When half-thawed, complete the defrosting in the lower part of the refrigerator well away from any other meats.

Giblets should be removed as soon as it is possible to loosen them from the cavity and all metal clips must be cut away before the bird is put into the microwave oven. Frozen turkey may be left in the plastic package (which should be slit underneath) standing in a shallow dish, in order to catch the juices.

Only the neck end of poultry should be stuffed and extra cooking time given if you prefer to use a sausage meat stuffing.

If more convenient, the turkey can be cooked in the conventional oven on 190°C/375°F/Gas Mark 5 for 3 hours 40 minutes or you can cook it in the microwave oven for three-quarters of the cooking time and then transfer to the conventional oven for 1–1¼ hours to complete cooking.

1. To make the stuffing, put the bacon in a 2 litre (3½ pint) bowl and cook for 1 minute. Stir in the butter, then mix in all the remaining stuffing ingredients.
2. Press the stuffing into the neck end of the turkey, then fold over the flap and secure firmly with wooden cocktail sticks by putting the wings over the flap to hold it in place. Tie the legs together with string. Do not use metal skewers.
3. Put the turkey, breast-side down, on to the largest shallow dish that will fit into the microwave oven. Cover with a large roasting bag slit lengthways and tucked under the sides of the dish to prevent the bag from blowing about.
4. Cook for 35 minutes on Maximum (Full), then leave the turkey to stand for 30 minutes. Provided the microwave oven is not required for anything else, it is hygienic to leave the turkey in the cavity during this time.
5. Carefully pull back the roaster bag covering on one side, and if possible spoon away any accumulated juices and reserve for use in gravy.
6. Turn the turkey over and rub the breast with the oil, paprika, salt and pepper. Shield any cooked parts with small pieces of foil, wrapping it firmly around the wing tips and legs, making sure that the foil is absolutely flat and does not protrude beyond the dish, where it might touch the metal sides or top of the microwave oven. Replace the roaster bag covering and cook for 25 minutes.
7. Remove any foil shielding, reduce the power to Medium Low (35%) and cook for 20–30 minutes or until the turkey is thoroughly cooked (when a thermometer inserted between the leg and the side or in the thickest part of the breast registers 85°C/185°F, or the juices run clear when the skin around the side is severed with a sharp knife).
8. Transfer the turkey to a hot serving dish and tent completely with foil or put into a hot conventional oven. Spoon away the fat from the dish and add the reserved juices. Blend the cornflour with the water and mix into

the juices. Put the dish in the microwave oven and cook on Maximum (Full) for about 3 minutes until the gravy thickens. Stir occasionally during cooking. To serve, garnish the turkey with watercress sprigs and serve with bacon rolls, if liked.

BREAD SAUCE

PREPARATION TIME: *5 minutes*
COOKING TIME: *7½ minutes, plus standing*
MICROWAVE SETTING: *Maximum (Full)*

3 bay leaves	*4 peppercorns*
450ml (¾ pint) milk	*75g (3oz) fresh*
1 medium onion, peeled	*breadcrumbs*
and sliced	*salt*
1 blade of mace	*25g (1oz) butter or*
2 cloves	*margarine*

1. Crumble one of the bay leaves. Combine the milk, onion, mace, crumbled bay leaf, cloves and peppercorns in a 2 litre (3½ pint) lipped bowl. Cook for 4 minutes or until the milk is steaming. Cover and leave at room temperature for 30 minutes.
2. Put the breadcrumbs into another similar sized bowl and strain in the infused milk. Add salt to taste, stir and cook for 2 minutes. Stir, then cook for a further 1½ minutes or until the breadcrumbs are well absorbed and the sauce is thick and soft. Stir in the butter or margarine. Garnish with the remaining bay leaves.

Turkey with chestnut stuffing; Bread sauce

ROAST POTATOES

See page 72
Allow 1½kg (3lb) potatoes weighed before peeling and cook in 8 tablespoons salted water for 18 minutes before roasting in the conventional oven.

BRUSSELS SPROUTS

PREPARATION TIME: *about 10 minutes*
COOKING TIME: *6–7 minutes*
MICROWAVE SETTING: *Maximum (Full)*

1 kg (2lb) firm even-sized Brussels sprouts; weight after trimming 450g (1lb)
6 tablespoons water
¾ teaspoon salt

Brussels sprouts will continue cooking in the residual heat left after they are removed from the microwave oven, so do not overcook. If the sprouts are to be set aside for later reheating, plunge them into cold water immediately after cooking, then drain and put into a cold covered casserole. Sprouts may be cooked conventionally, then reheated by microwave if preferred. Frozen sprouts may be substituted but the purchase weight will be only 450g (1 lb) and the cooking time similar. It is essential to use some water when cooking sprouts by microwave, otherwise they will dry out and become tough.

1. To trim the sprouts, remove the stem ends and any damaged outer leaves and soak the sprouts in cold salted water for about 10 minutes. Drain thoroughly.
2. Mix the water and salt in a large roaster bag or casserole, then add the sprouts. Loosely seal the roaster bag with an elastic band, leaving a gap at the top, or cover the casserole with the lid and cook for 3–4 minutes. Stir the sprouts or gently ease them into different positions in the roaster bag and cook for a further 3 minutes or until tender but firm. Drain and place in a covered casserole. Serve with butter curls, if liked.

CHRISTMAS PUDDING

PREPARATION TIME: *20 minutes, plus overnight standing*
COOKING TIME: *about 30 minutes, plus standing*
MICROWAVE SETTING: *Medium Low (35%)*

175g (6oz) currants	*¼ cooking apple, peeled, cored and finely chopped*
75g (3oz) sultanas	
75g (3oz) raisins	*1 teaspoon fresh lemon juice*
5 tablespoons medium sherry	
	1 tablespoon black treacle
2–3 tablespoons brandy	*75g (3oz) butter or margarine*
100g (4oz) muscovado sugar	
	75g (3oz) crumbs from a fresh granary loaf
¼ teaspoon ground nutmeg	
¼ teaspoon mixed spice	*2 eggs, beaten*
15g (½oz) mixed chopped nuts	*25g (1oz) plain flour*
	sprig of holly, to decorate

The pudding improves greatly with keeping. To store, overwrap in cling film and foil.

1. In a large bowl mix the dried fruit, sherry, 1 tablespoon of the brandy, sugar, spices, nuts, apple, lemon juice and treacle. Cover tightly and leave overnight.
2. Put the butter or margarine in a large mixing bowl and heat for about 1½ minutes until melted.
3. Stir in the crumbs, beaten eggs and flour. Add the fruit mixture a few tablespoons at a time, stirring thoroughly after each addition.
4. Well grease a 900ml (1½ pint) ovenglass pudding basin and place a 5cm (12 inch) disc of non-stick paper in the base.
5. Put the mixture into the pudding basin and cover with a plate greased underneath or with cling film vented. Cook on Medium Low (35%) for about 25 minutes. Cook only until the pudding is just dry on top. Leave for at least 10 minutes before turning out.
6. Pour over 1–2 more tablespoons of brandy and when this has been absorbed, the pudding may be served decorated with the holly sprig.

Brussels sprouts; Roast potatoes

BRANDY BUTTER

PREPARATION TIME: *about 5 minutes*
NO COOKING REQUIRED

100g (4oz) unsalted
butter
175g (6oz) icing sugar,
sifted
6 tablespoons brandy

1. Beat the butter until soft and almost white.
2. Gradually beat in the sugar and brandy, adding them alternately and a little at a time.
3. Pile the mixture into a pyramid shape in an attractive dish and ridge with a fork around the sides. Chill until cold.

CHOCOLATE TRUFFLES

MAKES ABOUT 16
PREPARATION TIME: *about 5 minutes*
COOKING TIME: *about $3\frac{1}{2}$ minutes, plus standing*
MICROWAVE SETTING: *Maximum (Full)*

Christmas pudding; Brandy butter; Chocolate truffles

3 tablespoons double
cream
2 teaspoons rum
3 egg yolks, threads
removed and lightly beaten
1 × 175g (6oz) bar dessert
chocolate, broken up
50g (2oz) chocolate
strands
50g (2oz) desiccated
coconut, toasted

To toast desiccated coconut, put the coconut into a dish and cook on Maximum (Full), stirring every 30 seconds until the coconut browns evenly, 50g (2oz) takes about 4 minutes.

1. Put the cream into a 1.2 litre (2 pint) basin and cook until boiling.
2. Stir in the rum and the beaten egg yolks
3. Put the chocolate into a jug or small basin and cook for 1 minute. Stir, then cook for a further $1-1\frac{1}{2}$ minutes, until the chocolate is shiny on top and beginning to melt. Stir and pour into the cream mixture. Beat thoroughly, then cook for 1 minute, beating every 15 seconds. Leave to stand for 10 minutes, then beat thoroughly once more. Chill until the mixture is completely cold and firm but not hard.
4. Put the chocolate strands into one small bowl or cup and the toasted coconut in another.
5. With lightly oiled hands shape the chocolate mixture into small balls, coating one at a time either in the chocolate strands or the toasted coconut. Refrigerate or freeze until required. (F)

DEVONSHIRE COUNTRY FARE

SMOKED MACKEREL PÂTÉ

HOT JOINT OF HAM AND CIDER GRAVY

POTATOES ANNA

BROCCOLI TUFTS

SPICED APPLE CRUMBLE WITH
DEVONSHIRE CREAM

Prepare the Smoked Mackerel Pâté a few hours ahead of time. The pâté may be frozen for up to 2 months but will require a thorough beating when thawed, which should be done at room temperature.
To prepare the Hot Joint of Ham and Cider Gravy, put the joint into the roasting bag and then into the dish 2 hours ahead of time, but leave in the refrigerator. Cook the gravy as in step 3 a few hours before serving. Cook the ham to coincide with your proposed time of serving the pâté, then complete the gravy, adding an extra 2 minutes on step 5. Tent the dish with foil and keep warm in the conventional oven.
Prepare the broccoli up to the end of step 3, then cook while serving the first course. Alternatively, cook conventionally or par-cook and refresh earlier in the day, then reheat on Medium Low (35%) for about 10 minutes.
Cook the Potatoes Anna before the meal and finish when needed. Either prepare the Spiced Apple Crumble up to the end of step 3 in advance, then cook for 12 minutes without turning the dish while eating the main course and brown under the grill while clearing the main course dishes; or pre-cook a few hours ahead and reheat in the microwave oven while clearing the dishes away. Allow about 4 minutes on Maximum (Full).

SMOKED MACKEREL PÂTÉ

PREPARATION TIME: *about 10 minutes*
COOKING TIME: *about 1½ minutes*
MICROWAVE SETTING: *Maximum (Full)*

350g (12oz) smoked mackerel fillet	*salt (optional)*
50g (2oz) butter	*freshly ground black pepper*
100g (4oz) curd cheese	
1 tablespoon lemon juice	*4–6 tablespoons single cream or top of the milk*
1 tablespoon mild creamed horseradish	*slices of lemon, to garnish*

1. Remove the skin and bones from the mackerel and put the flaked fish into a 1.2 litre (2 pint) basin. Cook for 1½ minutes or until the fish is warm.
2. Stir in the butter and pound until pulped, then work in the remaining ingredients, adding salt to taste if liked and pepper, then add sufficient cream to mix to a spreading

consistency. (For a smoother pâté, blend the mixture in the food processor.) (F)
3. Pile the pâté into a dish or individual ramekins and garnish with slices of fresh lemon. Serve with Melba or hot buttered toast.

Variation:
For a less rich-tasting pâté use cottage cheese instead of curd and blend in the food processor to produce a smooth texture.

HOT JOINT OF HAM AND CIDER GRAVY

PREPARATION TIME: *about 10 minutes*
COOKING TIME: *about 57 minutes*
MICROWAVE SETTING: *Maximum (Full); then Medium Low (35%); then Maximum (Full)*

1 × 1.5kg (3lb) joint unsmoked uncooked ham	*¼ teaspoon salt*
	450ml (¾ pint) dry cider
75–100g (3–4oz) dark soft brown sugar	*4 tablespoons seedless raisins*
2 tablespoons plain flour	*apple slices, to garnish*

Ignore any popping noises while the ham is cooking. This is due to the fat splattering and is not 'arcing'.

1. Put the joint into a roasting bag and seal with a large elastic band, leaving a gap for the steam to escape. Place the bag in a shallow dish. Cook on Maximum (Full) for 10 minutes, then turn the joint and bag over, reduce the setting to Medium Low (35%) and cook for 40 minutes or until a meat thermometer reads 60°C/140°F.
2. Carefully remove the elastic band and transfer the ham to a hot serving dish, leaving the juices in the roasting bag. Tent the ham to prevent it from cooling.
3. Combine the sugar and flour in a medium bowl or in the roasting dish, stir in the salt and gradually add the cider. Raise the setting and cook on Maximum (Full) for 4 minutes, stirring twice during cooking. Stir in the raisins.
4. Hold the roaster bag so that the juices are in one corner, snip off the bottom with scissors and allow the juices to drip into the sauce. As soon as the fat reaches the corner of the bag, flip it up with tongs or scissors and discard.
5. Stir the gravy thoroughly and cook on Maximum (Full) without covering for 2–3 minutes. Taste and adjust the seasoning. Pour into a jug and serve with the ham, garnished with apple slices.

Smoked mackerel pâté; Hot joint of ham and cider gravy

POTATOES ANNA

PREPARATION TIME: *about 15 minutes*
COOKING TIME: *about 12 minutes, plus grilling*
MICROWAVE SETTING: *Maximum (Full)*

1 kg (2 lb) medium even-shaped potatoes	*salt*
50 g (2 oz) butter	*freshly ground black pepper*

1. Peel the potatoes and slice as thinly as possible. Shake dry in a clean cloth.
2. Put the butter into a large bowl and cook for 30 seconds or until completely melted. Add the potatoes and toss until all the slices are evenly coated.
3. Arrange the potato slices in thin layers in a 23 cm (9 inch) round, shallow, flameproof dish and sprinkle each layer with salt and pepper. Make sure that the top layer is well coated with the melted butter, then press down firmly with a fish slice.
4. Cover the dish with cling film, pulling back one corner to vent and cook for about 6 minutes. Turn the dish round and cook for a further 6 minutes or until there is some give in the potatoes when pressed with a fork through the cling film. Leave to stand for about 5 minutes, then carefully remove the cling film.
5. Brown the potatoes under a preheated conventional grill.

BROCCOLI TUFTS

PREPARATION TIME: *about 10 minutes*
COOKING TIME: *about 7 minutes, plus standing*
MICROWAVE SETTING: *Maximum (Full)*

500 g (1¼ lb) broccoli, trimmed weight 375 g (13 oz)
8 tablespoons water
½ teaspoon salt

1. Trim the broccoli, remove the thick stalks. Rinse the florets in cold water, then using a potato peeler, peel the skin from the stalks.
2. Put the water and salt in a casserole and stir until the salt is dissolved.
3. Arrange the broccoli in the dish, the tufts towards the centre and the stalks towards the outside.
4. Cover the casserole and cook for 6–7 minutes or until the broccoli is tender. Leave to stand covered for 3 minutes before serving.

SPICED APPLE CRUMBLE WITH DEVONSHIRE CREAM

PREPARATION TIME: *about 15 minutes*
COOKING TIME: *about 11 minutes, plus grilling*
MICROWAVE SETTING: *Maximum (Full)*

50 g (2 oz) self-raising flour	*750 g (1½ lb) cooking apples, peeled, cored and finely sliced*
175 g (6 oz) wholemeal flour	*¼ teaspoon ground cloves*
125 g (4 oz) butter or soft margarine	*¼ teaspoon ground cinnamon*
75 g (3 oz) demerara sugar	*75 g (3 oz) caster sugar*
	300 ml (½ pint) Devonshire cream, to serve

1. Combine the flours in a mixing bowl and rub in the butter or margarine until the mixture resembles fine crumbs. Stir in 50 g (2 oz) of the demerara sugar.
2. Put the apples into a 1.2 litre (2 pint) oval pie dish. Stir in the ground cloves, cinnamon and caster sugar and mix thoroughly.
3. Spoon the crumble topping over the fruit and press down firmly. Sprinkle the remaining demerara sugar on top.
4. Cook for 6 minutes, then turn the dish round and cook for a further 5 minutes or until a round-bladed knife inserted into the topping comes out clean.
5. Brown the crumble under a preheated conventional grill, placing the dish 15–21 cm (6–8 inches) below the element or flame, or in a hot oven for 10 minutes. Serve hot with Devonshire cream.

Broccoli tufts; Potatoes Anna; Spiced apple crumble with Devonshire cream

Sprinkle the cheese evenly over the bread and cook for about 20 seconds or until the cheese melts.
5. Reheat the soup if necessary, pour into individual bowls and float a slice of cheesy bread on top. After a few seconds the bread absorbs the soup and becomes deliciously soft.

FRENCH FROLIC

SOUPE À L'OIGNON GRATINÉ

CANARD À L'ORANGE

POIREAUX BEURRÉS

POMMES PARISIENNES

PETITS MOUSSES AU CHOCOLAT

Prepare the Petits Mousses au Chocolat 2–3 days ahead and keep chilled.
Cook the soup one day ahead which will deepen and improve both texture and flavour, but dry the bread and melt the cheese just before serving. Cook for 2 minutes or until boiling.
Cook the leeks ahead of time and reheat just before serving the duck. Prepare the duck sauce up to the point at which the sugar is dissolved and set aside in a jug. Cook the duck just before dinner. Complete the sauce, allowing an extra 3 minutes to bring the sauce back to temperature, then cover the duck and sauce with foil and keep hot in the conventional oven while reheating the soup.
Reheat or complete the potatoes in the conventional oven while keeping the duck hot or keep hot in the conventional oven.

SOUPE À L'OIGNON GRATINÉ

PREPARATION TIME: *about 20 minutes*
COOKING TIME: *about 32 minutes*
MICROWAVE SETTING: *Maximum (Full)*

350g (12oz) onions, peeled and finely chopped	*150ml ($\frac{1}{4}$ pint) red wine*
1 small garlic clove, peeled and crushed	*salt*
	freshly ground black pepper
2 tablespoons salad oil	*3 slices French bread, halved*
2 tablespoons plain flour	
900ml (1$\frac{1}{2}$ pints) hot beef stock	*50g (2oz) grated Gruyère cheese*

1. Combine the onions, garlic and oil in a large 2.75 litre (5 pint) glass mixing bowl and cook for 15 minutes, stirring occasionally until the onion is soft.
2. Stir in the flour, then add 300ml ($\frac{1}{2}$ pint) of the hot stock and the wine. Cook, uncovered, for 5 minutes.
3. Add the remaining stock and salt and pepper to taste. Half cover with cling film and cook for a further 10 minutes.
4. Put the 6 half slices of French bread on a paper towel and cook for 1$\frac{1}{2}$ minutes or until the bread is crisp.

CANARD À L'ORANGE

PREPARATION TIME: *about 15 minutes*
COOKING TIME: *45–60 minutes, plus browning*
MICROWAVE SETTING: *Medium (50%); then Maximum (Full)*

1 × 2.5kg (5$\frac{1}{2}$lb) oven-ready duck or 6 × 400g (14oz) duck joints	*9 tablespoons caster sugar*
	6 tablespoons white wine vinegar
4 oranges	*1$\frac{1}{2}$ tablespoons arrowroot*
1 lemon	*watercress sprigs, to garnish*

1. Place the duck or joints on a rack in a deep dish and cook, uncovered, on Medium (50%) for 45–60 minutes or until the juices run clear when the flesh is pierced with a sharp knife. Reposition the pieces or turn the duck over 3 times during cooking. Half-way through, transfer the surplus juices and fat to a jug. Brown the cooked duck under a preheated conventional grill.
2. While the duck is baking, squeeze the juice from 2 of the oranges and the lemon, grate the zest of 1 orange, pare the lemon peel and cut it into thin strips. Peel and thinly slice the remaining oranges, removing the pips, and reserve.
3. About 15 minutes before the duck is ready, prepare the sauce. Put the lemon strips into a jug or bowl, barely cover with cold water and cook, uncovered, on Maximum (Full) about 2 minutes, until boiling. Cook for a further 1 minute. Drain and reserve.
4. Combine the sugar and vinegar in a 1.2 litre (2 pint) basin and cook for 2 minutes. Stir until the sugar is dissolved, then cook, uncovered, for about 7 minutes or until a purple-brown syrup forms.
5. Blend the arrowroot with 2 tablespoons of the duck juices and set aside.
6. Stir the remaining duck juices, about 300ml ($\frac{1}{2}$ pint), the fruit juices, about 200ml (7floz), the zest and strips into the syrup.
7. Add the blended arrowroot and cook for 3$\frac{1}{2}$ minutes or until the sauce thickens, stirring once during cooking.
8. Arrange the duck on a bed of orange slices and garnish with watercress. Spoon half the sauce over the duck and serve the remaining sauce separately.

Variation:
To roast the duck conventionally, cook the whole bird in a moderately hot oven 200°C/400°F/Gas Mark 6 for about 2 hours or cook duck joints at 190°C/375°F/Gas Mark 5 for 1 hour.

POIREAUX BEURRÉS

PREPARATION TIME: *about 10 minutes*
COOKING TIME: *about 17 minutes*
MICROWAVE SETTING: *Maximum (Full)*

750g (1½lb) leeks, trimmed to total weight 500g (1¼lb)	*½ teaspoon salt*
	¼ teaspoon freshly ground black pepper
6 tablespoons water	
15g (½oz) butter	

1. Cut the leeks into 5cm (2 inch) chunks, then slice lengthways into strips. Put into a colander and wash thoroughly under cold running water. Drain.
2. Put the leeks into a casserole with the water, cover and cook for 10 minutes.
3. Remove the leeks with a slotted spoon. Replace the casserole and cook, uncovered, for 4 minutes or until only about 2 tablespoons of the liquid remain.
4. Stir in the butter, salt and pepper, replace the leeks and toss thoroughly. Cover with the lid and cook for 3 minutes, stirring once during cooking.

Poireaux beurrés; Canard à l'orange with Pommes parisiennes; Soupe à l'oignon gratiné

POMMES PARISIENNES

PREPARATION TIME: *about 20 minutes*
COOKING TIME: *about 6 minutes, plus browning*
MICROWAVE SETTING: *Maximum (Full)*

1.5kg (3lb) large potatoes	*1 tablespoon plain flour*
5 tablespoons water	*25g (1oz) butter, for browning*
1 teaspoon salt	

1. Peel the potatoes and cut out small even-shaped balls with a Parisienne cutter (potato baller).
2. Put the water and salt into a large roasting bag and shake well to dissolve the salt.
3. Put the potatoes into the roasting bag and loosely seal with a large elastic band. Cook for 2½ minutes, then, using an oven glove, shake the bag gently to reposition. Cook for a further 2½–3 minutes, then drain thoroughly.
4. Sprinkle a clean teatowel with the flour and toss the potato balls, so that they are evenly coated.
5. Preheat a large browning dish according to the manufacturer's instructions. Quickly add the butter and toss in the potato balls, stirring them once.
6. Cook, uncovered, for 3 minutes, stirring briefly halfway through cooking. Transfer to a heated serving dish.

PETITS MOUSSES AU CHOCOLAT

PREPARATION TIME: *about 10 minutes*
COOKING TIME: *about 2 minutes, plus chilling*
MICROWAVE SETTING: *Maximum (Full)*

225g (8oz) plain dessert chocolate, broken into pieces	*15g (½oz) butter*
	4 large eggs, separated
	1 tablespoon brandy
3 tablespoons water	*double or whipping cream, whipped, to decorate*

1. Put the chocolate into a medium 2 litre (3½ pint) bowl with the water and cook for 1½ minutes until the chocolate melts. Beat vigorously to a smooth cream. Cook for a further 30 seconds, then beat again.
2. Beat in the butter and egg yolks one at a time, then stir in the brandy.
3. Using grease-free beaters in a clean bowl, whip the egg whites until stiff peaks form. Stir 1 generous tablespoon of the beaten egg white into the mixture, then fold in the remainder thoroughly. Pour into 6 individual ramekins, decorate with piped cream and chill for 3–4 hours.

Petits mousses au chocolat

ORIENTAL DELIGHT

FISH SOUP WITH BEAN CURD

ORIENTAL CHICKEN

PORK NOODLES

EGG FRIED RICE

STIR-FRIED VEGETABLES

TOFFEE BANANA FRITTERS

Fish Soup with Bean Curd can be prepared up to 24 hours in advance omitting the bean curd; add and cook this when reheating. The soup will take about 5 minutes on Maximum (Full), should be three-quarters covered and stirred once during reheating. Alternatively the soup can be reheated in a saucepan on the hob.
Cook the Oriental Chicken, planning to coincide with the intended serving time. The chicken can be cooked up to the end of step 5 before reheating the soup and the sauce completed in between the courses.
Reheat the Pork Noodles and Stir-Fried Vegetables together in the microwave oven on Maximum (Full) for 3 minutes while the soup is being eaten, but add the beansprouts to the vegetables to complete the recipe just before serving them. When reheating, you could stack the dishes so that the Pork Noodles are beneath the Stir-Fried Vegetables.
The Egg Fried Rice can be prepared up to 24 hours in advance and will reheat very quickly (about 3 minutes on full power). The rice can also be frozen, before the egg is added, for up to 2 months.
The Toffee Banana Fritters can be prepared in advance up to the end of step 5 but cooking must be completed after the main course.
If you prefer you can reheat the Pork Noodles, Vegetables and Rice consecutively in the microwave just before the meal and keep them hot in the conventional oven, but remember to cover with a lid not cling film.

FISH SOUP WITH BEAN CURD

PREPARATION TIME: *about 20 minutes*
COOKING TIME: *about 22 minutes*
MICROWAVE SETTING: *Maximum (Full)*

1 tablespoon vegetable oil	*1 tablespoon soy sauce*
1 celery stick, finely sliced	*salt*
1 shallot, peeled and thinly sliced	*freshly ground black pepper*
½ medium carrot, sliced diagonally, paper thin	*225g (8oz) fresh haddock fillets, skinned and boned and cut into 1 cm (½ inch) cubes*
3 thin slices root ginger	
900ml (1½ pints) chicken stock	*100g (4oz) block bean curd*
1 bunch watercress	

1. Combine the oil, celery, shallot, carrot and ginger in a 2 litre (3½ pint) bowl and cook for 5 minutes, stirring once.
2. Stir in the stock and watercress leaves (without stalks) and bring to the boil, about 10 minutes from cold.
3. Add the soy sauce and salt and pepper to taste. Stir in the fish and cook for 5 minutes.
4. While the fish is cooking, carefully cut the bean curd into 2 cm (½ inch) cubes, gently put into the soup and cook for a further 2 minutes.

ORIENTAL CHICKEN

PREPARATION TIME: *about 10 minutes*
COOKING TIME: *about 40 minutes, plus marinating and standing*
MICROWAVE SETTING: *Maximum (Full); then Medium Low (35%)*

6 tablespoons Hoisin sauce	1 tablespoon cornflour
2 tablespoons sesame oil	2 teaspoons cold water
½ teaspoon ground ginger	4 water chestnuts, finely sliced
½ teaspoon salt	
1 × 1.5 kg (3½ lb) oven-ready chicken, fully thawed if frozen	spring onions and tomato roses, to garnish

1. Combine the Hoisin sauce, sesame oil, ground ginger and salt in a small bowl or jug.
2. Put the chicken in a shallow dish and rub with the sauce mixture, spooning the remainder into the cavity.
3. Cover the chicken with a split roaster bag and leave in a cool place to marinate for 2 hours, basting occasionally.
4. Cook for 15 minutes on Maximum (Full), basting once during cooking, then reduce the setting to Medium Low (35%) and cook for 15–20 minutes, basting twice during cooking.
5. Remove the chicken from the dish and place on a hot serving dish, covering with an upturned bowl or foil to keep it warm.
6. Blend the cornflour and cold water together and stir into the juices left in the roasting dish. Add the water chestnuts and cook on Maximum (Full) for 1–1½ minutes or until the sauce thickens. Stir once or twice during cooking. Slice the chicken, pour the sauce over and garnish with the spring onions and tomato roses.

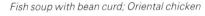

Fish soup with bean curd; Oriental chicken

PORK NOODLES

PREPARATION TIME: *about 10 minutes*
COOKING TIME: *about 20 minutes*
MICROWAVE SETTING: *Maximum (Full)*

225 g (8 oz) lean pork	1 medium onion, peeled and finely chopped
$\frac{1}{4}$ teaspoon ground ginger	
1 teaspoon cornflour	50 g (2 oz) mushrooms, sliced
salt	
freshly ground black pepper	175 g (6 oz) medium Chow Mein egg noodles
2 tablespoons sesame oil	spring onions, to garnish

Fresh noodles are ready as soon as the water reboils and need no standing time. Denser pastas such as spaghetti require a longer cooking time.

1. Trim away all fat and cut the pork into tiny dice.
2. Mix the ginger and cornflour together and add salt and pepper to taste. Add the pork and mix thoroughly.
3. Put the oil into a 2 litre ($3\frac{1}{2}$ pint) bowl and stir in the onion. Cook for 7 minutes, stirring once, until browned.
4. Immediately stir in the pork mixture, then cover with cling film and cook for 4 minutes stirring after 2.
5. Add the mushrooms, replace the cover and cook for 4 minutes. Leave to stand, covered.
6. Put the noodles into a large bowl or casserole and add sufficient boiling water to cover generously. Stir in $\frac{1}{2}$ teaspoon salt. Cook, uncovered, until the water returns to the boil, about 3 minutes, then cover and leave for 6 minutes or until the noodles are tender.
7. Drain the noodles thoroughly, mix in the pork mixture, then cover and reheat for 2–3 minutes. Garnish with the spring onions and serve.

EGG FRIED RICE

PREPARATION TIME: *about 5 minutes*
COOKING TIME: *about 11 minutes*
MICROWAVE SETTING: *Maximum (Full)*

2 tablespoons salad oil	1 tablespoon soy sauce
1 large onion, peeled and finely chopped	salt
	freshly ground black pepper
350 g (12 oz) cold cooked long-grain rice	
2 eggs	25 g (1 oz) butter or margarine

1. Put the oil in a 2 litre (.$3\frac{1}{2}$ pint) bowl and stir in the onion. Cook for $2\frac{1}{2}$ minutes, then stir and cook for a

further 2½ minutes or until the onion is soft.
2. Stir the rice into the onion mixture and cook for 5 minutes, stirring occasionally until the mixture is hot. (F)
3. Beat the eggs and soy sauce together, stir into the hot rice and cook for 1 minute or until the egg is cooked.
4. Sprinkle the rice mixture with salt and pepper to taste; then stir in the butter or margarine. Serve hot. If the egg fried rice is to be reheated, add an extra 15 g (½ oz) butter before serving.

STIR-FRIED VEGETABLES

PREPARATION TIME: *15 minutes*
COOKING TIME: *5 minutes, plus heating the browning dish*
MICROWAVE SETTING: *Maximum (Full)*

50 g (2 oz) butter or margarine	225 g (8 oz) fresh beansprouts
100 g (4 oz) mange-tout	1 tablespoon flaked almonds
1 green pepper, cored, seeded and finely sliced	salt
1 red pepper, cored, seeded and finely sliced	freshly ground black pepper
4 tablespoons soy sauce	1 tablespoon sesame seeds
1 teaspoon sherry	

1. Preheat a large browning dish to the maximum recommended by the manufacturer.
2. Immediately add the butter and stir in the mange-tout and sliced peppers, continuing to stir until the heat dies down.
3. Stir in the soy sauce, sherry, beansprouts and almonds and cook, uncovered, for 5 minutes, stirring once or twice during cooking.
4. If necessary, add a little salt and a good shake of pepper. Stir, sprinkle with sesame seeds and serve hot.

TOFFEE BANANA FRITTERS

PREPARATION TIME: *15 minutes, plus chilling*
COOKING TIME: *30 minutes*
MICROWAVE SETTING: *Maximum (Full)*
MAKES 15–18

Batter:	oil for deep frying
1 egg	Syrup:
150 ml (¼ pint) cold water	225 g (8 oz) caster sugar
150 g (5 oz) plain flour	225 ml (8 fl oz) cold water
3 firm medium-sized bananas	1 teaspoon salad oil

1. Half fill a large bowl with cold water and chill in the refrigerator or add 10–12 ice cubes.
2. To make the batter, beat the egg and water together in a mixing bowl, then gradually beat in the flour until the mixture is smooth.
3. Peel the bananas, cut them into 2½ cm (1 inch) slices and immerse them in the batter.
4. On the conventional hob, fill a deep frying pan one third full of oil, heat and deep-fry the bananas a few at a time until pale golden. Drain on paper towels.
5. To make the syrup, combine the sugar and water in a 2 litre (3 pint) ovenglass bowl. Cook on Maximum (Full) for 3 minutes, then stir until the sugar is dissolved.
6. Stir in the oil and cook, uncovered, for 17 minutes or until the syrup is thick and brown and has reached the hard ball stage. (A hard ball should form when a few drops are dropped into a saucer of cold water.)
7. Dip the bananas in the syrup so that they are fully coated and immediately plunge them into the chilled bowl of iced water. Remove with a slotted spoon, drain briefly and serve immediately.

Left to right: Pork noodles; Egg fried rice; Stir-fried vegetables; Toffee banana fritters

COST CUTTER

SPINACH AND ANCHOVY PÂTÉ

MINCE GOULASH WITH DUMPLINGS

CABBAGE AND CARAWAY SEEDS

APPLE CRUNCH WITH YOGURT TOPPING

Prepare the pâté up to the end of step 3 earlier in the day and divide between the individual ramekins. Cover with cling film and leave at room temperature. Complete 35 minutes before serving time.
Prepare the sauce for the cabbage up to the end of step 1 ahead of time. Prepare and arrange the cabbage in the salted water in advance and keep covered. Cook the cabbage and reheat with the sauce during the standing time for the pâté, then cover and keep warm.
Prepare the Apple Crunch with Yogurt Topping up to the end of step 2 a few hours ahead of time and keep apples and topping separately, covered. Make the yogurt topping (step 5) ahead of time. If the dessert is to be served cold, it may be entirely completed a few hours in advance but if serving hot, put the biscuit crumbs on top of the apples and add the melted butter. Cook without turning while eating the main course. After adding the yogurt topping, reheat on Medium Low (35%) for about 5 minutes.
The meatballs for the Mince Goulash can be shaped (step 3) and the sauce made (steps 5–6) ahead of time. Just before the meal, complete the dish, allowing an extra 5 minutes on Maximum (Full) to heat the sauce. After the dumplings are cooked, cover and keep hot in the conventional oven.

SPINACH AND ANCHOVY PÂTÉ

PREPARATION TIME: *about 10 minutes*
COOKING TIME: *20 minutes, plus standing*
MICROWAVE SETTING: *Maximum (Full); then Medium Low (35%)*

350g (12oz) fresh spinach leaves; bought weight 750g (1½lb)	*1 small onion, peeled and finely chopped*
1 × 50g (1¾oz) can anchovy fillets	*¼ teaspoon freshly ground black pepper*
1 tablespoon oil from anchovy fillets	*3 eggs*
	100g (4oz) fresh breadcrumbs
	cucumber slices, to garnish

1. Wash the spinach leaves and put in a roaster bag with only the water left after draining. Seal with an elastic band, leaving a gap in the top for the steam to escape. Cook on Maximum (Full) for 5 minutes. Drain.
2. Combine the oil and onion in a basin and cook for 1½ minutes, then stir and cook for a further 1½ minutes until the onion is soft.
3. Purée all the ingredients in the liquidizer, adding the breadcrumbs last.
4. Divide the mixture between 6 individual ramekins, covering each with cling film. Reduce the setting to Medium Low (35%) and cook for 6 minutes. Give each dish a half-turn and cook for a further 6 minutes or until the mixture is set. Leave for 20 minutes. Garnish with cucumber and serve warm with hot buttered toast.

MINCE GOULASH WITH DUMPLINGS

PREPARATION TIME: *about 20 minutes*
COOKING TIME: *about 20 minutes*
MICROWAVE SETTING: *Maximum (Full)*

Minced beef balls:	Sauce:
750g (1½lb) lean minced beef	*2 medium onions, peeled and finely chopped*
4 slices bread, crusts removed and diced	*2 tablespoons vegetable oil*
1 medium onion, peeled and grated	*3 tablespoons plain flour*
1 medium carrot, peeled and grated	*2 tablespoons paprika*
1 teaspoon salt	*5 tablespoons tomato purée*
½ teaspoon freshly ground black pepper	*1 teaspoon sugar*
½ teaspoon caraway seeds (optional)	*750ml (1¼ pints) hot beef stock*
2 eggs	**Dumplings:**
	50g (2oz) soft margarine
	1 large egg
	100g (4oz) plain flour
	5–6 tablespoons milk

1. Put the meat in a solid handleless plastic colander and set over a large bowl. Cook for 4 minutes, stirring every minute until the meat changes colour and the fat and some of the juices have dripped into the bowl. Carefully lift out the colander and place on a plate to catch any further drips.
2. Spoon away the surplus fat from the bowl and stir the bread into the residual juices, leaving them until all the juices have been absorbed.
3. Add the grated onion and carrot, the minced beef, salt, pepper, caraway seeds if used and eggs and mix thoroughly together. Shape the mixture into 12 even-sized balls.
4. Arrange the meatballs in a circle in a large casserole. Cover and cook for 1½ minutes. Turn the dish round and cook for a further 1½ minutes. Leave to stand while preparing the sauce.
5. To make the sauce, combine the chopped onion and oil in a large bowl and cook for about 3 minutes or until the onion is golden. Stir once or twice during cooking.

6. Stir in the flour, paprika, tomato purée and sugar and when these are well blended, add the beef stock. Cook for 2 minutes, then add salt and pepper to taste. Stir thoroughly, cover and cook for about 5 minutes, stirring once during cooking.
7. Meanwhile, prepare the dumplings. Beat the margarine, egg and one tablespoon of the flour together until smooth and creamy and stir in a pinch of salt.
8. Add alternate spoonfuls of the remaining flour and milk until the mixture will drop easily from the spoon.
9. Place 6 spoonfuls of the dumpling mixture around the edges of the hot sauce, cover and cook for 3 minutes or until the dumplings are no longer liquid on top.
10. Carefully place the meatballs in the centre of the sauce and spoon the sauce over both the dumplings and the meat. Cover and cook for 1 minute or until the meat is hot.

CABBAGE AND CARAWAY SEEDS

PREPARATION TIME: *10 minutes*
COOKING TIME: *about 12 minutes*
MICROWAVE SETTING: *Maximum (Full)*

15g (½oz) butter or margarine	salt
1 tablespoon plain flour	freshly ground black pepper
150ml (¼ pint) chicken or beef stock	3 tablespoons water
1 tablespoon caraway seeds	450g (1 lb) trimmed cabbage, washed and cut into 6 wedges

1. Put the butter or margarine into a 1.2 litre (2 pint) basin and cook for 30 seconds or until melted. Stir in the flour until smooth, then stir in the stock and caraway seeds. Blend thoroughly.
2. Cook for 1 minute, then stir and cook for a further 1–1½ minutes or until the sauce thickens. Add salt and pepper to taste. Cover and keep warm.
3. Put the water into a dish and add salt to taste. Arrange the cabbage wedges in a single layer in the dish. Cover with cling film and cook for 4 minutes, then reposition the cabbage wedges, so that those on the outside are moved to the inside. Cover and cook for a further 4 minutes.
4. Remove the cabbage from the dish and stir the sauce into the remaining liquid. Replace the cabbage, spooning the sauce over the top and reheat for 1 minute.

Spinach and anchovy pâté; Mince goulash with dumplings; Cabbage and caraway seeds

APPLE CRUNCH WITH YOGURT TOPPING

PREPARATION TIME: *about 15 minutes*
COOKING TIME: *about 17 minutes*
MICROWAVE SETTING: *Maximum (Full); then Medium Low (35%)*

750g (1½ lb) cooking apples, peeled, cored and thinly sliced

175g (6 oz) soft dark brown sugar

130g (4½ oz) digestive wheatmeal biscuits

75g (3 oz) butter or margarine

150ml (¼ pint) plain unsweetened yogurt

1 teaspoon cornflour

demerara sugar, to decorate

1. Place the apples in a 900ml (1½ pint) pie dish. Cook on Maximum (Full) for 3 minutes until the apples soften.
2. While the apples are cooking, put the sugar in a bowl, add the biscuits and coarsely crush with the head of a rolling pin.
3. Spread the mixture on top of the apples.
4. Put the butter in the bowl and cook for 30–45 seconds on Maximum (Full) until melted. Pour evenly over the biscuit mixture. Cook for 3 minutes, then give the dish a quarter turn and cook for a further 3 minutes. Leave to stand while preparing the topping.
5. To make the topping, mix the yogurt and cornflour in a small bowl and stir until well blended. Reduce the microwave setting to Medium Low (35%) and cook for 7 minutes, stirring frequently until the mixture thickens to the consistency of half-whipped cream.
6. Pour the yogurt topping over the apple pudding, sprinkle over the demerara sugar and serve hot or cold.

Apple crunch with yogurt topping

ПEPTUПE DIППER

EGG MAYONNAISE WITH CAPERS

BAKED SALMON TROUT

NEW POTATOES

PETITS POIS AND SPRING ONION COMPOTE

STRAWBERRY AND ORANGE MALLOW

Cook the eggs and prepare the mayonnaise ahead of time. Coat and decorate within half an hour of serving, otherwise the mayonnaise will develop a skin.

The Strawberry and Orange Mallow may be prepared up to 3 days in advance and will set more firmly if refrigerated during this time. The mallow does not freeze well.

If the Salmon Trout is to be served cold, it may be prepared in advance. If serving hot, cook it when ready to eat. The salmon will keep warm if it is tented in foil. Although it can be reheated, the results will be patchy.

Scrape the potatoes and keep immersed in cold water about 2 hours ahead of cooking and cook while you are skinning the salmon.

The Petits Pois and Spring Onion Compote can be cooked up to 1 day in advance. Reheat, covered, for about 3 minutes on Maximum (Full) as soon as the potatoes are cooked.

EGG MAYONNAISE WITH CAPERS

PREPARATION TIME: *about 10 minutes*
COOKING TIME: *about 30 seconds*
MICROWAVE SETTING: *Maximum (Full)*

Mayonnaise:
300ml (½ pint) good quality salad oil
2 egg yolks
¼ teaspoon salt
¼ teaspoon white pepper
¼ teaspoon dry mustard

2 tablespoons fresh lemon juice
1 tablespoon capers, finely chopped
3 tablespoons single cream
6 hard-boiled eggs

To garnish:
crisp lettuce leaves
cress

1. Put the oil in a jug and heat for 25–30 seconds until just warm to the touch.
2. Using an electric whisk, beat the egg yolks, salt, pepper and mustard together until foamy and thick.
3. Slowly pour in the oil drop by drop, beating continuously until the mayonnaise begins to thicken.
4. While still beating, add the lemon juice to thin, then the remaining oil, pouring it in in a steady stream.
5. Stir in the capers and the cream.
6. Arrange the lettuce on individual serving plates. Peel the eggs, halve lengthways and arrange 2 halves curved side up on each plate. Spoon the mayonnaise over the eggs to coat well and garnish with the cress.

Egg mayonnaise with capers

BAKED SALMON TROUT

PREPARATION TIME: *about 5 minutes*
COOKING TIME: *about 30 minutes*
MICROWAVE SETTING: *Medium Low (35%)*

4 bay leaves	*salt*
1 × 1.75 kg (3 lb 12 oz) whole salmon trout, washed and gutted but with the head attached	*freshly ground black pepper*
	15 g (½ oz) butter
	cucumber and lemon slices, to garnish

If you prefer to cook the salmon without the head which weighs approximately 200 g (7 oz), the cooking time can be reduced by about 5 minutes. The salmon does not need to be covered during cooking as the skin takes the place of a cover, sealing in the juices. If you prefer the fish to be firmer when cooked, slash the skin in several places before cooking. It should not stick to the oven floor or turntable but if it does, try a little fat to grease.

1. Insert the bay leaves inside the salmon along the flap and sprinkle with salt and pepper.
2. If the salmon will not fit in flat, curve around the edge of the turntable or on the oven shelf and rub with butter.
3. Wrap the head in foil and overwrap with a double layer of cling film. Repeat with the thin end of the tail (the foil must not touch the sides of the oven).
4. Cook the salmon trout on Medium Low (35%) for 20 minutes, then remove the cling film and foil from the tail end and cook for a further 10 minutes. To test for cooking, insert a knife through the skin along the backbone of the fish; it should lift evenly away from the flesh.
5. To serve, remove the head if preferred, remove the skin and take out the bay leaves. Garnish with cucumber and lemon slices. Serve hot or cold.

NEW POTATOES

PREPARATION TIME: *about 10 minutes*
COOKING TIME: *about 11 minutes, plus standing*
MICROWAVE SETTING: *Maximum (Full)*

8 tablespoons water	*1 kg (2 lb) new potatoes, scrubbed and well scraped*
½ teaspoon salt	*butter (optional), to serve*

1. Put the water into a casserole and stir in the salt until dissolved. Add the potatoes. Cover the casserole and cook for 7 minutes.
2. Reposition the potatoes and cook for a further 4 minutes, then leave to stand covered for 4 minutes. Test to see if they are cooked, then drain and serve. (A dab of butter may also be added; it will melt quickly and easily.)

PETITS POIS AND SPRING ONION COMPOTE

PREPARATION TIME: *about 5 minutes*
COOKING TIME: *15 minutes*
MICROWAVE SETTING: *Maximum (Full)*

500 g (1¼ lb) frozen petit pois	*salt*
5 spring onions, skinned, trimmed and finely sliced	*freshly ground black pepper*
8 tablespoons well-flavoured chicken stock	*15 g (½ oz) butter*
	7 g (¼ oz) flour

There is only sufficient sauce in this dish to thicken slightly.

1. Combine the peas, onions and stock in a 1.2 litre (2 pint) casserole, cover and cook for 10 minutes.
2. Add salt and pepper, then cook, uncovered, for 3 minutes or until the liquid boils. Meanwhile, blend the butter and flour together.
3. Using oven gloves, tip the dish so that the liquid collects at one end and beat in the butter paste.
4. Stir to mix the vegetables with the liquid and cook for 2 minutes or until the sauce thickens.

STRAWBERRY AND ORANGE MALLOW

PREPARATION TIME: *5 minutes*
COOKING TIME: *2 minutes, plus setting*
MICROWAVE SETTING: *Maximum (Full)*

350 g (12 oz) fresh or frozen strawberries, thawed	*50 g (2 oz) ground almonds*
175 g (6 oz) marshmallows	*150 ml (¼ pint) whipping cream, whipped*
juice of 1 orange (4 tablespoons)	

1. Reserve 6 strawberries for decoration. Combine the remaining strawberries and marshmallows in a 2 litre (3½ pint) bowl and cook for 2 minutes or until the marshmallows melt and the mixture starts to puff up. Stir and set aside in a cool place.
2. When the mixture begins to set, beat in the orange juice and ground almonds, then chill until cold.
3. To serve, spoon the mallow into individual dishes, top with whipped cream and decorate with the reserved strawberries.

Petits pois and spring onion compote; Baked salmon trout; New potatoes; Strawberry and orange mallow

POACHER'S PRIDE

CORN ON THE COB

CASSEROLED RABBIT IN RED WINE

SWEDE AND ORANGE PURÉE

APRICOT PARFAIT

Prepare the Apricot Parfait several days in advance and chill or freeze for up to 3 months. If frozen, leave at room temperature for about 20 minutes before serving or in the refrigerator for about 1 hour.
Prepare the Swede and Orange Purée several hours in advance or freeze if preferred. If frozen, store for up to 3 months, then remove from the freezer a few hours in advance and reheat on Maximum (Full) for about 6 minutes, stirring occasionally, then cover and transfer to the conventional oven to keep hot.
Cook the rabbit up to 12 hours ahead of time, cool rapidly and refrigerate. Remove just before the meal and reheat on Maximum (Full) for 10–15 minutes, repositioning once. Leave to stand, covered, while eating the first course.
Cook the Corn on the Cob about 45 minutes before the meal is to be served, then tent with foil and keep hot in a cool conventional oven. If you anticipate that the first course will take 25 minutes, it is possible to cook it just before preparing the rabbit.

CORN ON THE COB

PREPARATION TIME: *5 minutes*
COOKING TIME: *15 minutes, plus standing*
MICROWAVE SETTING: *Maximum (Full)*

6 corns on the cob, weighing about 350g (12oz) each
butter, to serve
salt
freshly ground black pepper

1. Wipe the husks and remove the silks at the end. Pile the corn cobs in a large shallow dish. (If preferred, the husks and corn silk can be removed and the cobs can be wrapped individually in greaseproof paper.)
2. Cook for 5 minutes, then reposition the corn cobs, putting the warm cobs on the top of the pile. Cook for a further 5 minutes, then reposition once more. Cook for a further 5 minutes and give the dish a half-turn, then leave to stand for 5 minutes before serving.
3. To serve, remove the husks and silk, put the corn on individual heated plates, top with a dab of butter and sprinkle with salt and pepper.

CASSEROLED RABBIT IN RED WINE

PREPARATION TIME: *10 minutes*
COOKING TIME: *50–55 minutes, plus thawing and standing*
MICROWAVE SETTING: *Maximum (Full)*

1½kg (3lb) frozen rabbit joints
1 medium carrot, peeled and trimmed
1 medium onion, peeled and finely chopped
1 stick celery, finely sliced
25g (1oz) butter
3 tablespoons plain flour
½ teaspoon dried rosemary
300ml (½ pint) medium red wine
salt
freshly ground black pepper

1. Thaw and rinse the rabbit joints.
2. Cut the carrot into 5cm (2 inch) lengths and make grooves down the lengths of each chunk at regular intervals. (A canelle knife is useful for this.) Slice up the chunks to make flowers.
3. Combine the carrot, onion, celery and butter in a large, deep casserole and cook for 3 minutes. Stir, then continue cooking for a further 5 minutes or until the onion is brown.
4. Stir in the flour, herbs and wine and cook for 2 minutes, stirring every minute. Season to taste with salt and pepper.
5. Put the rabbit portions into the sauce. Cover with the lid and cook for 40–45 minutes or until just tender. Reposition the pieces 4 times during cooking. Leave to stand, covered, for 15 minutes before serving.

SWEDE AND ORANGE PURÉE

PREPARATION TIME: *5 minutes*
COOKING TIME: *10 minutes*
MICROWAVE SETTING: *Maximum (Full)*

1 × 550g (1¼lb) swede
150ml (¼ pint) water
4 tablespoons orange juice
salt
freshly ground black pepper
strips of orange peel and parsley sprig, to garnish

1. Scrub the swede and prick deeply in several places. Put into a roaster bag and add the water. Seal loosely with an elastic band, leaving a gap in the top, and cook for 10 minutes or until the swede feels soft when squeezed.
2. Carefully remove the elastic band, take out the swede and place it on a board. Peel, using a sharp knife and a fork. Cut the swede into several pieces, place in the food processor bowl, add the orange juice and process until puréed. Add salt and pepper to taste. (F)
3. Pour the purée into a suitable serving dish, cover and reheat for 2–3 minutes. Stir once before serving, garnished with the orange strips and parsley.

APRICOT PARFAIT

PREPARATION TIME: *about 15 minutes*
COOKING TIME: *about 5 minutes, plus setting*
MICROWAVE SETTING: *Maximum (Full)*

about 100 g (4 oz) cooking chocolate, broken into pieces	*1 × 400 g (14 oz) can apricots, well drained*
150 ml (¼ pint) milk	*300 ml (½ pint) double cream, beaten until peaks form*
25 g (1 oz) sugar	
2 egg yolks	*1 tablespoon Apricot Brandy or Orange Curaçao*
few drops almond essence	

For a special occasion the parfait can be decorated with piped cream and apricot slices.

1. Chill a 900 ml (1½ pint) basin until it is cold to the touch.
2. Place the chocolate in a small jug and cook for 1 minute. Stir, then cook for a further 30 seconds or until the chocolate is shiny on top. Stir until evenly melted.
3. Pour the melted chocolate into the chilled basin and swirl, so that the bowl is completely coated. Make sure that the chocolate comes right to the top of the basin. Replace the basin in the refrigerator. (If the chocolate begins to roll away from the top of the basin, add a second coat when the first is set. This may require the melting of a little more chocolate.)
4. Stir the milk and sugar together in a lipped bowl and cook for 1 minute. Stir again.
5. Beat the egg yolks and almond essence together, and stir into the warm milk. Cook for about 30 seconds, then stir and cook for a further 30–40 seconds until the custard is hot but not boiling (or curdling will occur). Cover and leave until cold.
6. Purée the apricots and beat in the cream, then beat in the cooled custard and the liqueur.
7. Pour the mixture into the chocolate-lined pudding basin and place in the freezer for a minimum of 2 hours. (F)
8. To turn out, dip the basin into a bowl of very hot water for 15–20 seconds, then dry and turn out on to a serving dish. Leave for 10 minutes before cutting and serving.

Casseroled rabbit in red wine; Swede and orange purée; Corn on the cob; Apricot parfait

PARTY MENUS

All the recipes are planned for six to twelve on the basis that few partygoers will have more than one item from each dish. In keeping with other chapters you can include dishes from another menu if you wish.

It goes without saying that the Bazaar selections have good keeping qualities and even the Lemon Curd can be refrigerated for a week or two and frozen for up to 3 months. The Drinks and Dunkers party needs a little more care. The Aubergine Dunk is best eaten fairly soon after preparation but the Cheese Fondue freezes and reheats very well.

Vol-au-vents and tartlet cases keep well in a tin and can also be frozen. Peanut Brittle softens and becomes sticky after a few days – and of course you can vary the fillings for the jam tartlets as blackberry jam, for example, cooks just as well as strawberry. You could use tuna instead of prawns in the tartlets and change the vol-au-vents fillings as you will.

You also don't have to have a barbecue to enjoy the Barbecue Party in this section as instructions are also given for cooking everything completely in the microwave and, if you wish, you can have one big come-and-try party using all thirty-seven recipes.

```
COFFEE MORNING PARTY
```

DEVIL'S FOOD CAKE

SQUARE BROWN SCONES

LEMON TEABREAD

GINGERBREAD

FLORENTINES

SHORTBREAD FANS

The Scones, Lemon Teabread and Gingerbread can be prepared ahead of time and stored in the freezer. Store the scones for up to 6 months, the teabread and gingerbread for up to 6 weeks. Thaw at room temperature, unwrapped.
The Shortbread Fans will keep well for at least 1 week in an airtight container.
The Florentines keep well in an airtight container in the refrigerator or freezer but should be layered between sheets of greaseproof paper.
The Devil's Food Cake keeps well in an airtight container, but must be left at room temperature for about 2 hours before serving to enable the icing to attain a crust.

DEVIL'S FOOD CAKE

PREPARATION TIME: *about 20 minutes*
COOKING TIME: *about 4 minutes, plus standing (cake); about 8 minutes (icing)*
MICROWAVE SETTING: *Maximum (Full)*
MAKES 1 RING CAKE

75 g (3 oz) plain flour	75 g (3 oz) golden syrup
35 g (1¼ oz) cocoa powder	25 g (1 oz) ground
¼ teaspoon bicarbonate of soda	almonds
	American frosting:
85 ml (3 fl oz) milk	175 g (6 oz) granulated
75 g (3 oz) softened butter or margarine	sugar
	100 ml (3½ fl oz) cold water
75 g (3 oz) caster sugar	1 egg white
2 large eggs	¼ teaspoon cream of tartar

1. To make the cake, lightly grease a 1 litre (1¾ pint) plastic ring mould, alternatively put a glass in the middle of an ordinary dish.
2. Sift the plain flour and cocoa powder together in a mixing bowl. Blend the bicarbonate of soda with the milk and add to the flour. Add the butter or margarine, caster sugar, eggs, syrup and almonds, beating for 1–2 minutes until smooth.
3. Pour the cake mixture into the prepared ring and cook for 2 minutes. Turn the dish round and cook for a further 2

minutes or until the cake is just dry on top. Leave to stand for 4–5 minutes before turning on to a wire tray. Place the wire tray over another tray and leave the cake until cool but not cold.
4. Meanwhile, make the American frosting. Mix the sugar and water together in a medium ovenglass bowl. Cook for 3 minutes, then remove the bowl and stir until the sugar is completely dissolved.
5. Return the bowl to the microwave oven and cook for 5 minutes without stirring until the soft ball stage is reached, 115°C (238°F) – a few drops of the syrup should form a soft ball when dropped into ice-cold water. When the ball is removed from the water, it should immediately lose its shape. Remove the bowl and beat the mixture with a wooden spoon until cloudy.
6. Using clean beaters in a grease-free bowl, beat the egg white until stiff peaks form.
7. Add the cream of tartar and pour the hot syrup into the beaten white. Continue beating as the mixture cools.
8. Pour or spoon the frosting over the cake and leave uncovered until the icing crisps on the surface.

Variation:
The cake can be decorated with a drizzle of melted chocolate if preferred.

SQUARE BROWN SCONES

PREPARATION TIME: *about 10 minutes*
COOKING TIME: *about 3 minutes*
MICROWAVE SETTING: *Maximum (Full)*
MAKES 9

225 g (8 oz) wholemeal plain flour	75 g (3 oz) butter or margarine
4 teaspoons baking powder	25 g (1 oz) dark soft brown sugar
pinch of salt	75 g (3 oz) sultanas
	5 tablespoons milk

Provided the scones are kept covered, they will stay fresh for several hours. The scones spread sideways but do not rise very much, so do not overcook in anticipation that they will grow taller.

1. Mix the flour, baking powder and salt together, then rub in the butter or margarine until the mixture resembles crumbs.
2. Stir in the sugar and sultanas. Add the milk and mix to a soft dough.
3. Do not knead the dough but shape into a square 2½ cm (1 inch) thick on a floured surface. Cut into 9 squares and arrange in a circle on a paper towel.
4. Cook for 3 minutes or until a cocktail stick comes out clean. Do not overcook or the scones will become solid. Leave to cool. (F)
5. Serve warm, split and filled with butter or cream and jam.

Square brown scones; Devil's food cake; Lemon teabread

LEMON TEABREAD

PREPARATION TIME: *about 20 minutes*
COOKING TIME: *about 12½ minutes*
MICROWAVE SETTING: *Maximum (Full); then Medium (50%)*
MAKES 1 LOAF

grated rind of 1 lemon	pinch of salt
about 3 tablespoons lemon juice	75 g (3 oz) butter
75 g (3 oz) currants	100 g (4 oz) dark soft brown sugar
100 g (4 oz) raisins	1 egg, beaten
25 g (1 oz) sultanas	3 tablespoons milk
225 g (8 oz) plain wholemeal flour	¼ teaspoon bicarbonate of soda
½ teaspoon baking powder	15 g (½ oz) mixed peel

If you prefer to eat the teabread cold, it should be wrapped tightly in cling film immediately after its standing time. To eat hot, it may be reheated on Maximum (Full) for about 30 seconds.

1. Combine the lemon rind, juice, currants, raisins and sultanas in a basin and cook on Maximum (Full) for 1½ minutes or until the mixture boils. Leave standing, covered, until all the juice is absorbed. Leave for a few minutes to cool down.
2. Sift the flour with the baking powder and salt into a mixing bowl and rub in the butter until the mixture resembles breadcrumbs. Stir in the sugar.
3. Beat the egg, milk and bicarbonate of soda together and pour into the flour mixture. Mix thoroughly, then fold in the mixed peel and the fruit mixture.
4. Put the mixture into a loaf-shaped container about 20 × 13 × 10½ cm deep (8 × 5 × 3 inches). Reduce the setting to Medium (50%) and cook for 11 minutes or until the mixture is just dry on top. Leave the teabread in the cooking container for 5 minutes before turning out on to non-stick silicone paper. Immediately reverse to prevent the top of the cake from being damaged. (F) Serve warm, slicing with a sharp knife.

GINGERBREAD

PREPARATION TIME: *about 15 minutes*
COOKING TIME: *about 8½ minutes, plus standing*
MICROWAVE SETTING: *Maximum (Full); then Medium (50%)*
MAKES ABOUT 12 SLICES

50g (2 oz) butter or margarine	1 teaspoon ground ginger
50g (2 oz) dark soft brown sugar	1 teaspoon cinnamon
	1 egg
3 tablespoons black treacle	5 tablespoons milk
75g (3 oz) plain flour	½ teaspoon bicarbonate of soda
	crystallized ginger, to decorate

1. Combine the butter or margarine, sugar and treacle in a 1.5 litre (2½ pint) mixing bowl and cook for 45 seconds or until the butter is melted. Stir to dissolve the sugar. Sift in the flour, ginger and cinnamon, stir, then mix in the egg.
2. Put the milk in a cup or glass and cook for 30 seconds until steaming but not boiling. Stir in the bicarbonate of soda. Pour the milk into the flour mixture and beat thoroughly to the consistency of a thin batter.

3. Grease and line the base of a plastic rectangular shape about 18 × 15 × 5 cm (7 × 6 × 2 inches) deep. Pour in the batter, reduce the microwave setting to Medium (50%) and cook for 3½ minutes. Turn the dish round and cook for a further 3½ minutes or until just dry on top. Leave to cool.
4. Turn out on to a sheet of non-stick silicone paper and immediately reverse to ensure that the top is undamaged. Leave whole, wrap in cling film and store for a few days for an even better flavour. (F) Alternatively, cut into about 12 squares, top with a piece of crystallized ginger and serve at once.

FLORENTINES

PREPARATION TIME: *about 10 minutes*
COOKING TIME: *about 8 minutes, plus cooling*
MICROWAVE SETTING: *Maximum (Full)*
MAKES ABOUT 20 PIECES

50g (2 oz) butter	50g (2 oz) chopped mixed peel
50g (2 oz) sugar	10 glacé cherries, chopped
40g (1½ oz) chopped walnuts	1 tablespoon double cream
40g (1½ oz) flaked almonds	225g (8 oz) plain dessert chocolate

When making Florentines, use oven gloves, place dishes on a dry board or heatproof surface. Prepare only when you have the time to stay close to the microwave oven during cooking as recipes based on sugar syrups burn easily.

1. Line the base of two 23 cm (9 inch) round ovenglass dishes with circles of non-stick silicone paper.
2. Put the butter in a 1.2 litre (2 pint) basin and cook for about 1 minute or until melted.
3. Remove the bowl and add the sugar, stirring until it is dissolved and the mixture slightly thickened. Return the bowl to the microwave oven and cook for 2 minutes until the mixture is creamy yellow and syrupy and large bubbles form.
4. Carefully remove the bowl and place on a dry board or heatproof surface. Stir in the walnuts, almonds, peel, cherries and double cream.
5. Spoon half the mixture into each ovenglass dish, placing it in the centre and spreading only slightly. Cook each dish separately for 2–2¼ minutes or until the mixture spreads and is golden brown. Switch off if the centre of the nut mixture becomes dark brown.
6. Remove the first dish and place on a heatproof surface. Wait for 5 minutes for the base plate in the microwave oven to cool, then cook the second florentine mixture (this will take less time than the first as the temperature in the cabinet will be higher and the base plate warm). Remove the second dish.
7. Leave both florentines to cool down for 5 minutes or until they stiffen, then carefully reverse them on to a flat surface lined with greaseproof or non-stick silicone paper.
8. Break up the chocolate, put into a jug and cook for 1 minute. Stir, then cook for a further 30 seconds or until the chocolate is shiny on the surface and is beginning to melt. Complete the melting process by stirring.
9. Pour the melted chocolate over the smooth surface of the florentines and leave until nearly set. Swirl with a fork to form ridges. Leave until the chocolate is firm. To serve, break into uneven wedges.

SHORTBREAD FANS

PREPARATION TIME: *about 15 minutes*
COOKING TIME: *about 4 minutes, plus standing*
MICROWAVE SETTING: *Maximum (Full)*
MAKES 16 PIECES

100 g (4 oz) softened butter or soft margarine	*175 g (6 oz) self-raising flour, sifted*
25 g (1 oz) caster sugar	*caster sugar, to decorate*
1 egg yolk, beaten	

1. Put all the ingredients together in a mixing bowl and work with the hands until a soft dough is formed. Shape into a 20 cm (8 inch) round between 2 sheets of greaseproof paper. Remove the top sheet of greaseproof paper but leave the dough in position on the lower sheet.
2. Using a 5 cm (2 inch) cutter, remove a round from the centre of the dough and cut this round into 8 triangles.
3. Mark the large circle into 8 wedges and prick thoroughly with a fork. Place one of the small triangles on the outer edge of each section.
4. Carefully lift the greaseproof paper and dough into the microwave oven, making sure that the paper is not too large to impede the process if the oven is fitted with a turntable.
5. Fill an individual paper cake case with baking beans and insert into the centre of the dough. Cook for 4 minutes or until the shortbread is just dry on top. Test with a cocktail stick to make sure that it is set. Leave for a few minutes before removing the paper and shortbread from the microwave oven.
6. Remove the paper case and baking beans and sprinkle the top of the shortbread with sugar. Cut into sections before the shortbread is quite cold.

Left to right: Gingerbread; Florentines; Shortbread fans

BUMPER BAZAAR

COCONUT ICE
CHOCOLATE NUT FUDGE
PEANUT BRITTLE
FRESH LEMON CURD
LEMON, LIME AND ORANGE MARMALADE
TOMATO AND PEPPER CHUTNEY

Coconut Ice keeps well in an airtight container and becomes drier. It is best to leave it out, covered in muslin, to dry completely before storing. Turn the pieces over frequently.
Chocolate Nut Fudge keeps well in an airtight container.
Lemon Curd will keep for up to 2 weeks in the refrigerator or 3 months in the freezer.
The marmalade keeps well provided it is sealed properly.
Tomato and Pepper Chutney improves with keeping but tends to get harder. Stir in 1 tablespoon boiling water if the chutney has become too hard and repot.
Store Peanut Brittle in an airtight container between sheets of non-stick silicone paper. The peanut brittle tends to become soft and bendy after about 2 weeks' storage.

COCONUT ICE

PREPARATION TIME: *about 10 minutes*
COOKING TIME: *about 7 minutes, plus setting*
MICROWAVE SETTING: *Maximum (Full)*
MAKES ABOUT 500g (1¼lb) or 32 PIECES

450g (1 lb) sugar	100g (4oz) desiccated coconut
pinch of cream of tartar	
65ml (2½ floz) evaporated milk	3 drops red food colouring
65ml (2½ floz) water	3 drops raspberry flavouring

Always use oven gloves when making confectionery in the microwave oven due to the high temperature reached by the sugar.

1. Combine the sugar and cream of tartar in a large bowl. Add the milk and water and mix thoroughly. Cook for 2 minutes.
2. Shake the bowl to dissolve the sugar but do not stir. Cook for about 4 more minutes until a few drops of the syrup form a soft ball when dropped into a glass of cold water (188°C/238°F).
3. Immediately stir in the coconut, beating thoroughly until the mixture thickens and becomes opaque. Pour half

of the mixture into a ungreased foil container measuring about 15 × 10cm (6 × 4 inches) and spread smoothly.
4. Beat the food colouring and flavouring into the remaining mixture, then pour carefully on top. Smooth with a palette knife. Leave until set, then turn out on to a board and leave until the coconut ice is dry on top.
5. When completely set, cut into bars.

CHOCOLATE NUT FUDGE

PREPARATION TIME: *about 5 minutes*
COOKING TIME: *about 3 minutes, plus setting*
MICROWAVE SETTING: *Maximum (Full)*
MAKES 50 PIECES

100g (4oz) plain dessert chocolate	275g (10oz) icing sugar, sifted
50g (2oz) butter	75g (3oz) chopped mixed nuts
2 tablespoons milk	
1 teaspoon vanilla essence	

1. Lightly grease an 18cm (7 inch) square tin.
2. Break up the chocolate, cut the butter into 5 or 6 pieces and place both in a large bowl. Cook for 1 minute, then stir. Cook again for about 1½–2 minutes until bubbling.
3. Remove the bowl and stir in the milk and vanilla essence. Mix in the icing sugar, a spoonful at a time, then blend in the nuts.
4. Spoon the mixture into the prepared tin and smooth the surface with a palette knife. Leave until cold, then cut into squares.

PEANUT BRITTLE

PREPARATION TIME: *about 10 minutes*
COOKING TIME: *about 9 minutes*
MICROWAVE SETTING: *Maximum (Full)*
MAKES ABOUT 350g (12oz)

2 tablespoons water	150g (5oz) salted peanuts
5 tablespoons glucose syrup	¼ teaspoon vanilla essence
175g (6oz) caster sugar	1 teaspoon cold water
25g (1oz) butter or hard margarine	1 teaspoon bicarbonate of soda

1. Put the 2 tablespoons water, glucose syrup and caster sugar in a large 2.75 litre (5 pint) ovenglass bowl and cook for 2 minutes. Stir until the sugar has dissolved, then stir in the butter or margarine. Cook for 1 minute. Stir to make sure that the butter has melted.
2. Mix in the peanuts and, without stirring, cook for 5½–6 minutes until the mixture is foamy and light brown underneath (you can see this through the bottom of the glass bowl).

Peanut brittle; Chocolate nut fudge; Coconut ice

3. Mix the vanilla essence with 1 teaspoon cold water. During the last minute of the cooking period, add the bicarbonate of soda to the vanilla essence mixture and blend thoroughly.

4. Using oven gloves, remove the bowl with the peanut mixture and immediately pour in the blended mixture. Beat thoroughly with a wooden spoon for 1 minute or until the mixture bubbles up into a honeycomb (this is important to ensure that the brittle will be hard enough).

5. Grease a long-handled palette knife. Put a sheet of non-stick silicone paper on a heat-resistant surface and

pour on the hot peanut mixture. Using the palette knife, smooth the mixture to a 5 mm ($\frac{1}{4}$ inch) thickness. Leave for at least 3 minutes, allowing just enough time for the mixture to cool down, as handling at this stage would burn your fingers.

6. Cover with a second sheet of non-stick silicone paper and flip over. The brittle will look rather flat on this side.

7. As soon as the mixture is cool enough to touch, stretch with your fingers to a 28 × 20 cm (11 × 8 inch) rectangle.

8. Leave until cold, then break up into pieces and store in an airtight container.

FRESH LEMON CURD

PREPARATION TIME: *about 10 minutes*
COOKING TIME: *about 12 minutes*
MICROWAVE SETTING: *Maximum (Full)*
MAKES ABOUT 1.5kg (3½lb)

10 lemons
8 eggs
450g (1 lb) caster sugar
225g (8oz) unsalted butter

1. Squeeze the juice from 8 of the lemons. Grate the rind from the remaining 2 lemons and segment and chop the flesh.
2. Beat the eggs and lemon juice together and strain into a 2.75 litre (5 pint) bowl. Stir in the sugar, then add the butter cut into 10 or 12 small pieces. Cook for 8 minutes, stirring after 4 minutes, then stir once or twice during the remaining cooking period or when you see the curd thickening around the edges of the bowl.
3. Add the reserved rind and chopped lemon and cook for a further 3–4 minutes, stirring once or twice during cooking.
4. Remove the bowl and stir for 30 seconds. Allow the lemon curd to cool, then spoon into clean dry jars. Seal and label. (F)

LEMON, LIME AND ORANGE MARMALADE

PREPARATION TIME: *about 20 minutes*
COOKING TIME: *60 minutes*
MICROWAVE SETTING: *Maximum (Full)*
MAKES 1.5kg (3lb)

3 large oranges, washed and dried	*2 limes, washed and dried*
3 large lemons, washed and dried	*900ml (1½ pints) boiling water*
	1 kg (2 lb) sugar
	knob of butter

The total weight of the fruit should be about 1.25 kg (2½lb).

1. Pare away the zest from the fruit and remove as much pith as possible. Shred the zest finely. Set aside.
2. Finely chop the pared fruit, pips and pith and put into a large ovenglass bowl. Add the boiling water. Cook, uncovered, for 20 minutes, stirring once during cooking.
3. Strain the liquid into another similar-sized bowl, pressing the pulp to extract all the liquid. Discard the pulp.
4. Stir the shredded rind into the hot liquid and cook for

20 minutes, stirring once or twice during cooking until the rind is tender. Remove the shredded strips with a slotted spoon and set aside.
5. Stir the sugar into the hot liquid until it has dissolved. Three-quarters cover with cling film and cook for 10 minutes. Stir, add the reserved shreds and cook for 5 minutes. Add the butter and cook for 5 minutes or until setting point is reached. A spoonful of the mixture, dropped on to a cold plate, should wrinkle when pushed with the back of a spoon.
6. Pot in hot sterilized jars, seal and label.

TOMATO AND PEPPER CHUTNEY

PREPARATION TIME: *about 15 minutes*
COOKING TIME: *about 45 minutes*
MICROWAVE SETTING: *Maximum (Full)*
MAKES 1 kg (2lb)

750g (1½lb) very ripe soft tomatoes	*100g (4oz) soft dark brown sugar*
1 red pepper, cored, seeded and finely chopped	*1 tablespoon salt*
1 green pepper, cored, seeded and finely chopped	*200ml (7fl oz) malt vinegar*
225g (8oz) onions, peeled and finely chopped	*15g (½oz) ground ginger*
	¼ teaspoon paprika
100g (4oz) sultanas	*½ teaspoon mustard powder*

Make this chutney a few weeks in advance as the flavour improves on keeping.

1. Combine all the ingredients in a 2.75 litre (5 pint) bowl, three-quarters cover with cling film and cook for about 45 minutes, stirring every 5 minutes to prevent burning.
2. When the chutney is thick and all the liquid has been absorbed, stir thoroughly, then allow to cool. Spoon into clean dry jars, seal and label.

Fresh lemon curd; Tomato and pepper chutney; Lemon, lime and orange marmalade

FINGER AND FORK FOOD

FARMER'S TERRINE

PRAWN TARTLETS

GARLIC CHEESE BREAD

SMOKED CHICKEN VOL-AU-VENTS

RICE AND RAISIN SALAD

APRICOT TARTINES

CHESTNUT ICE CREAM NESTS

This menu will serve 10–12

Make the Chestnut Ice Cream Nests up to several weeks ahead and store in a closed container in the freezer. Make the meringue nests up to three weeks in advance and store in an airtight container.

The Farmer's Terrine can be prepared ahead of time, wrapped and frozen for up to 2 months.

Prepare the Apricot Tartines ahead of time and store in an airtight container.

For the Prawn Tartlets prepare the pastry cases to the end of step 4 in advance and store in an airtight container. Make up the filling a few hours ahead of time. Fill and complete the cooking. They can be served either warm or cold.

Prepare the Garlic Bread ahead of time up to the end of step 4.

Make the filling for vol-au-vents up to the end of step 2 a few hours ahead of time, cover and keep chilled.

Reheat on Maximum (Full) for 2 minutes, then stir thoroughly and fill the heated cases just before serving.

Prepare the Rice and Raisin Salad ahead of time, cover and chill.

FARMER'S TERRINE

PREPARATION TIME: *about 20 minutes*
COOKING TIME: *about 18 minutes, plus standing*
MICROWAVE SETTING: *Maximum (Full)*
MAKES A 1 kg (2 lb) LOAF

225 g (8 oz) pig's liver, trimmed and sinews removed	*½ teaspoon freshly ground black pepper*
225 g (8 oz) lean pork, minced	*1 egg (size 1)*
	4 tablespoons brown ale
100 g (4 oz) raw lean beef, minced	*1 tablespoon flour*
	100 g (4 oz) butter or margarine
1 medium onion, peeled and finely grated	*100 g (4 oz) fresh breadcrumbs*
1 garlic clove, peeled and crushed	**To garnish:**
	red pepper rings
1 teaspoon salt	*watercress sprigs*
	cucumber slices

The quantities may be doubled or trebled but the meat loaves should be cooked separately for the time recommended.

1. Chop the liver finely, then mix with the pork, beef, onion, garlic, salt, pepper, egg, ale and flour. Cover and set aside.
2. Put the butter or margarine in a loaf-shaped dish, about 20 × 13 × 10½ cm (8 × 5 × 3 inches) and cook for 2 minutes or until melted. Stir in the crumbs. Cook for about 6 minutes, stirring every 2 minutes until the crumbs are golden brown.
3. Spoon out half the crumbs and set aside. Press the remaining crumbs into the base of the dish. Cover with the meat mixture, pressing it well down, then add the remaining crumbs to form a crisp topping.
4. Cook for 10 minutes, giving the dish a quarter turn every 2 minutes until the meat loaf is firm. Leave to stand in the dish for 5 minutes, then turn on to a wire tray. Leave until cold. (F)
5. Cut into slices, garnish with the red pepper, watercress and cucumber and serve with white or brown bread.

PRAWN TARTLETS

PREPARATION TIME: *25 minutes, plus chilling*
COOKING TIME: *about 60 minutes*
MICROWAVE SETTING: *Maximum (Full) or Medium Low (35%)*
MAKES 40

Pastry:	*1 garlic clove, peeled and crushed thoroughly*
175 g (6 oz) cream cheese	
4 tablespoons double cream	*1 tablespoon fresh or 1 teaspoon dried lemon thyme leaves*
275 g (10 oz) butter, softened	
	75 g (3 oz) Cheddar cheese, grated
350 g (12 oz) plain flour, sifted	
	175 g (6 oz) peeled cooked prawns
1 teaspoon salt	
Filling:	*pinch of freshly ground black pepper*
250 ml (8 fl oz) double cream	
	salt
2 large eggs	*chopped fresh parsley, to garnish*

Fresh prawns, lettuce and cucumber slices give an extra flourish to the presentation.

1. Beat the cream cheese, cream and butter together.
2. Work in the flour and salt to a smooth, soft dough. Form into a ball with floured hands, wrap in cling film and chill for 30–60 minutes.
3. Roll out the pastry on a floured surface and use to line 40 individual patty tins or the appropriate number of patty trays (suitable for conventional baking).
4. Prick the pastry thoroughly, fill with dried beans and

bake blind in a conventional oven preheated to 180°C, 350°F, Gas Mark 4 for 20 minutes. Remove the baking beans and transfer to a wire tray.

5. To prepare the filling, stir the cream and eggs together until well blended. Mix in the remaining ingredients, but taste before adding the salt, as the cheese may be sufficiently salty.

6. Divide the filling between the pastry cases (not more than three-quarters full). Put a piece of paper towel on the turntable or oven base and gently place 4 of the filled tartlets on the paper, spacing them out well but not putting any in the centre.

7. Cook each batch on Maximum (Full) for 1½–2 minutes, removing the tartlets as soon as the mixture begins to bubble. Over-cooking will cause the filling to curdle and toughen. Repeat the process with the remaining tartlets (if the first batch has curdled, microwave successive batches on Medium Low (35%), allowing 4½–5 minutes for each batch).

8. Using a fish slice, transfer the tartlets carefully to the serving dish and eat hot or if preferred, leave to cool. Garnish with chopped parsley.

GARLIC CHEESE BREAD

PREPARATION TIME: *about 5 minutes*
COOKING TIME: *about 3½ minutes, plus crisping*
MICROWAVE SETTING: *Medium Low (35%)*
SERVES 10–12

2 small French loaves, not more than 33cm (13 inches) long	*2 × 70g (2¾oz) packets garlic and herb cheese*
	100g (4oz) butter

1. Slash the loaves as far as, but not through, the bottom crust at 4cm (1½ inch) intervals.

2. Put the cheese into a small bowl and heat on Medium Low (35%) for 30 seconds until soft and beginning to melt.

3. Beat in the butter until the mixture is smooth.

4. Spread the mixture between the bread slices, then reform each loaf, pressing the slices together tightly and wrap in white paper napkins or a paper towel

5. When required, heat on Medium Low (35%) for 5 minutes, rearranging the loaves halfway through. Carefully unwrap and transfer to a hot flameproof serving dish or baking tray and flash under a preheated conventional grill.

Prawn tartlets; Garlic cheese bread; Farmer's terrine

SMOKED CHICKEN VOL-AU-VENTS

PREPARATION TIME: *about 10 minutes*
COOKING TIME: *about 8 minutes*
MICROWAVE SETTING: *Maximum (Full)*
MAKES 18

15g (½ oz) butter	225g (8 oz) smoked
50g (2 oz) button	chicken, chopped
mushrooms, chopped	18 medium vol-au-vent
15g (½ oz) plain flour	cases, ready baked
150ml (¼ pint) milk	lettuce leaves, to serve

Fresh cooked chicken may be used if smoked is
unavailable.

1. To make the filling, put the butter and mushrooms into
a 1.2 litre (2 pint) basin and cook for 2 minutes. Stir, then
cook for a further 1½ minutes or until the mushrooms are
soft.
2. Stir in the flour until well blended, then gradually mix
in the milk. Cook for 1½ minutes, then stir and cook for a
further 2 minutes or until the sauce thickens. Stir in the
chicken.
3. To serve cold, leave the chicken mixture to cool then fill
the vol-au-vent cases up to 30 minutes before serving. To
serve hot, place the vol-au-vent cases on paper towels
and heat for about 1 minute. Alternatively, warm up in a
conventional oven. Fill with the chicken mixture before it
has cooled and serve, garnished with lettuce leaves.

RICE AND RAISIN SALAD

PREPARATION TIME: *about 10 minutes*
COOKING TIME: *about 12 minutes, plus standing*
MICROWAVE SETTING: *Maximum (Full)*
SERVES 10–12

225g (8 oz) easy-cook	freshly ground black
long-grain rice	pepper
salt	12 medium tomatoes,
675ml (just over 1 pint)	washed and dried
boiling water	1 × 75g (3 oz) piece of
50g (2 oz) seedless raisins	cucumber, peeled and
3 tablespoons salad oil	diced
1 tablespoon red wine	To garnish:
vinegar	shredded lettuce
1 tablespoon chopped	sprig of watercress
fresh basil or 1 teaspoon	
dried basil	

1. Combine the rice, 1 teaspoon of salt and boiling water
in a large 2.75 litre (5 pint) bowl and stir in the raisins.
Cover the bowl with cling film, pulling back one corner to
vent and cook for 12 minutes. Leave to stand for 10

minutes until all the liquid has been absorbed. Uncover
and fluff up with a fork.
2. Stir the salad oil, vinegar and basil into the warmed rice
and add salt and pepper to taste. Cover and leave to cool.
3. While the rice is cooking, cut a slice from the top of
each tomato and set aside. Scoop the flesh from the
tomato and save for a soup or sauce recipe. Sprinkle the
inside of the tomato shells with salt, then turn upside
down on a plate and leave to drain.
4. Mix the diced cucumber into the rice and fill the tomato
shells with the mixture. Replace the reserved lids and
arrange the tomatoes on a bed of shredded lettuce and
garnish with the watercress. Serve cold.

APRICOT TARTINES

PREPARATION TIME: *about 15 minutes*
COOKING TIME: *4 minutes, plus standing*
MICROWAVE SETTING: *Maximum (Full)*
MAKES 12

Frangipan filling:	100g (4 oz) self-raising
50g (2 oz) soft butter or	flour
margarine	4 teaspoons demerara
50g (2 oz) caster sugar	sugar
50g (2 oz) stale cake	To decorate:
crumbs	12 teaspoons apricot jam
50g (2 oz) ground	150ml (¼ pint) double
almonds	cream, whipped
2 large eggs	12 apricot halves, canned
½ teaspoon almond essence	or fresh, skinned
½ teaspoon lemon juice	pieces of glacé cherry and
Streusel:	apricot, to decorate
50g (2 oz) butter or hard	
margarine	

1. Prepare 12 individual paper cake cases, using a double
or triple thickness of paper for each tartlet to ensure a
good shape. The outer case can be re-used.
2. Beat the butter and sugar together until light and fluffy.
3. Stir in the cake crumbs and ground almonds and beat
in the eggs, almond essence and lemon juice.
4. To make the streusel, rub the butter or margarine into
the flour in a mixing bowl, until the mixture resembles
fine crumbs. Stir in the sugar.
5. Half-fill each cake case with the frangipan mixture and
arrange in batches of 6 in a circle on the microwave oven
shelf. Cook each batch for 1 minute, then remove and
press the streusel on top to reach to the top of the paper
case. Cook each batch for a further minute.
6. Leave the cakes to stand for 5 minutes, then remove
from the paper cases and place upside down on a wire
tray. Spread a spoonful of apricot jam on the top of the
cakes and spread the cream around the sides.
7. Drain the apricots thoroughly and place 1 apricot half,
cut side down, on top of the jam. Arrange on a serving
platter, decorated with cherry and apricot pieces.

Smoked chicken vol-au-vents; Rice and raisin salad; Chestnut ice cream nests; Apricot tartines

CHESTNUT ICE CREAM NESTS

PREPARATION TIME: *about 5 minutes*
COOKING TIME: *about 5 minutes, plus cooling and freezing*
MICROWAVE SETTING: *Maximum (Full)*
MAKES 1.5 LITRES (2½ PINTS)

300ml (½ pint) milk	600ml (1 pint) double
225g (8oz) sugar	cream, half whipped
4 egg yolks	**To decorate:**
½ teaspoon vanilla essence	grated chocolate or
1 × 450g (1 lb) can	crushed chocolate flake
chestnut purée	meringue nests
	wafers

To make meringue nests, use leftover egg whites, allowing 50g (2oz) sugar for each egg white, to make a firm meringue. Pipe into nests about 7cm (2½ inches) wide, using a rose nozzle, or spoon into mounds, depressing the centres. You will get about 6 nests from 1 egg white.

1. Mix the milk and sugar together in a 1.2 litre (2 pint) basin and cook for 2 minutes, stirring once during cooking. Then stir until the sugar is dissolved.
2. Beat the egg yolks and vanilla essence together and stir into the sugar mixture. Cook for 2 minutes, then stir and

cook for a further 2 minutes or until the custard thickens slightly. The custard will be a thin pouring consistency.
3. Blend in the food processor or liquidizer with the chestnut purée. (This may need to be done in 2 batches, depending upon the size of the bowl or goblet.) Leave until cold.
4. Fold the half-whipped cream into the chestnut custard, then pour into a large container or individual ramekin dishes. Freeze until firm, then cover.
5. Just before serving transfer the ice cream from the freezer to the refrigerator and leave for 15 minutes. Alternatively, portions of the ice cream from the freezer can be softened in the microwave for 10 seconds on Maximum (Full).
6. Scoop or pipe into meringue nests. Top with grated chocolate and serve with ice cream wafers.

BARBECUE PARTY

SALAMI PATTIES
GLAZED CARROT BARRELS
PORK ÉLITE WITH HOT AND PEPPERY BARBECUE SAUCE
PAPRIKA POTATOES
BARBECUED LAMB CHOPS
TANDOORI CHICKEN

This menu will serve 6–8
Barbecued Lamb Chops can be prepared up to the end of step 2 and kept for 1–2 days in the marinade in the refrigerator before cooking. The flavour will be better if the lamb is freshly cooked rather than reheated.
The Glazed Carrot Barrels can be cooked ahead of time. Reheat, covered, on Maximum (Full) for about 5 minutes.
The Paprika Potatoes can be made in advance and kept chilled. Reheat, uncovered, 6 at a time on Maximum (Full), allowing about 5 minutes and rearranging the potatoes once or twice during reheating. Keep warm on the side of the barbecue or in the conventional oven.
The Salami Patties may be shaped and cooked ahead of time up to the end of step 2. Reheat in the same way as the potatoes, allowing about 3 minutes, then continue on the barbecue or in the conventional oven.
Pork Elite can be completely cooked in advance and kept chilled. Reheat thoroughly in the microwave, rearranging the roll-ups during reheating and basting with the barbecue sauce. Keep hot in a conventional oven or complete on the barbecue.
Tandoori Chicken: the chicken may be marinated (to the end of step 2) for as long as is required. If cooked thoroughly by microwave, the chicken can be reheated in the microwave, allowing 4–5 minutes on Maximum (Full) and rearranging once or twice. Brown under the grill after reheating or continue on the barbecue. However, the chicken will be more flavoursome if it has been freshly cooked.

The recipe may be doubled or trebled, the burgers should be cooked in batches of 6.

1. Mix all the ingredients, except the salami slices, thoroughly together and shape into six 6 cm (2½ inch) rounds.
2. Sandwich each patty between 2 salami slices and arrange in a shallow dish. Cook, uncovered, for 4 minutes, then remove with a slotted spoon and drain on paper towels. Leave to stand for 5 minutes before serving. Garnish with onion rings and serve on lettuce leaves and tomato slices.
3. To barbecue, brown the patties on a metal tray over the hot barbecue.

HOT AND PEPPERY BARBECUE SAUCE

PREPARATION TIME: *about 5 minutes*
COOKING TIME: *about 10 minutes*
MICROWAVE SETTING: *Maximum (Full); then Medium Low (35%)*
MAKES 150 ml (¼ pint)

5 tablespoons water	1 tablespoon Worcestershire sauce
2 tablespoons Muscovado sugar	1 teaspoon chilli powder
5 tablespoons tomato ketchup	small piece of onion, finely chopped until the juices flow
5 tablespoons cider vinegar	

1. Combine the water and sugar in a 1.5 litre (2½ pint) bowl and stir until the sugar is dissolved.
2. Add all the remaining ingredients and cook on Maximum (Full) for 3 minutes or until the sauce boils.
3. Reduce the setting to Medium Low (35%), three-quarters cover with cling film and cook for a further 5 minutes or until the sauce is thick.

SALAMI PATTIES

PREPARATION TIME: *about 10 minutes*
COOKING TIME: *4 minutes*
MICROWAVE SETTING: *Maximum (Full)*
MAKES 6

450g (1 lb) raw lean minced beef	½ beaten egg
25g (1 oz) fresh breadcrumbs	salt
2 teaspoons chopped fresh parsley	freshly ground black pepper
1 tablespoon tomato purée	12 × 6 cm (2½ inch) diameter slices salami, skins removed
½ teaspoon fresh lemon juice	onion rings, to garnish

GLAZED CARROT BARRELS

PREPARATION TIME: *about 10 minutes*
COOKING TIME: *about 13 minutes*
MICROWAVE SETTING: *Maximum (Full)*
SERVES 6

450g (1 lb) slender carrots, peeled	1 tablespoon fresh lemon juice
1 tablespoon honey	4 tablespoons medium sherry
½ teaspoon salt	chopped fresh parsley, to garnish
1 teaspoon grated lemon rind	

This recipe may be doubled if preferred, in which case the carrots need to be cooked for twice as long at each stage.

Glazed carrot barrels; Salami patties; Pork élite with Hot and peppery barbecue sauce

1. Cut the carrots into 2 cm (¾ inch) lengths and shape into barrels using a sharp paring knife.
2. Put the honey, salt, lemon rind, juice and sherry into a 1.2 litre (2 pint) basin, add the carrots, then cover with cling film and cook for 8 minutes until just tender, stirring once during cooking.
3. Remove the carrots with a slotted spoon, cover and keep warm. Replace the basin of cooking liquid and cook, uncovered, for 4 minutes, until syrupy.
4. Return the carrots to the bowl, stir and cook for 1 minute.
5. Put the carrots into a dish suitable for the barbecue, cover and keep hot on the side of the barbecue. Serve garnished with chopped parsley.

PORK ÉLITE

PREPARATION TIME: *about 20 minutes*
COOKING TIME: *about 6 minutes*
MICROWAVE SETTING: *Maximum (Full)*
MAKES 6

350g (12oz) pork fillet	*salt*
175g (6oz) skinless sausages	*freshly ground black pepper*
3 tablespoons very finely chopped onion	*150ml (¼ pint) Hot and Peppery Barbecue Sauce (see opposite)*
½ teaspoon lemon thyme leaves	*cucumber slices, to garnish*
1 teaspoon marjoram leaves	

The recipe may be doubled. Allow 10–12 minutes total cooking time.

1. Cut the pork into 6 thin slices. Trim and beat flat.
2. Mix the sausages, onion and herbs together and add salt and pepper. Divide between the pork slices and roll each into a parcel. Secure each with a cocktail stick.
3. Dip each roll-up into the barbecue sauce and place in a round shallow dish, arranging them in a circle. Cook, uncovered, for 3 minutes, then turn the roll-ups over and cook for a further 2–3 minutes or until the sausages are cooked. Do not overcook the sausage or it will become spongy. Serve garnished with cucumber slices.

PAPRIKA POTATOES

PREPARATION TIME: *about 5 minutes*
COOKING TIME: *about 13 minutes, plus standing*
MICROWAVE SETTING: *Maximum (Full)*

3 × 225g (8oz) jacket potatoes, scrubbed, dried and pricked thoroughly	*50g (2oz) butter*
	2 tablespoons milk
2 teaspoons paprika	*1 small red pepper, cored, seeded and cut into rings*
½ teaspoon salt	
½ teaspoon freshly ground black pepper	*50g (2oz) Cheddar cheese, grated*

1. Put the potatoes in a circle on a paper towel and cook for 5 minutes. Turn the potatoes over and cook for a further 5 minutes or until they are fairly soft. Wrap in a clean cloth and leave to stand for 10 minutes.
2. Halve the potatoes, scoop out the centres and mash with the paprika, salt, pepper, butter and milk. Taste and add more salt and pepper if required. Fill the potato shells with the mixture.
3. Spread out the red pepper circles on a plate, cover and cook for 1 minute. Drain and cut the circles in half. Arrange 4 of the most curved pieces flat on top of each potato.
4. Sprinkle with the cheese, pressing it well down. Transfer the potatoes to a grill pan and brown under a preheated conventional grill. Serve as they are, or, to barbecue, wrap in a tent of foil before browning and heat in the coals or on the grid skin-side down.

BARBECUED LAMB CHOPS

PREPARATION TIME: *about 10 minutes*
COOKING TIME: *about 15 minutes, plus marinating*
MICROWAVE SETTING: *Maximum (Full)*
SERVES 5–6

4 tablespoons salad oil	*1 tablespoon tomato purée*
8 tablespoons red wine	*½ teaspoon freshly ground black pepper*
1 garlic clove, peeled and crushed	
1 teaspoon grated onion	*5–6 trimmed lamb chops, total weight 450g (1lb)*
½ teaspoon salt	*sprigs of rosemary and onion rings, to garnish*
1 tablespoon Worcestershire sauce	

1. Mix the salad oil, wine, garlic, onion, salt, Worcestershire sauce, tomato purée and pepper together in a 2 litre (3½ pint) bowl. Cook for 3 minutes or until the onion is tender. Stir well.
2. Put the lamb chops into the liquid in the bowl, cover and marinate for 2 hours, basting occasionally.
3. To prepare for cooking on the barbecue, put the chops

in a shallow dish and microwave for 2 minutes. Brush with the marinade and barbecue over hot coals.
4. If not using a barbecue, the dish can be completed in the microwave oven. Remove the lamb from the bowl and blot with paper towels.
5. Heat a large browning dish to the maximum recommended by the manufacturer and quickly add 2 tablespoons of the oil from the surface of the marinade. Immediately add the lamb chops, pressing them down well with a fish slice. Turn them over quickly and press down once more. Cook for 4½ minutes or until the chops are tender. Remove from the dish and keep hot.
6. Pour the marinade into the juices remaining in the browning dish and skim as much of the oil and fat from the surface as possible. Cook, uncovered, for 4 minutes, until about 4 tablespoons of the juice and sediment remain. Spoon the sediment over the hot chops and serve at once, garnished with sprigs of rosemary and onion rings.

Barbecued lamb chops; Paprika potatoes; Tandoori chicken

TANDOORI CHICKEN

PREPARATION TIME: *about 15 minutes*
COOKING TIME: *about 30–35 minutes, plus marinating*
MICROWAVE SETTING: *Maximum (Full)*
SERVES 4–8

8 × 250g (10oz) chicken breasts on the bone	1 teaspoon ground cumin
3 tablespoons lemon juice	1 teaspoon ground coriander
2 teaspoons salt	2 teaspoons ground turmeric
150ml (¼ pint) unsweetened yogurt	½ teaspoon ground ginger
2 tablespoons salad oil	orange and red food colouring (see below)
4 garlic cloves, peeled and crushed	bay leaves and cucumber slices, to garnish
2 teaspoons paprika	

The length of cooking time will depend upon the starting temperature of the chicken and if the cooking is to be completed on the barbecue, the microwave cooking time can be reduced and the barbecue cooking time increased.

Powdered food colouring is more satisfactory than liquid but is more difficult to obtain. You may need 1–2 teaspoons liquid food colouring.

1. Skin the chicken and cut off the wing tips at the last joint. Reserve both skin and tips for making stock. Rinse the chicken pieces in cold water, then pat dry. Slash the chicken pieces deeply in about 3 or 4 places.
2. Mix the remaining ingredients together in a large bowl, adding sufficient colouring to produce a deep orangey-red mixture. Add the chicken pieces one at a time, rubbing the mixture well in. Cover the bowl and marinate for 10–12 hours in the refrigerator, turning and basting the chicken pieces occasionally.
3. Put a rack into a large shallow dish and stack up the chicken pieces in the same way as toast in a toast rack. Cook, uncovered, for 25–30 minutes, repositioning halfway through, so that the inside pieces are moved to the outside and the pieces are also turned over.
4. Test for cooking, then transfer the chicken to a wire tray over a metal baking tin and brown under the grill or on the barbecue grid over hot coals. Serve garnished with bay leaves and cucumber.

CHILDREN'S PARTY

EGG SANDWICHES

MINI SAUSAGES ON COCKTAIL STICKS

CHEESE STRAWS

FLAPJACKS

CHOCOLATE CUP CAKES WITH FUDGE ICING

STRAWBERRY JAM TARTS

This menu serves 6
Chocolate Cup Cakes may be prepared ahead of time. Store in a single layer in an airtight container but not in the freezer.
Strawberry Jam Tarts: both the jam and the tarts may be made in advance and assembled when convenient.
Egg Sandwiches may be prepared in advance.
Flapjacks: prepare ahead of time and store in an airtight container. If the flapjacks have gone soft during storage, crisp in the microwave oven for 1–2 minutes only.
Store Cheese Straws in an airtight container. Crisp in the microwave.
Mini Sausages should be prepared just before the party or served cold. While it is better not to reheat the sausages, this can be done in the microwave oven, taking care that they are completely reheated but are not so hot that they will burn the children's mouths.

EGG SANDWICHES

PREPARATION TIME: *about 10 minutes*
COOKING TIME: *10 minutes*
MAKES 24

4 eggs	freshly ground black pepper
15g (½ oz) butter	
1 teaspoon salad cream (optional)	12 slices bread from a sliced loaf
salt	cress, to serve

Eggs in their shells must not be cooked in the microwave oven as the build-up of pressure inside would cause the egg to burst. Hard-boiled eggs should also not be reheated in the microwave, even without their shells.

1. Hard boil the eggs in boiling water on the conventional hob for 10 minutes. Carefully remove the eggs with a slotted spoon and plunge into cold water. Shell the eggs.
2. Mash the warm eggs with the butter and salad cream if used, adding salt and pepper to taste. Spread the mixture on one side of each of 6 slices of bread, then cover with the remaining slices. There is no need for additional butter on the bread. Cut into quarters either square or diagonally. Serve on a bed of cress.

MINI SAUSAGES ON COCKTAIL STICKS

PREPARATION TIME: *about 5 minutes*
COOKING TIME: *about 4 minutes, plus standing*
MICROWAVE SETTING: *Maximum (Full)*
MAKES 12

12 cocktail sausages

A browning dish is needed for this recipe. The recipe may be doubled if required, adding one-third extra cooking time.

1. Separate the sausages and put into a large browning dish. Cook for 1½ minutes, turning frequently.
2. Remove the sausages from the dish with tongs or a slotted spoon, leaving the fat in the browning dish. Keep the sausages warm.
3. Return the browning dish to the microwave oven and heat for 2 minutes or until the fat is sizzling.
4. Quickly return the sausages to the dish and brown by tossing along the surface of the dish, pressing them down as you do so. Cook uncovered for 30 seconds, then leave to stand for 2 minutes.
5. Remove the sausages with a slotted spoon or tongs, drain on paper towels and spear with cocktail sticks.

CHEESE STRAWS

PREPARATION TIME: *about 10 minutes*
COOKING TIME: *about 3 minutes*
MICROWAVE SETTING: *Maximum (Full)*
MAKES ABOUT 24

50g (2 oz) plain flour	⅛ teaspoon freshly ground black pepper
25g (1 oz) butter or margarine	
25g (1 oz) grated cheese	about 2 teaspoons cold water
⅛ teaspoon salt	

1. Sift the flour into a mixing bowl and rub in the butter or margarine until the mixture resembles breadcrumbs.
2. Stir in the cheese, salt and pepper and add the cold water. Mix to a manageable but not stiff dough with a palette knife, adding extra water if necessary.
3. Form the pastry into a ball. Roll out on a floured surface to a rectangle about 5mm (¼ inch) thick. Cut into strips about 5cm (2 inches) long and 1cm (½ inch) wide.
4. Carefully place the strips on a piece of greaseproof paper and cook for 2½ minutes. Remove any straws that are slightly brown on the sides. Cook the remainder for a further 30 seconds. Leave until cool and crisp, then store in an airtight container.

Egg sandwiches; Cheese straws; Mini sausages on cocktail sticks

FLAPJACKS

PREPARATION TIME: *about 5 minutes*
COOKING TIME: *about 7 minutes*
MICROWAVE SETTING: *Maximum (Full); then Medium Low (35%)*
MAKES 12

50g (2oz) butter or margarine	*2 tablespoons golden syrup*
50g (2oz) demerara sugar	*150g (6oz) rolled porridge oats*

1. Put the butter or margarine in a large bowl and cook for 30–60 seconds or until melted.
2. Stir in the remaining ingredients, mixing thoroughly.
3. Turn into a rectangular container, approximately 18 × 15 × 2½cm (7 × 6 × 1 inches). Press the mixture down firmly and to an even thickness and cook on Maximum (Full) for 1 minute.
4. Turn the dish and reduce the setting to Medium Low (35%). Cook for 5–6 minutes until the mixture is set and leaves no impression when pressed gently with a wooden spoon. Take care not to overcook as flapjacks tend to burn in the centre of the mixture.
5. Leave to cool in the dish before turning out. Cut into 12 bars and leave until cold. Store in an airtight container.

CHOCOLATE CUP CAKES WITH FUDGE ICING

PREPARATION TIME: *about 10 minutes*
COOKING TIME: *about 2½ minutes*
MICROWAVE SETTING: *Maximum (Full)*
MAKES 12

50g (2oz) soft margarine	**Chocolate fudge icing:**
50g (2oz) caster sugar	*50g (2oz) butter*
1 large egg	*2 tablespoons cocoa powder, sifted*
75g (3oz) self-raising flour	*1 tablespoon boiling water*
½ teaspoon baking powder	*175g (6oz) icing sugar, sifted*
1 tablespoon sifted cocoa powder	*assorted sugar-coated chocolate sweets, to decorate*
1 tablespoon water	

1. Mix the margarine, sugar, egg, flour, baking powder, cocoa powder and water together in a bowl and beat for 2 minutes.
2. Divide the mixture between 12 double thickness small paper cake cases. Arrange 6 at a time in a circle and cook

Flapjacks; Strawberry jam tarts; Chocolate cup cakes with fudge icing

each batch for 1 minute. Test with a cocktail stick which should come out clean.
3. Put the butter in a medium-sized basin and cook for 30 seconds or until melted. Stir in the cocoa powder and boiling water, then work in the icing sugar to a smooth paste.
4. Spread the chocolate fudge icing over the freshly made, warm cakes, top with a sweet and leave to set. Before serving, remove the outer paper cases.

STRAWBERRY JAM TARTS

PREPARATION TIME: *5 minutes (jam); 10 minutes (pastry)*
COOKING TIME: *21 minutes, plus setting and cooling*
MICROWAVE SETTING: *Medium Low (35%); then Maximum (Full)*
MAKES 12

Jam:	Pastry:
225g (8oz) strawberries, hulled	*225g (8oz) plain flour*
200g (7oz) caster sugar	*pinch of salt*
1 tablespoon lemon juice	*100g (4oz) soft margarine*
½ teaspoon butter	*50g (2oz) desiccated coconut*
	2 tablespoons ice-cold water

1. To make the jam, mix the strawberries, sugar and lemon juice in a large 2.75 litre (5 pint) ovenglass mixing bowl. Three-quarters cover with cling film and cook on Medium Low (35%) for 12 minutes, stirring every 4 minutes. Stir gently until the sugar is dissolved, taking care not to break up the strawberries.
2. Raise the setting, pull back the cling film covering, so that the bowl is only half covered and cook on Maximum (Full), without stirring, for 7 minutes. Test for setting by dropping a teaspoon of the syrup on to a cold plate; it should wrinkle slightly when pushed with the handle of a spoon. You could chill the plate in the refrigerator to speed up the setting. Do not overcook as the jam sets firmly on cooling.
3. Stir the butter into the hot jam, cover and leave to cool.
4. To make the pastry, sift the flour and salt into a mixing bowl and work in the margarine with a fork or round-bladed knife. Stir in the coconut. Add the water and mix to a soft dough.
5. Roll out the pastry on a lightly floured surface to a 3mm (⅛ inch) thickness.
6. Cut 12 rounds to fit over the outside of two 6-hole microwave-proof bun trays or the backs of small ramekins, and press the pastry round the sides, so that it fits snugly. Prick with a fork, then cook, 6 at a time, on Maximum (Full) for 2 minutes or until the pastry is set. Leave until cool, then loosen the pastry shells with the back of a knife and remove when cold.
7. Spoon the jam into the tart cases, place on a paper towel and heat, 6 at a time, on Maximum (Full) for 30 seconds or until the jam bubbles. Leave until cold.

DRINKS AND DUNKERS

LIQUEUR COFFEE
CHOCOLATE FONDUE WITH FRESH FRUIT
MULLED WINE
CHEESE FONDUE
SALTED SPICY ALMONDS
AUBERGINE DUNK

This menu will serve 12–14
Liqueur Coffee may be made ahead of time up to the end of step 1 and reheated for 3 minutes just before completing the recipe and serving.
The Chocolate Fondue may be made in advance but if a long standing time is expected, add extra milk. Resoften on Maximum (Full) for about 2 minutes, stirring once or twice during reheating.
Mulled Wine may be prepared in advance. Reheat to steaming but not boiling point, about 5 minutes.
The Salted Spicy Almonds and Aubergine Dunk can be prepared ahead of time. Stir the dunk thoroughly before serving.
The Cheese Fondue can be prepared 24 hours ahead of time. Cover and keep chilled. To serve, reheat on Medium Low (35%) for 10–12 minutes, stirring every 2 minutes.

LIQUEUR COFFEE

PREPARATION TIME: *10 minutes*
COOKING TIME: *9 minutes*
SERVES 6

300ml ($\frac{1}{2}$ pint) water	600ml (1 pint) extra strong hot black coffee
3 tablespoons sugar	
6 cloves	6–12 tablespoons brandy
3 strips orange peel	300ml ($\frac{1}{2}$ pint) double cream
3 strips lemon peel	
$\frac{1}{2}$ teaspoon ground cinnamon	

To make double the quantity, at step 1 cook initially for 5 minutes until boiling, then for a further 5 minutes.

1. Combine the water, sugar, cloves, orange and lemon peel and cinnamon in a large jug or lipped bowl. Cook for 3 minutes or until boiling. Stir and cook for a further 5 minutes. Strain, return to the jug and reheat for 1 minute.
2. Pour the coffee into 6 heated cups, then stir 3 tablespoons of the infusion into each. Carefully pour 1–2 tablespoons brandy over the rounded bowl of a warmed teaspoon held over the coffee. Ignite carefully at once.
3. Stir 1–2 tablespoons cream into each cup and serve.

CHOCOLATE FONDUE WITH FRESH FRUIT

PREPARATION TIME: *about 15 minutes*
COOKING TIME: *about 5 minutes*
MICROWAVE SETTING: *Maximum (Full)*
SERVES 6

assortment of fresh fruit including pineapple, peaches, strawberries, bananas, apricots or other fruits that are not too juicy	1 × 400g (14oz) can condensed milk
	2 tablespoons water
	$\frac{1}{2}$ teaspoon vanilla essence
	2 tablespoons Crème de Cacao liqueur
200g (7oz) plain dessert chocolate	single cream, to decorate

The dip can be kept warm on Low (10%) for about 20 minutes. Add a little extra water or fresh milk if necessary. If doubling the quantities, cook for 2$\frac{1}{2}$ minutes at step 2. At step 3 cook initially for 1$\frac{1}{2}$ minutes, stir, then for a further 2 minutes. Allow half a fruit per person.

1. Prepare the fruit and cut into chunks. Cover and set aside.
2. Break up the chocolate, put into a medium bowl and cook for 1 minute. Stir, then cook for a further minute or until the chocolate is shiny on top.
3. Stir in the milk, water and vanilla essence and cook for 1$\frac{1}{2}$ minutes. Stir, then cook for a further minute until the sauce is hot. Stir in the Crème de Cacao. Pour into a fondue pot or place the bowl over a basin of hot water to keep it warm. Decorate with a swirl of cream.
4. To serve, provide forks to spear and dip the fruit.

MULLED WINE

PREPARATION TIME: *about 5 minutes*
COOKING TIME: *about 5 minutes*
MICROWAVE SETTING: *Maximum (Full)*
SERVES 6–8

1 litre (1$\frac{3}{4}$ pints) red wine	grated rind and juice of 1 lemon
1 teaspoon grated nutmeg	
1 teaspoon ground cinnamon	about 15 cloves
	3 tablespoons brown sugar

If making double the quantity, cook for 10 minutes.

1. Combine all the ingredients in a large bowl and stir until the sugar is melted.
2. Cook for 5 minutes or until the wine is steaming but not boiling. Drain into a heated bowl.

Chocolate fondue with fresh fruit; Mulled wine; Liqueur coffee

CHEESE FONDUE

PREPARATION TIME: *10 minutes*
COOKING TIME: *about 11 minutes*
MICROWAVE SETTING: *Maximum (Full); then Medium Low (35%)*
SERVES 12–14

450ml (¾ pint) good quality dry white wine	*2 tablespoons Kirsch*
	salt
450g (1lb) Emmental cheese, grated	*freshly ground black pepper*
1 garlic clove, peeled and finely crushed	*small chunks of fresh French bread*
25g (1oz) cornflour	

1. Reserve 4 tablespoons of the wine and put the remainder into a 2 litre (3½ pint) bowl.
2. Stir in the cheese and garlic and cook on Maximum (Full) for 1 minute. Stir, then cook for a further minute or until the cheese is melted.
3. Blend the cornflour with the Kirsch and remaining wine and stir into the cheese mixture. Reduce the setting to Medium Low (35%) and cook for about 9 minutes, stirring every 3 minutes, until the mixture thickens. *The fondue must not boil.* Add salt and pepper to taste.
4. Pour the mixture into a fondue pot over a low flame or into a bowl over a basin of hot water. To eat, spear a piece of French bread with a fondue fork and dip and twirl in the cheese mixture. Should the fondue cool and become thick, transfer it to a suitable bowl and heat on Medium Low (35%) until the mixture is liquid once more.

SALTED SPICY ALMONDS

PREPARATION TIME: *about 5 minutes*
COOKING TIME: *about 4 minutes*
MICROWAVE SETTING: *Maximum (Full)*
MAKES 225g (8oz)

225g (8oz) blanched skinned almonds	*few grinds pepperander (a mixture of white and black peppercorns and coriander)*
15g (½oz) butter	
coarse salt	

1. Put the almonds and butter in a shallow round ovenglass dish and cook for 4 minutes, stirring every minute. (The almonds will brown inside although this may not be visible without cutting one in half.) Test to make sure that they are not beginning to burn.
2. Spoon the almonds into a serving dish lined with a paper towel. Sprinkle generously with the coarse salt and add the pepperander. Toss to mix thoroughly, then remove the paper towel.

AUBERGINE DUNK

PREPARATION TIME: *about 5 minutes*
COOKING TIME: *about 5 minutes*
MICROWAVE SETTING: *Maximum (Full)*
SERVES 6–8

1 × 350g (12oz) aubergine	*50g (2oz) cream cheese*
4 sprigs parsley	*150ml (¼ pint) soured cream*
3 tablespoons fresh chives	*crisp raw vegetables (e.g. carrot, cucumber, green pepper, mushrooms) or Emmental cheese, to serve*
1 teaspoon fresh lemon juice	
¼ teaspoon salt	
¼ teaspoon freshly ground black pepper	

1. Cut away the stalk and wrap the aubergine in cling film. Cook for 5 minutes or until the flesh feels soft. Leave until cold. Remove the cling film and scoop out the flesh, discarding the skin.
2. Cut up the aubergine and purée in the liquidizer with the parsley, chives and lemon juice. Add the salt and pepper, cheese and soured cream and purée briefly. Taste and adjust the seasoning if necessary.
3. Spoon into a serving dish. Cut up a selection of crisp raw vegetables or cheese into fingers and serve as dunks for the dip.

Cheese fondue; Salted spicy almonds; Aubergine dunk

INDEX

ACKNOWLEDGEMENTS

Photography:
    Ian O'Leary
Photographic styling:
    Sue Brown, Paula Lovell
Preparation of food for photography:
    Judy Bugg, Jacqui Hine, Cecilia Norman, Clare Gordon-Smith
The publishers would also like to thank the following companies for the loan of props for photography:
Anchor Hocking Corporation, 271 High Street, Berkhamsted, Herts;
Corning Ltd, Wear Glassworks, Sunderland;
Dickins & Jones, 224 Regent Street, London W1;
Fieldhouse, 89 Wandsworth Bridge Road, London SW6;
David Mellor, 26 St James Street, London WC2;
Toshiba UK Ltd, Toshiba House, Frimley Road, Frimley, Camberley, Surrey
Triangle Designs, 202/208 New North Road, London N1